JAMES PATTERSON

& ROBISON WELLS

The Warning

arrow books

1 3 5 7 9 10 8 6 4 2

Arrow Books
20 Vauxhall Bridge Road
London SW1V 2SA

Arrow Books is part of the Penguin Random House group of companies
whose addresses can be found at global.penguinrandomhouse.com

Penguin
Random House
UK

First published by Arrow Books in 2019

www.penguin.co.uk

A CIP catalogue record for this book is available from the British Library

ISBN 9781787462298
ISBN 9781787462304 (export edition)

Printed and bound in Great Britain by Clays Ltd, Elcograf S.p.A.

THE WARNING

THE MAGAZINE

CHAPTER 1

Jordan

"WELL, THE TOWN doesn't *appear* to be glowing."

Mom kept her eyes on the road. The silence lingered until Charlie blurted out, "Crickets!"

I laughed and angled toward the back seat. "Where'd you get *that* from?"

"You, you big dummy!" Charlie cackled. He was six. "'Awkward silence equals crickets,' you said."

I gave his knee a squeeze. Mom had traveled this route thousands of times but not in the past eleven months and never as part of a bumper-to-bumper convoy that stretched on for miles toward the outskirts of town. "I just don't think it's funny is all," she said.

"I don't, either," I said. "I'm the one who was in the hospital."

She shot me a glare, then returned her attention to the rear bumper of a black Toyota SUV with the number 80 affixed to its license plate. "Not from radiation, though."

"That's true," I said. "The meltdown played no role in my accident."

Mom gripped the steering wheel tighter. The accident was a sticky subject.

"It wasn't a meltdown," she said.

"Right," I said. "It was an explosion at a nuclear plant that caused the evacuation of an entire population. Nothing to see here."

"I didn't hear a boom," Charlie chimed in. "Explosions go boom."

"I didn't hear a boom, either," I said. "We'll have to ask Dad whether there was one."

Dad worked for the Mount Hope Nuclear Power Plant and stayed there while we were relocated to a refugee camp.

Mount Hope, South Carolina, is tucked into a valley between two mountain ranges. It's accessible only by two roads, one from the north and one from the south. Likewise, there were two refugee camps, the main one north of town and the so-called sick (code for radiation exposure) camp to the south. Mom, Charlie, and I were in the latter one, thanks to my accident. Most folks I knew—including almost every other kid—were in the healthy-people camp, though even they were quarantined.

And now we were all getting to go home at last.

"Dad says it's not going to be safe to live in Chernobyl for twenty thousand years," I said. "So we've got a 19,999-year jump on them."

Mom wasn't having it. "And I say this wasn't Chernobyl. It was more like Three Mile Island, if you want to start comparing nuclear-plant incidents."

"I was thinking *The China Syndrome*," I said.

"This happened in China, too?" Charlie asked.

"How do you even *know* that movie?" Mom asked.

"I have my ways," I said, detecting what, for the first time in a while, appeared to be the crack of a smile on my mom's face.

She can't help it. She's amused that I drop references to movies from her era and before. People don't realize there's this thing called the internet—and YouTube and On Demand, for that matter.

Speaking of which, I checked my phone again. Still no signal.

At the camp, there was no cell-phone service, and our data was limited. We could send and receive emails—no attachments, of course—but getting onto a website? Fugged-aboutit.

"You know who says it's safe?" Mom asked. "Your father."

"Right. Dad," I said. "I remember that guy."

"Jordan, don't."

"No, it'll be nice not to be in a single-parent household. Truly."

Crickets.

"Will Daddy still have a sunburn?" Charlie asked.

"Good question," I said. "Maybe he's catching up to me on the shade scale."

We were able to talk to Dad a couple times on the camp landline—he had clout enough to arrange that—and he told us about the radiation burns he'd received. Normally his skin was on the light-but-not-too-light side that would make people wonder whether he was Italian or Middle Eastern or even...*black*? Mom brought the darker cocoa to the mix, which explained why Tico liked to call me Latte.

Our beat-up Nissan sedan inched forward, with Mom

keeping a healthy distance behind car No. 80. Our SUV was totaled in the accident.

The town alarms had sounded, and the evacuation was shifting into high gear. And so, apparently, was Hank Bradshaw's Ford F-350. Mom was rushing to pick up Dad at the plant, not knowing that he wouldn't be joining us after all. She certainly didn't know that we'd sustain a direct hit to the passenger-side door and would all wind up in the hospital and then the so-called sick camp.

Her right leg got snapped like a wishbone, though now she not only was walking without a limp but had resumed her morning jogs. Charlie took some flying glass in his left arm and across his forehead but otherwise, miracle of miracles, was in tip-top shape. As for me, well...

Like I said, we were gone for eleven months. I remember ten of them. I was in pretty bad shape, or so they tell me. Mom tallied the surgeries for me: seven. Her tearstained face was what I saw when I finally came out of the coma-slash-delirium that the docs had me in. Being a mom isn't the easiest job, and I admit I'm no walk in the park.

"How's your head?" she asked now, eyes fixed on the road.

"Fine," I replied, though it had been aching over the past few days. I reached up and touched the scar on the back of my scalp. I'd never been able to adjust the mirrors in the hospital or our trailer to get a full view, but my phone camera captured the spiderweb of pink scar tissue that contrasted brightly against my smoky skin.

My skull had been fractured in three places, though doctors said there had been zero lasting damage. I couldn't say the same about my right arm, which had a zipper running lengthwise along its underside. It was full of pins and screws and always felt a little numb. My right knee had a neat circle drawn around the cap, and my chest wounds looked as if they were outlining pectoral muscles that I was just starting to develop. The four broken ribs on my right side hurt whenever I did anything athletic, which was going to be a problem when I tried out for football.

Mom breathed in and out through her mouth, in the shape of an "o," then said, "What if our house was looted?"

"*That's* what you're worried about?" I laughed.

"It's been sitting there for almost a year. You never know."

She stretched an arm to the back-seat floor to grab a cigarette pack in her purse.

"No," I said.

She'd quit smoking before I was born but started again after the evacuation. She went from smelling like lavender shampoo to stinking of stale smoke, but at least she smoked only outside. She knew better than to make Charlie and me suffer in the car.

"Sorry," she said, dropping the pack back into her purse. "It's just, they said at the camp that we shouldn't get our hopes up that everything is going to be perfect. Why would they say that if there wasn't going to be a lot of damage?"

"If someone messed with our house," Charlie declared, "I'll hunt them down and pop a cap in their ass!" Mom almost swerved off the road before shooting me an accusatory look.

"I might have been quoting *Pulp Fiction* to him again," I muttered.

"Don't worry, Mom," Charlie said. "I'm trying real hard to be the shepherd."

Mom's right foot alternated between the gas and brake

pedals. We were moving that slowly. But soon I saw the green sign that read WELCOME TO BOXSMITH COUNTY, and I knew we were close. Everything looked more familiar now, even the trees, which had grown especially lush since we left.

"Do you know when you're going back to work?" I asked Mom.

"Doug emailed me that the bank may open as soon as tomorrow because people want to check on their money."

The caravan meandered along the south road beside the Sweetbay River.

I checked my phone again. Still no signal.

Mom turned on the radio, and a deep, authoritative voice intoned, "…continue along your directed route. When you reach Mount Hope town limits, military police will direct you further. Please continue along your directed route…"

It was a loop. I punched the button for the classic-rock station, but the message was there, too. It was everywhere, up and down the dial, AM and FM. Mom turned it off.

"Do you think everything will look the same?" Charlie asked.

"We'll know soon enough," I replied.

CHAPTER 2

Jordan

EVERY HALF MILE or so, a military Jeep was parked on the side of the road with camouflage-clad officers monitoring the caravan with walkie-talkies pressed to their faces. One especially muscle-bound guy fixed his steely eyes on me until we moved past him.

My head hurt even more until I saw the Tastee Freeze. The sign's hundreds of little lightbulbs were all lit, perhaps for the first time ever.

"Let's get ice cream!" Charlie announced.

"It won't be open now," Mom said. "It's ten in the morning, and people are just getting back."

"But it *is*. Look!"

Sure enough, a line of about twenty smiling people snaked from the pickup window around the corner into the parking lot.

"Huh," she said again, guiding the car past the courthouse and library, their lawns full, green, and perfectly manicured. As we paraded up Main Street, the storefronts and sidewalks all looked power-washed, their windows glinting in the late-morning sunlight.

"What town is this?" Mom asked. "It's a little too perfect, isn't it?"

As she turned onto Oak, the traffic dispersed, and we had a clear shot home. But when we arrived at a stop sign, I announced, "You know what? I'm gonna get out here if you don't mind."

"Are you crazy, Jordan?" Charlie barked, but Mom had a knowing look on her face.

"Tell Maggie we say hi," she said.

"Sure thing," I said, chagrined, as I closed the door behind me and was immediately overwhelmed by the scent of freshly mown grass and flowers in full bloom. Since when did Mount Hope smell like a greenhouse at peak season?

Mom lowered the passenger-side window. "Please be back soon to help unpack. I may need your help figuring out what was looted."

"Ha," I said. "Okay."

"Give your girlfriend a big KISSY!" Charlie chimed in.

"She's not my girlfriend," I muttered as they pulled away. I pulled up her number on my phone, but still . . . no service.

Maggie and I weren't dating. She'd been my best friend since we were little, and I didn't want to mess up a good thing. She was one of those girls who's better-looking than she realizes—or if she did realize it, she never let on. Her blond hair had a life of its own. So did her hazel eyes.

Yet, if anything, we had grown closer while we were away at our separate camps. Her emails were the one thing that kept me from going crazy at a place where the only people my age wore military uniforms.

"Where are you going?" a raspy voice behind me called as I walked down a quiet sidewalk beside weedless lawns, immaculate houses, and even a few new white picket fences. I turned to see a soldier with stubble on his baby face and a large rifle at his side.

"Just headed to my friend's house," I said. "We were in different camps."

"The town of Mount Hope is currently under martial law," he said with a robotic intonation. "You must heed the curfew rules until the emergency protocols are lifted."

I fast-walked in the other direction, not looking back until I hit a dirt path. The empty lot next to Redmond's Lumberyard was a shortcut to Maggie's house. The grass and weeds were almost as tall as I was.

As I made my way through the thicket, I heard a growl.

You know how something might sound large or small to you? Whatever made this noise did *not* sound small.

It was not a cat.

It was not a dog.

I froze.

There it went again, louder. It reminded me of when I visited the Charleston zoo, and a lion roared and the bars seemed to shake.

And there it was, about thirty feet away, standing up on its haunches amid the weeds.

A bear. A ten-foot-tall bear.

I remembered from Boy Scouts that brown bears attacked when they were hungry, but grizzlies liked to fight for the sake of it. This bear was black.

I knew there was a hole in the lumberyard's chain-link fence halfway down. The bear was right behind me, snorting like a bull just before it charges.

Now I wasn't running; I was *flying,* going faster than I'd

ever gone in a football game. I ducked behind an old red cedar tree next to the fence and—*shit*. The fence had been fixed, the hole gone. Thanks, do-gooding military.

Not looking back, I latched onto the limbs of the cedar and started climbing, my old sneakers scraping against the loose bark of the branches.

I made it up that tree in an instant and dropped to the ground on the other side of the fence, sticking the landing with my knees bent, including the surgically reconstructed one. It didn't even hurt. I looked back at the bear halfway up the tree, grabbed a piece of loose lumber off the ground, and heaved it like a javelin.

Bam! That wood got a snoutful of bear, knocking the animal off the tree and back onto the path on the other side of the fence. It landed with a squeal and an *ummph*.

CHAPTER 3

Maggie

NERF WAS THE sweetest golden retriever ever. He didn't walk so much as hop on his paws. His ears would prick up, his brown eyes would brighten, and he'd let out a gentle *"Aarf! Aarf!"*

Now Nerf was slamming his face against his kennel cage, lunging, barking, and trying to gnaw through the plastic bars. He had murder in his eyes, and those eyes were aimed at me.

"What is *wrong* with him?" I asked my mom again, crouched on the floor of her veterinary office.

"I gave him a sedative," she said. "He should be calming down soon."

"He should've calmed down already."

Mom let out a dramatic sigh. On the drive back from camp, the McAlisters rear-ended the Mitchells about twenty-five miles from town. There must've been fifty soldiers on the scene within thirty seconds.

"Could this be a reaction to the radiation?" I asked from the floor. "It's like he got infected the moment we were back in town."

"No," Mom said, stepping into the entryway to pick up a suitcase. "Radiation doesn't work like that. And that's all gone, anyway, remember?" She lugged the bag upstairs.

I looked back at Nerf.

"Hey, boy!" I said in my sweetest voice.

He smashed his face into the bars, jolting me backward again. The collision didn't faze him at all as he growled and reared back on his haunches. I worried he was going to concuss himself. He barked savagely.

"Mom, Nerf is freaking me out!" I grabbed my two duffels and joined Mom upstairs.

I tossed my bag onto my bed and looked around. Our living space was basically a studio apartment, the attic of the vet practice. Any money we had went for what Mom, Dr. Renee Gooding, called "infrastructure improvements," most recently, twenty thousand dollars into an X-ray machine.

I pulled out my phone and looked for a text. Jordan and I had emailed about getting together when we both arrived in town, but the phone was showing no bars.

"Did the accident do something to the cell towers?" I asked.

"The phone companies probably haven't reactivated the towers yet. Bureaucracy."

Emails came through, though. Most of my friends were in the camp, so we didn't email much, but from the moment I sent a message to Jordan, way over in the "sick" camp, I started checking my in-box compulsively. And when "Jordan Conners" popped up in my in-box, I smiled.

I felt even closer to him many miles apart than I did growing up with him in Mount Hope.

I also missed him.

After his injuries, how would he look now?

I checked my phone again. No signal.

Ring. Ring. Ring.

I turned from Mom to hide the smile breaking across my face, and I scrambled down the stairs. I ducked into the office to check myself in the mirror.

"Are you playing hard to get?" Mom called down.

"Aooooo!" Nerf howled from the other room.

I took a breath, straightened my posture, and opened the door.

Jordan burst in, slammed the door behind him, locked the bolt, and peered back out through the blinds. His shirt was drenched in sweat, and he was gasping for breath.

"Jordan! Great to see ya!" I announced. "Which bank did you rob?"

"I must have lost it," he said, his eyes still directed through the front window.

"What?"

"The bear."

"Oh, the bear," I said.

"Hi, Maggie," he said with a sheepish smile. "I was chased here by a giant black bear. Sorry."

He wrapped me in a hot, damp hug.

"Eeesh," I said. "You *smell* like a giant black bear."

"More like a panther," he said, and let go of me, crossed the room, and picked up the phone at the receptionist's desk. "No dial tone."

"Go figure."

He returned to the blinds and scanned the neighborhood.

"I missed you, too," I deadpanned.

Jordan flashed that grin I'd missed so much. "Maggie, it

was an *actual bear.*" As I stepped toward the door, a loud *clang* burst from inside the office.

"What the hell was *that*?" Jordan asked.

"C'mere," I said, and led him to the cage where Nerf was growling, teeth bared.

"Spooky," Jordan said as Nerf hurled himself toward us.

"What?"

"That's the look the bear was giving me."

CHAPTER 4

Maggie

THE BEAR HAD moved from Redmond's lot onto a quiet county road by the time we pulled up, but as we cruised the town in Deputy Ruby's squad car, we couldn't miss the massive furry black animal lumbering down the center of the woods-lined County Road J.

Holy crap, that thing was huge and *not* friendly-looking. No wonder Jordan worked up such a sweat.

"That's some bear," Deputy Ruby said as we crouched behind his car.

Mom got out the tranquilizer gun and rested the barrel atop the car's hood.

The bear was loping along in the opposite direction, getting smaller and smaller. Mom steadied her aim and squinted.

And fired.

We were too far away. The dart skidded by the bear's feet. The bear looked down, then whipped back toward us.

Oh, shit.

"Maggie," Jordan said as the four of us ducked behind the squad car.

"Not now, Jordan!" I hissed.

We heard scraping on the gravel. Then it stopped, then started again.

It was getting closer.

Then heavy wheezing, growing louder.

Mom was sitting with her back to the car door, the tranq gun cocked and loaded. She spun around, held the barrel over the hood, and...

Whack! The bear slapped away the gun, which then skittered to the edge of the woods. The bear roared, loudly, and we heard a screeching of metal. As we bolted away from the car, I looked back to see the bear hoisting the passenger-side door over its head and then flinging it our way like an oversize Frisbee.

"Look out!" I cried, and Deputy Ruby dove to his left to avoid decapitation.

The bear was now atop the car's roof, stomping it down into the cabin, shattered glass from the windows and flashing lights spraying onto the road. The tranquilizer gun had come to rest just beyond the road's shoulder. I was the closest to it and could get there faster than the bear—I thought.

"Maggie!" Jordan shouted as I scrambled toward the gun.

The bear was taking giant strides, closing the gap. In one fluid motion, I grabbed the gun and whirled toward the charging animal, which was two steps from me, claws out.

Zap! The dart hit it right between the eyes, and the bear spilled over backward.

"*Damn!*" Jordan cried. "Nice *shot!*"

I blew into the muzzle and smiled.

"That's my girl," Mom said as she and Jordan jogged toward me and wrapped their arms around my shoulders. "I'm not sure how to get it back to the clinic for an exam."

"Well, it's not going in that squad car," I said, nodding toward the pile of twisted metal and scattered glass in the middle of the road.

I looked at Jordan and put on my sweetest voice: "So what were you trying to tell me?"

"I was wondering how effective a tranquilizer that didn't work on Nerf would be on a raging ten-foot-tall bear."

The smile on my face froze. I turned toward the bear just as it was launching itself back onto its feet, towering above me.

"Maggie!" Mom cried.

Blam! Blam! Blam! Blam! Blam! Blam! A crouching Deputy Ruby emptied his pistol chamber into the animal, red patches oozing in its fur. The bear *roared*—and bolted toward the deputy, who fell over backward, his hands in front of his face.

As the bear arched over him, snarling, teeth out, I saw a flash from inside the woods and heard a *voop!*

The bear *exploded,* and the sky was filled with raining clumps of fur and bear meat.

Four young military officers stepped out of the woods, one hoisting a grenade launcher.

"The situation has been neutralized," the officer with the launcher said. "Please proceed back into town."

Mom's face was as white as the newly painted stripes on the road.

"Don't worry," I said, rubbing her shoulder blades. "We'll find another bear for you to examine."

"Thanks," she coughed out.

Jordan extended a hand to pull a bloodied Deputy Ruby to his feet.

"That was some bear," the deputy grunted, and we all started walking back to town.

CHAPTER 5

Jordan

CHARLIE SCREAMED WHEN I stepped in the door.

"Don't worry," I said. "It's not my blood."

Wearing a horrified expression, Mom leaned in and plucked something off my forehead.

"Is that fur?" she asked, holding up a sticky strip.

"Not mine, either," I said.

"You smell like charred meat," she said.

"Mind if I shower?"

Mom backed away with her hands up. She wasn't going to argue with that.

"Tico came by," she called up as I headed to the bathroom.

"Cool."

The house hadn't been looted. Actually, it looked fantastic.

"Mom, have you been dusting?" I asked when I reemerged, looking and smelling human again.

Mom walked to the big front window. "Who painted the house and planted the vegetable garden?"

"Maybe Dad got his army pals to make it look like new. Whatever. A few hours ago you were worried that the house would be looted and trashed. Now you're riled up that it looks too nice."

"I don't believe in perfect," Mom said.

With the phones out—cell and landline—I couldn't call Tico back, which was too bad. I missed him and his dry wisecracks. But I'd done quite enough walking on this day, thank you very much. I'd have to wait till football practice bright and early the next morning to talk to him.

When I saw him out on the field, he looked a bit chunkier around the middle, though he was still a crafty little guy. "Too much sitting around at camp," he complained, patting his stomach.

I didn't have that problem, having spent so much time rehabbing.

Tico was a speedy defensive back. I was a less speedy linebacker, though now when the coach called for team sprints, I found myself in the unusual position of leading the pack.

"I think that bear made you run faster, son," Coach Garner said, clapping me on the shoulder. "Maybe it taught you how to move—how to draw up all that energy inside and *go*."

"Yes, sir," I said.

Who told him about the bear?

"Aw, man, everyone knows about the bear. Are you kidding?" Tico said during a break. "I'm just glad animal control was able to shoo the thing out of town."

"Well, that's not what really—" I was interrupted by the coach's whistle to start the next set of drills.

Football practices usually began in August, a month earlier, so we had to get right to it. Classes started next week.

Coach Garner, a wiry man with a whistle always close to his mouth, ran a tight ship, with little chitchat on the field, just a lot of huffing, grunting, and thudding. Not long into the practice, he pulled me aside and said, "I want you to train with Coach Winters."

"But he's offense," I said. "I play linebacker, sir."

"I want to try you on offense. Running back, maybe. Run through the drills."

"Yes, sir."

Coach Winters, who was built like a defensive lineman, started me with more sprints, running alongside guys I'd never played with. Starters like them and benchwarmers like me rarely interacted. Yet I beat them with every sprint, every plant-and-cut, every stance-and-start. I was faster and more agile, turning on a dime. Every footstep was precise, and I felt like I never felt before: born to play. Usually I got winded easily, but not today. I was tearing it up.

To add to this surge of good feelings, I spotted Maggie sitting in the bleachers, witnessing the football clinic I was putting on. Even though we emailed a lot from our respective camps, I didn't know where we'd stand once we were back home. That she wasn't sick of me after yesterday's bear adventure was a good sign.

"Conners!" Coach Winters barked as we finished a cut-block drill.

"Yes, sir?" I said, jogging over to him.

"Bowman?" he called toward the hulking blond guy nearby.

"Yeah, Coach," said Luke Bowman, the starting running back.

"I've got a problem," the coach said. "I've got too many running backs and not enough quarterbacks. I want you both to join their drills and show me if I'm crazy or if one of you can throw as well as you run."

"Yes, sir," we both said.

Luke wasn't just the starting running back; he was the team's star, a ripped gym rat with calves like Virginia hams. A year ahead of me, he was a senior who'd made all–South Carolina last year and had been attracting recruiters before our season was cut short.

"Luke," Coach Winters said, and nodded toward the bleachers, "those guys here for you?"

Two men in suits were sitting and watching.

"Couldn't say, sir," Luke said.

"Well, play your ass off, just in case."

He motioned for us to go, and we jogged off toward the quarterbacks.

"You're better than last year," Luke said as we ran. "But I've been practicing all year for this. Do not screw me."

"Just playing the game," I said lightly.

"Part of the game is that I look good in front of those scouts."

"Look, man," I said with a straight face, "they're here to scout *me*. They heard I'm back in town, bringing the Chocolate Lightning."

Luke looked puzzled. "Yeah, right."

I laughed. "C'mon, Luke, they're not scouts. We've been in quarantine, remember? No one could even get in here."

"Then who the hell are they?"

I put my finger to my lips. "You ever see *The Matrix*?"

He scowled.

I never thought of myself as a quarterback. My arm strength was just okay, and I took too long to read the field.

Yet today, once again, I could do no wrong. Everything felt easier, like I was watching perfectly executed football from above. In a distraction drill, I couldn't be distracted. In an off-balance drill, I never got off balance.

We ran a few plays, some with me as the quarterback and some with me as the running back, and we did the same with Luke. Aiden Cole, the presumed starter after our previous QB graduated, got some reps, too, though they were unremarkable. I completed seven of nine passes, and Luke hit six of ten, not that I was counting.

I heard Maggie cheer whenever I completed a pass or got in a good run. The book on her lap remained closed.

Despite all this activity, my ribs didn't ache. The doctors at the sick camp had cleared me with no restrictions, even football and mountain biking. They said I'd be fine.

Coach Garner whistled us all together for a six-on-six scrimmage. With Aiden under center, Luke pounded through the line for five and eight yards. Then the coach called me in for a couple of running plays. I managed to get seven yards on the first attempt and broke away for a 41-yard touchdown on the second.

I looked at the bleachers and saw Maggie standing and cheering. I winked at her, not that she could see my eyes from behind my helmet.

Next, Luke was in at quarterback, me still at running back. I knew he would try to keep the ball out of my hands. But on the third play, he got ready to snap it, he audibled, and then he turned back to me to say he'd hand it off. I was ready.

Just like all my plays that day, this one seemed to unfold in slow motion. Luke jammed the ball into my rib cage, and

I darted toward where the hole was supposed to open up in the line. But no one on my team was blocking. Instead, the offensive line let everyone pass, and six guys, most of them mammoth, bore down on me in unison. I had nowhere to juke, nowhere to spin, nowhere to move. They led with their helmets, and I was pummeled—in my ankles, knees, torso, and, with a blazing, blinding crash after my feet lifted off the ground, my head.

I went down, face grinding into the dirt, the crush of bodies steamrolling over me and staying there. I tried to yell but had no air in my lungs. I gasped beneath a thousand-plus pounds of sweaty football players and their bulky equipment.

Then all went dark.

Where was I? I was still on the field, but now it looked postapocalyptic: torn up, parched, overgrown with weeds in a hazy rusty light, as if the sun couldn't make it past clouds of dirt in the air. Then came a twinge of déjà vu and a foggy speck emerging in the middle of my vision. The speck grew, moved closer, accompanied by a sound that suggested both laughing and crying. Voices came from all around me, behind me, where I couldn't turn to look.

The spot got bigger and brighter and morphed into a face: male, but with skin pulled back and stretched out like shrink-wrap. He was grinning a big, wide, evil grin—like Jack Nicholson in *The Shining,* like Jack Nicholson as the Joker, like Jack Nicholson as the Green Goblin.

No, the Green Goblin wasn't Jack Nicholson. That was Willem Dafoe. Or James Franco. Or Dane DeHaan.

For God's sake, Jordan, focus!

The face, so close in front of me, began to burn along its jaw, flickers moving upward, the skin blackening and crisping before actual flames appeared. Blisters rose and grew and popped.

Gross.

The creature laughed, his eyes the only things unaffected by the heat.

Then the fire spread to...*me.* Arms, legs, head...it was white-hot and excruciating and...

Darkness. Again.

CHAPTER 6

Maggie

JORDAN DIDN'T MOVE. He was out.

I ran down from the bleachers, ducking through the fence to get onto the football field. Those assholes. It was obvious what had happened: Luke called a screen to the team but told Jordan it was a draw, so when the play started, the offensive line let the defenders past them, and Jordan got hammered and went airborne. The crack of the helmet-to-helmet contact was loud and sickening.

The coaches jogged out to him, and I tried to join them, but one of the boosters—Mr. Kilpack, the local pharmacist—intercepted me.

"Let them do their work," he said, wearing a Mount Hope Gladiators polo shirt.

"Luke did that on purpose," I seethed.

"Looked like a broken play from here," Mr. Kilpack said. "Football is dangerous. But your fella will bounce right back."

My *fella*?

"Concussions can mess up someone for life," I muttered

to Mr. Drugstore, not that he heard me as he walked away. Given all his other injuries, should Jordan even be playing football?

Jordan's buddy Tico, who hadn't been part of the play, emerged from the crowd in the middle of the field and trotted my way.

"He's got little birds chirping around his head, but he's okay," Tico said, holding his helmet at his side.

"Thanks, Tico," I said. "That Luke is a piece of garbage."

"Well, I'm sure the recruiters were impressed by his decision-making skills," Tico said, nodding toward the bleachers on the opposite sideline. Two men in suits just stood there, arms at their sides. We'd had our share of players picked up by big schools over the years, so scouts weren't an uncommon sight, but no one would wear a suit in September in South Carolina. I was in shorts and a sleeveless top and could feel the sweat trickling down my back.

Through a gap in the crowd, I spotted Jordan slowly rising onto his elbows, his helmet off, his head swaying from side to side. One of the assistant coaches supposedly had a degree in sports medicine, but this town could have used a real doctor at this point. Who could examine him if anything really was wrong?

Mom always had wanted to be a doctor—a people doctor—but she fell in love with my dad and quit school. It wasn't until I was born and Dad left us that she went back to school to become a vet. Her recent medical experience was greater with horses than humans.

I looked back to the bleachers, and the recruiters were gone. Practice was nearing its end, and Coach Garner ordered the players to run a few laps around the field before he helped Jordan to his feet. Jordan took a few steps and wasn't favoring either leg. He also wasn't holding his arms gingerly or wincing at all. The coach held Jordan's helmet, and the two walked off the field. Finally, he slapped Jordan on the butt—I've never understood that particular ritual— and handed him his helmet.

"You looked great out there, kid," Coach Garner said.

"Aside from imitating a crash-test dummy, sure," Jordan replied with a forced laugh.

The coach took off, and Jordan made his way toward me with a wide, bright smile.

"You okay?" I asked, wanting to sound less concerned than I was.

"You should've seen the other guy," he said, rubbing his hand over the back of his head.

"I did. He seemed fine."

"Well," Jordan said, "looks can be deceiving."

I laughed and raised my hand—I wanted to rub his upper arm, tell him I was worried about him, but then the coach yelled over. "Hit the showers, Conners!"

"Yes, sir!" Jordan said.

"See you later?" I asked.

"Sure," he said. "I've got to help my mom clean up the garden this afternoon, but maybe we can go get ice cream tonight?"

"I'd like that," I said.

I thought of giving him a hug but opted instead to stand there awkwardly.

"Well, bye," he said, and as he turned to walk toward the locker room, I noticed something I'd missed yesterday: the scar on the back of his head, about three inches of pink snaking through his hair like a river in a dense forest, with a few spindly streams heading off to the sides.

How much surgery had he had? What did they do? And whatever was done, could he now withstand such blows to the head? Could *anyone*? I might have to break it to him over ice cream that I wasn't so sure about this him-playing-football thing.

But he wasn't the only one who was damaged goods.

I had convinced myself that I had cancer.

No one had diagnosed me, but there was a lump in my breast that wasn't there before we'd all been irradiated. That's a bad sign, right?

I didn't tell my mom because I wasn't sure about it and didn't want to freak her out. We were far from rich, and if I let my mom know about the lump, she'd max out her credit cards trying to get every available test.

Besides, sixteen was too young for breast cancer, wasn't it? I didn't know how my breasts were *supposed* to feel anyway. I hadn't had them that long, relatively speaking, and I'd heard that one might be a bit different from the other. It's not like while I was in camp I could read all about it on the internet. Now that I was back in town, I still couldn't.

Then again, anyone who researches *any* symptom online will conclude that she or he has cancer, so maybe I wasn't missing much.

Still, we lived in the latest place with a name that had become a synonym for nuclear disaster. Just because I wasn't in the sick camp didn't mean that I—or anyone else— wasn't sick.

Well, this was a cheerful train of thought that I was riding. I'd have been better off worrying some more about Jordan and his surgically repaired, battered head, poor guy. And thinking about his smile.

And then his frown when he learned that *I have cancer and might die.*

Maybe we could watch *The Fault in Our Stars* together.

Get ahold of yourself, Maggie. You've got a plan to diagnose yourself without bankrupting your mom. No point in doing anything or telling anyone till you're sure.

I'd never wanted to be less sure of anything in my life.

CHAPTER 7

Jordan

THE WATER FELT good on my muscles and not only because they'd just *been on fire*. Seriously, what was up with that? I'd been hammered before but never with the side effect of a freaky flaming face setting me ablaze. That didn't feel like a vision. It felt like . . . *a freaky flaming face setting me ablaze.*

As I came to on the field, what felt like fire gave way to the regular ol' heat of the late-morning sun. I'd never been happier to view the sight of six guys who'd just pummeled me into oblivion.

My shower was long and hot. Usually I wasted no time getting in and out of the locker room—I wasn't crazy about the whole communal-cleansing thing—but the other guys were still running laps.

In the sick camp, I had been cleared for exercise three months earlier but didn't do much more than running. I yearned for a weight room so I could gain some bulk for football, but there was no gym. The physical therapy consisted mostly of stretching and running; I circled the camp's perimeter over and over, gaining speed and endurance. I worked on my sprinting, though given that I was running alone, I wasn't measuring myself against anyone else.

After finishing my shower, I examined my scars in the mirror. The one on the right side of my chest, where they'd gone in to fix my punctured lung and do whatever they did to my ribs, seemed to be glowing. Normally when ribs break, you don't do anything for them. Two seasons ago, Lance Butler cracked a couple and was back before the final game. But when you puncture an organ or two—aside from my lung, the ribs gouged my liver—they have to open you up and put everything back where it's supposed to go.

The zipper on my left arm ran from the elbow to the wrist, and the one around my knee was bright pink. My scars looked *fresh*. My mom told me that if I'd been in a real hospital trauma center, the doctors would have minimized the scarring, but apparently not military surgeons. Fat chance of finding a plastic surgeon at sick camp.

I was standing in my boxers by my locker when the rest of the team tromped in, their cleats clonking against the tile floor.

"Well, look who's upright," drawled Troy Cameron as he stopped between the banks of lockers. I'd known him since elementary school. He was a short, fat kid with a red bowl cut who'd grown up to be a tall, stocky kid with a red bowl cut. I once tried and failed to argue him out of pulling the legs off a frog.

Now I said nothing.

Luke stood next to Troy, both in full pads, helmets in their hands. "Maybe Jordan doesn't know," Luke said with pretend concern. "Troy here is the one who nailed you with that sweet head shot."

"Knocked you clean out," Troy chimed in.

Allow me to pause here and point out the obvious. I'm black—mixed race, actually, but to these folks, black. Luke and Troy are white. We're in South Carolina. Mount Hope has a long, complicated history when it comes to race, and I'm sure you could read about it online, assuming where you live didn't experience a nuclear meltdown and internet access isn't cut off for no apparent reason. My town is home to a lot of white people and a fair number of black people, with some Hispanics, such as Tico's family, thrown in to boot. We've all been living together for a long time, and sometimes "issues" come up, but mostly everyone knows who's who and what's what and gets on with life.

That is to say that these two big white dudes giving this charming black brother some grief wasn't a racial issue. They were just mouth-breathing motherfuckers.

I turned toward Troy and said in my most sincere voice, "I forgive you."

"*Forgive* me?" Troy said. "Oh, ho, I'm not looking for forgiveness."

"Aw, I've seen you at church with your family in your cute suit and bow tie," I said. "I'm sure God will understand."

"God is telling me to splatter your brains across the floor, Conners," he huffed.

Jesus, this guy. "Have a blessed day." I smiled.

Luke stepped forward, his lips curling upward. "Do you forgive *me*?"

"Hey, man," I said, "I know quarterback isn't your position, so I can't blame you for calling a shitty play that got your teammate injured. I'm sure those scouts won't hold it against you, either."

"You listen to me, you little bitch," Luke said. "I don't know what your problem is, but today was *my* day. They were here to see *me*. I've started at running back since I was a sophomore, and you're not going to take that away from me."

"You *did* pull off that nice scamper into the end zone, though. Oh, wait, that was . . . me."

"Oh, man," he said, licking his lips like he was about to eat a whole pig with the skin still on. "I'm gonna enjoy this." He handed his helmet to Troy, took a step toward me.

The other players were all clustered around us now.

"You gotta be kidding, man," Tico said. "My guy was just out cold and is standing there in his underwear, and now you're gonna fight him?"

"Shut the fuck up, Tico," Luke barked.

"Take off your pads at least, pretty boy," Tico returned.

That's my man—not about to back down.

Luke turned toward him, weighing whether he wanted to fight this battle on two fronts.

"Thanks, Tico, but I got this," I called out, directing Luke's attention back to me. I didn't know what inspired me to do that or, then, to position myself with one foot forward, the other back, and my hands hanging down.

There wasn't much room with lockers on both sides of us and a bench down the middle. Luke shuffle-stepped toward me, and I backed up.

Images of where I could hit him flooded my head, as if I'd made anatomical notes: ankles, knees, hips, stomach, elbows, throat, chin, face, ears.

He swatted out with one hand, trying to grapple my arm, and I angled out of reach, bouncing on the balls of my feet.

An odd calm came over me. I wasn't thinking about how much I hated Luke right now or how badly Troy had hurt me. I just was observing Luke's body, the way it moved, his stance, his center of gravity—and how slow he seemed.

When he swatted again, I grabbed his hand and yanked him toward me, and with my other hand, I thrust the tips of my fingers into the spongy base of his throat, lightning-fast. I let go just as quickly, and he stumbled to the floor, hacking a pained cough.

Luke wasn't about to admit defeat, though. Instead, he returned to his fighting crouch. *Fine.* I whipped the side of my foot into his cheekbone, and he flopped onto the bench.

Troy jumped forward but couldn't get around his big dumb friend to reach me. Instead, he threw the helmets at me, one after the other, leaving dents in the lockers behind me as I easily dodged them.

Luke rose up again. What a dummy.

He stood on my side of the bench, while Troy crouched opposite us. Troy wore a tentative expression, like a confused ox. Luke looked pissed and uncorked a right hook. I leaned away from it, let it pass, and pivoted to smash his fist into the lockers. He howled, then tried to grab me with his other hand, but I stepped backward again. I had room to do that one more time before I was up against the wall.

Luke moved to get alongside me, and I didn't want that to happen. I was tired of fighting this guy. I leaped forward and kicked, the top of my foot colliding with the side of his knee. He fell, screaming, his leg bending in the wrong direction.

I turned just as Troy lunged toward me, so I dropped down and punched him between his chest pads and his belt. He gasped, and as he grabbed his stomach, I threw an uppercut and felt and heard the crunch of his shattering jaw. He started making noises like a wounded large animal that needed to be put down.

I popped back up into ready stance, but there was no need.

"What the hell did they teach you over in the sick camp, Conners?" Coach Garner asked as he broke through the crowd. "Some kind of special-forces crap?"

I relaxed my muscles.

"He didn't start it, sir," Tico said over Luke's shrieks and Troy's moaning.

"No shit," Coach Garner said through gritted teeth. "Who starts a fight in their boxers?"

"I broke Troy's jaw," I said, to myself as much as the coach. It was dawning on me that I was in deep shit. "And something tore in Luke's knee, maybe his ACL."

"Ya think, Conners? See, and I thought he was showing us a new yoga position."

Coach Garner turned to Coach Winters. "Call an ambulance, if you can figure out how."

He pivoted back to me: "In my office. Dressed. *Now.*"

CHAPTER 8

Maggie

WE HAD TO put Nerf down. The way he kept banging his face against the cage bars, he was going to destroy himself anyway. He just wouldn't stop.

I'd lived in a vet's office long enough to see dozens of animals put to sleep. But keeping it together for Nerf was tough.

I threw some treats out to him in the backyard, and as he nibbled at them, Mom slipped a catchpole, with a loop of cord at one end, over his head and pinned him to the ground. While he thrashed around, I held the syringe and looked for an opening. I had to move quickly as I injected him with a sedative and backed away. This potent medicine calmed him down enough to let us finish the job, with Mom handing me the catchpole as she applied a syringe of pentobarbital.

I whispered to him every loving thought in my head as his breathing slowed and eventually stopped, a puddle of urine spreading in the dirt as his muscles loosened.

If we buried every animal we had to put down, our whole yard would be a cemetery. We didn't make an exception for

Nerf. Mom had a deal with the mortuary to send animals there for cremation, so she and I picked up Nerf's still-warm body and deposited it into a plastic bag. We said nothing as we took care of business—no words of farewell or anything—but after she and I went inside to wash up, Mom put her arms around me, and I sobbed inconsolably over that doofy dog.

That evening Mom went down to the Savannah Grill, which serves okay food but mainly functions as the town bar. She'd gone there the previous night, too, and I wondered whether she was meeting someone. Well, she was allowed. My dad hadn't been in the picture since I was two, and Mom deserved to have some kind of social life.

I jumped at an unfamiliar sound: the office phone ringing.

"Hello, Mount Hope Veterinary Hospital," I answered.

"Hey, Maggie," Jordan said, and immediately I detected some sort of question mark in his voice.

"Hey, Jordan," I said. "How's your head feeling? You okay?"

"Yeah, sure, weirdly. You want the good news or bad news first?"

"Does this involve our ice-cream date tonight?"

"No."

"Then bad news first."

"Okay, but first some good news: The phones are working again."

I laughed, pacing the office floor. "No shit."

"Landlines only and no long-distance, but still."

"Right, and the nonfunctioning cellular networks are the bad news."

"No, the bad news is I got suspended from school."

"Wait, what?" I stopped pacing. "School hasn't even started yet."

"I know, and the suspension starts immediately and will be over by the time classes begin next week, so it's kind of bullshit. But here's the thing: I got in a fight in the locker room."

"Right after I saw you? When you were going back there to recuperate from that . . . ?" The image flashed in my mind and stirred up my stomach: Jordan flying, taking a brutal head shot, and crashing to the ground.

"That would be when," he said.

"You've got to be kidding. Have you ever even been in a fight? Who were you fighting?"

"Troy Cameron and Luke Bowman."

"Oh, fuck."

"What?"

"Nothing." I don't drop many f-bombs, but with those two thugs, this couldn't have ended well. "Are you okay? Did you get in any good shots at least? Are you in the hospital?"

"*Someone* is," he responded, and let out the weirdest little laugh.

I tried to process all of this. He certainly sounded okay.

"All right, Jordan, what gives?" I asked. "How big of a brawl was this, and how did you survive?"

"Honestly, I don't know," he said. "It was the two of them against me. But this was the kind of fight that you fantasize about."

"I don't fantasize about fights."

"I broke Troy's jaw. They're wiring it shut right now at the army hospital. Luke tore his MCL and meniscus. I was a machine. They couldn't touch me."

"They couldn't touch you on the football field, either— until they did."

"I'm telling you, it wasn't me doing the kicking and punching. I mean, it was, but I knew stuff that I shouldn't know, like I'd been trained by a fighting master but didn't remember it."

"You've watched *The Matrix* too many times. I hope you don't have to dodge any bullets."

"You think you're being funny, but everything really did slow down for me."

I seated myself in the rickety wooden swivel chair behind the office's main desk.

"Jordan," I said, "you just beat up Troy Cameron and Luke Bowman, two of the biggest douchebags in school. You're going to be hero of the nerds. So suspension aside, that can't be the bad news."

"Well, I probably have a target on my back now if I ever show my face on the south side of town. Fortunately, I'm not visiting the Mansions of Mount Hope anytime soon."

"How about the Tastee Freeze?"

"Uh, rain check?"

"Sure," I said, trying to keep the disappointment out of my voice.

"But, yeah, the bad news for Luke is that after what I did to his knee, he's out for the season. And the good news for me is that just before he suspended me, Coach made me the new starting quarterback."

CHAPTER 9

Maggie

AFTER I HUNG up with Jordan, I kicked myself for wimping out about not telling him *my* bad news. I'd thought of revealing it over ice cream, not that that wouldn't have been awkward, too. I almost called him back, but now wasn't the time. I needed to confirm that it actually was bad news.

My mind racing, I walked into the exam room, turned on the light, and stepped over to the new X-ray machine. We'd installed it only a few months before the evacuation, and it was one of the first things Mom checked on when we came back. It was super expensive, and the bills for it had been piling up. One good thing about the evacuation was that the government stepped in to freeze all of Mount Hope residents' payments: cars, mortgages, X-ray machines...

I slipped a CD into the old boom box sitting beside a yellowed lamp. We didn't have a lot of music choices among the discs stacked crookedly on the shelf, but Devo's *Freedom of Choice* had become a personal favorite and not just because of the band's red flower-pot hats. It's hard to feel completely forlorn when listening to Devo and that herky-jerky beat.

"She's just the girl, she's just the girl..."

I took off my hoodie, leaving on my "I Can't Believe It's Not Butter!" T-shirt, which I found in a thrift store and couldn't resist. I'd taken X-rays before but only on animals. Their fur was thicker than my shirt, so I figured this would work.

I switched on the machine, and it shot a square of light onto the table. I lay on my back and angled my left breast into the square.

Our town had been irradiated; how much was unclear, but I knew it was super rare for someone my age to get breast cancer. In one of my mom's books, I read that 80 percent of lumps were benign and that teenage breasts can be lumpy. Well, that was exactly the sexiest thing I'd ever heard.

So why was I scared shitless?

The machine didn't have a timer—it wasn't designed for taking your own X-rays—so this would be tricky. Through trial and error, I learned that there was a three-second delay between hitting the button and the machine taking a picture.

For the first effort, I didn't make it back onto the table fast enough, and the image was a blur. The second attempt was decent, if a bit fuzzy, but the third looked good, as did the fourth, which I took just in case.

Back on the office computer, I pulled up the images after moving them into a folder titled "Maggie Homework" and deleting the originals from the X-ray machine. I pulled out Mom's medical encyclopedia and looked up a "normal" chest X-ray.

That image was clear. Mine was cloudy. Some of the clouds were low, down by my liver and spleen. I couldn't see even an outline of my breasts, and I wondered: *If X-rays go through skin and tissue, would they show a tumor?* The medical encyclopedia made me think they would, at least to some extent.

On my images, I could see a blob that looked similar to the encyclopedia's tumor pictures, but it was hard to be sure. Even doctors often needed to refer such matters to specialists.

I pulled up the first two X-rays I'd taken, the ones that didn't come out right. The first was a mass of clouds, no doubt stemming from my movement as I tried to position myself on the table. The other one was a little clearer but showed the right side of my body: arm, shoulder, and collarbone.

Wait, what was that?

Leaning closer to the screen, I stared at a single spot of bright white on my upper arm. I'd seen such things in veterinary X-rays, when dogs still had their collars on. A spot like that would have to be something dense, like metal or plastic. Maybe something on the table or my T-shirt got in the picture?

None of the other three images showed that arm.

The clock read 8:00 p.m. Mom wouldn't be home for another hour at least. I went back into the exam room and looked all over the table for something that might leave that pill-like mark. Nothing. Maybe I'd knocked the object off the table when I was rushing to get back under the X-ray beam, but I found nothing on the floor, either.

I took two more X-rays of my upper arm, breathing deep and trying to be as motionless as possible. When I opened these images, it was clear that something was in my right deltoid.

I dug through the medical encyclopedia again, looking for an X-ray image that might match. One person had swallowed a key, another a wedding ring. A kid had gulped down a penny, and another had jammed a pearl way up his nose. There also were X-rays in which people had inserted more bizarre objects into more bizarre places. I moved quickly past those.

Nothing matched what I had.

Then I remembered: That shoulder was where I had gotten my most painful flu shot ever, at the army clinic in the evacuation camp. It had ached for days and left a large red spot. Flu shots had never left any kind of lasting mark. Mom got one, too. Everyone had. The flu vaccine wouldn't look like a pill, of course.

I needed to tell someone. I picked up the phone to call Jordan but stopped myself. When he asked why I was X-raying myself, I'd have to tell him about the lump and my suspicion that I had cancer. I wasn't just afraid that he'd freak out. I also didn't want to talk to him about my breasts. I *liked* this guy and was hoping we might reach a romantic place before we started getting all clinical.

I *should* have told my mom, but she'd kill me for X-raying myself—six times. Patients were supposed to wear lead blankets that covered everything but the areas being filmed, and the technician was supposed to stand behind the protected partition.

As for the lump, where would she take me? To the army doctors? They're the ones who had given us the "flu shots" in the first place.

I needed another way to find out: What the hell was in my arm?

CHAPTER 10

Jordan

MOM WAS, SHALL we say, displeased about my suspension.

"You *what*?" she snapped, stepping away from the pot of jarred spaghetti sauce that she had freshened up with mushrooms, onions, peppers, and tomatoes from our garden. The lines at the grocery store were so long, she'd said, that she was going to cook what we had for now. "Getting suspended before classes start is impressive even for you."

"On the bright side," I said, "I won't actually miss any school."

"Well, how is it a suspension, then?"

"I'm barred from the school for now, including practices. But, hey, guess who's the new starting quarterback?"

"You play DEE-fense!" Charlie chimed in.

"Well, now I play OFF-fense!" I responded. "I'll be dishing it out."

"Sounds like you got off to an early start," Mom grumbled, giving the sauce a stir.

"And I won't miss any games," I continued, ignoring Mom while Charlie ran upstairs.

Actually, I wasn't sure about that—not about just me but

the whole team. Our main rival, the Canville Badgers, already had canceled their game against us for health concerns, and I wasn't sure whether the army was allowing any outsiders into Mount Hope yet. Our first game was scheduled for a week from Friday.

"Hey, Mom," I said, "have they opened up the roads? Can people come into town?"

"No," she said, putting the sauce on simmer and stepping into the living room to sit in the easy chair across from me on the couch. Both of us faced the TV, which, of course, wasn't working.

"You'd think we could get some kind of news," she said irritably, hitting a button on the remote and watching an error message pop up on the screen. "Why should the power-plant problems—which supposedly were *solved*—affect our satellite?"

"I'm sure things will be fine," I said. "They said everything should be up and running in a week or so."

"*They* fed us that line in the camp, too," she grumbled. "It was always 'next week' and 'shortly' and 'as soon as possible.' Oh, yeah? Define 'possible.' We haven't seen your father in four months, and I had to jump through hoops to get one phone conversation with him every week. Now we're back, and there's supposedly no radiation, and everything is safe, so where is he? Why's he still living at the nuclear plant? It's a fifteen-minute drive."

"Well, we *did* get to come home," I said. "They didn't lie about that."

"They also didn't tell us that everything in our house and in town would be fixed. They're very selective about what they tell us."

"Yeah, it's terrible that everything got fixed up," I said.

Mom slapped her hand against the end table. "Okay, smart boy who was chased by a bear and just put two kids into the hospital, *you* tell *me* that everything is normal."

"Everything is normal," I said.

She shook her head.

"I do what my mother tells me to do!" I protested, putting on a smile and waving jazz hands at her.

"You beat up two big-time athletes from the south side and ended their seasons. You know who else lives on the south side? All the bosses: my boss, your father's boss, and anyone who has any influence in this town. So keep joking your way through this, and see how that works out."

Sometimes my mom is where fun goes to die.

"Okay, fine, I feel like crap now," I said, putting my feet up on the ottoman as Dad usually did when he sat in that chair. "Happy? They started the fight. I defended myself. Would you feel better if I were in the hospital now instead of them?"

"Of course not, you nitwit," Mom spat out. "And the coach said you didn't start it. But he also told me you were overly violent and cruel, and that's not how we raised you."

"Mom," I said, holding my hands up, "when have I ever been in a fight before? Do you think I did this on purpose?"

"I think you were tired of those boys bothering you your whole life, and you wanted to hurt them," she said, popping up the recliner's footrest.

I sighed. If I'd had time to think about it, I might have reached that very conclusion. But I didn't have time. They came after me, and I eliminated them as threats, with unplanned/planned precision. It was as simple as that.

Mom was quiet, her head back against the absurdly

cushioned chair, her eyes half closed. "Jordan, this is how you're going to face those bullies: You will apologize."

"What?"

"You'll do it because you're the bigger man. They may spit in your face, but it doesn't matter. You'll apologize and mean it."

"And if I don't?"

"You will," Mom said. "Or *I'll* make you sorry."

I let out a long, slow breath in the manner of the meditation exercises we'd both learned. Whether she would follow through on such a threat didn't matter. She knew I could never defy her. I said nothing, which for me amounted to surrender.

Mom's expression softened. "You know they'll talk about this being two white boys."

"You mean two big white boys bullying a slender black kid in his skivvies?"

She snorted out a laugh. "'Skivvies.' You and your vocabulary. Yes, that. But, no, not really."

"People don't have to turn everything into a racial thing."

"Just like you and Maggie."

If I could've shot laser beams from my eyes, Mom's head would have been soot by the time I said, "What *about* me and Maggie?"

"Come on, people talk about you and your pretty little blond girl."

"And?"

"And we're still not living in a post-racial society no matter what some people want to believe."

"You should know," I shot back. We almost never talked about the fact that Mom was black and Dad was a quadroon or octoroon or whatever he was that allowed him to "pass" in certain situations and gave me my warm, Obamaesque skin tone.

"I *do* know," she said—and might as well have dropped the mic right there.

"Mom," I said, "Maggie and I have been friends forever, and nothing has ever happened between us."

She arched her eyebrow at me.

"Look, I wish I had something more salacious to report on this subject," I added.

"Do you?"

Yeah, I did. At some point I might even have to act on this feeling, because, damn, what was the point of being gossiped about if you weren't actually getting to enjoy the thing you were supposedly guilty of? Also, I really liked Maggie, and there was something pathetic about my having the courage to beat the shit out of those two jock assholes while being petrified of, I don't know, holding her hand. I bet it would be warm and soft, too.

"Just be careful," Mom said.

"I'm the most cautious dude in town," I said with my most charming smile, then muttered under my breath, "Maybe other people shouldn't fuck with me. Bears, neither."

"What?"

"Nothing."

"You said *something*."

I didn't know where that had come from, actually. I never talked to myself, out loud or in my head, with that kind of aggression.

"Must've been the concussion talking."

Mom got up and placed her hand on my forehead. It felt good.

"When you get hit and lose consciousness, that's a traumatic brain injury," she said. "You'll have to take it easy for a few days and see how you feel."

"I will, Mom. Love you."

That night the burning face came back to me in my dreams. I was tied down to a table, with restraints on my arms and legs and a metal collar around my neck. As I struggled to get loose, I saw a pair of hands peel open my abdomen as if it were a box and then start pulling my organs out and placing them onto a metal table.

I didn't see the face until I turned my head to the left and was confronted by a huge, unnaturally wide smile with rows of razor-sharp teeth that gleamed like metal in the faint light. Then his head started to burn, and I couldn't look away as he laughed, the flesh blackening, cracking, blistering, and popping.

Even at this moment of horror, I tried to make a wisecrack— something about how this was what happened when Rice Krispies went to hell (no one said jokes have to make sense in dreams)—but couldn't get any words out. Then I saw my dad standing a foot from me in his white lab coat, and from deep inside me erupted a howl for help. I howled and howled, and he did nothing.

Just stood there as the flaming man's hands tore me apart.

CHAPTER 11

Maggie

I JOLTED UP in bed and looked at the clock. 4:14 a.m. What had awakened me? Nerf?

No, not Nerf. Ugh.

Mom's voice was coming from downstairs. What was she doing up so early? Some animal emergency, no doubt.

I got out of bed and stretched one arm, then the other, over my head, my oversize Pure Prairie League T-shirt (I was a killer thrift-store shopper) flapping against my waist. The air felt humid and stuffy, which was usually the case when we had no animals inside; Mom liked to save on air-conditioning bills when she could. In her view, having a cat in the kennel was good reason to cool the place, but having a daughter upstairs was not.

I descended the stairs softly to find Mom in the front doorway leaning against the jamb, her arms folded. She was wearing shorts and a wrinkled button-up, as if she'd gone to sleep in her clothes.

"That's ridiculous," she said, sounding tired and resigned.

"I swear on a stack of Bibles," responded a raspy female voice from outside.

"Hey," I said.

Mom looked up at me with red eyes, something I hadn't seen for a long time.

"You know Rachel," she said, and looked out the door. I peered out and saw Rachel Anderson smoking a cigarette in the dark. She lived a few blocks down, in a house where they kept goats.

With the nearest streetlight a block away on Main, most of the light outside came from our yellow "24-Hour Emergency" neon sign. I stepped outside, if for no other reason than to get into the cooler air.

"Rachel's sheepdog, I think you've seen him," Mom said. "He had to get stitches last year. Anyway, I just put him in the back. Same condition Nerf had."

"He's been a good dog," Rachel said. "Had him seven years, maybe longer. He went after the goats as soon as we got back from the camp. I had to put one of them down. Neck wound." She took a long pull on her cigarette.

"I swear," Mom said, "something's in the air."

"Radiation," I said, and Mom shook her head.

"An army guy showed me his Geiger counter," she said. "The levels are safe."

Rachel dropped her cigarette butt and mashed it into the concrete with the tip of her shoe. "Then why won't they let us out?"

"Aren't we out now?" I asked.

"Not out of the camps," she said. "Out of town. Head south, and Jefferson Bridge is out. They've been working on it since before the evacuation."

"Well, yes," Mom said, "but we can still go north up through Canville."

"Closed off," Rachel said. "Kent drove there just this last evening—he was headed up to the gun show—and he said they've got a tank on the road and a bunch of barricades. He was told we could get shipments in, and we won't run out of food, but no one can go in or out for now."

"How long is that going to go on?" Mom asked.

"Who knows? It's not like we can check online or the TV for updates."

"How about the *Sentinel*?" I asked. "That should be back, right?"

Mom waved a hand. "That's hardly a paper. It's Ronnie Stevenson's two-page diary with ten pages of ads."

Rachel lit up another cigarette. "So, they haven't taken away freedom of the press, just access to the worthwhile press."

"How is this not a big story?" I asked. "A whole town under lockdown, with no way to communicate with the outside world. You'd think *Dateline* or somebody would be out here with news vans and helicopters."

"Right," Mom said. "Send 'em an email."

Mom wasn't usually the sarcastic type. She seemed rattled.

"But, hey," she said, stepping out from the door and onto the concrete, "they fixed our sign."

I glanced up at it. The "u" had been burned out for years, so it had read "24-Ho r Emergency."

"We never did get to experience a twenty-four-whore emergency," Mom said.

Rachel laughed—a coarse, tobacco laugh. "If Mount Hope is going to be our lifelong prison, you two will be good cellmates."

I smiled for the first time since waking up, but this nice

moment was interrupted by a spasm of barking from inside. Rachel's dog was waking up.

"Do you want the ashes?" Mom asked Rachel. "Some people do."

"No," Rachel said, tapping out her cigarette. "Dispose of him how you like. Tiger's never been a pet; he's a workin' dog. Chasing the goats, rounding them up. We'll get a new one. I heard Eugene out by the drive-in just had a litter of border collies. We'll pick one up and get him to work."

Mom nodded. "I delivered those pups. They'll be good, not a runt in the bunch."

"Well," Rachel said, "thank you for this." She held out her forearm, marked by a dog bite, deep and ugly, that Mom apparently had stitched up. "You'll send me a bill? I'm sorry to get you up in the middle of the night."

"That's why we're here, Rachel," Mom said.

After an exchange of handshakes, Rachel gathered up her rope and muzzle, loaded them into her pickup, and drove off.

"I hope we're not trapped in this town. What if we have a medical emergency?" I asked. I still hadn't decided to tell her what I thought was going on with me.

She shrugged. Apparently, we were on our own.

CHAPTER 12

Jordan

WHEN I WOKE up and looked at my watch, I was surprised to see it already was 9:45 a.m. I didn't usually sleep that late. Well, I had a concussion—and my head ached like a guy suddenly cut off from a heavy coffee habit—so maybe that was a factor.

Coffee sure would have hit the spot around now, preferably something made with freshly ground beans (light roast, please; African origins preferable to South American) in a French press or a pour-over. I was a connoisseur, so I suffered in the camps as they used up what must've been a stash of Maxwell House cans dating back to the 1960s. ADHD medication is basically a stimulant, and I had found that a good, tall morning mug of coffee—with that oh-so-popular stimulant, caffeine—helped me to focus. Right now, I certainly needed to do that.

When I opened my bedroom door, I didn't smell coffee but something even more pleasing: bacon. Fatback. That could mean only one thing.

I didn't bother getting dressed, just ran down the stairs

in my T-shirt and basketball shorts and rounded the kitchen door to see...

"Dad!"

There he sat at the kitchen table. He'd shaved his head and had lost the close-cropped beard he'd worn ever since I could remember. He was clean-cut, like a different person. Mom stood at the stove, three frying pans going, a cast-iron family heirloom in the back with slices of fatback sizzling and popping.

Dad stood up and wrapped his arms around me. I shook off my recollection of the nightmare and rubbed his bald head. "Please don't tell me this is from the radiation," I said.

"Radiation gives you cancer," he said seriously as he sat back down at the table. "Chemotherapy is what makes you lose your hair. I've never had my radiation tag go off, and I've certainly not been prescribed chemo."

Charlie spoke up. "Dad said that he's on R and R. Rock and roll!"

Dad smiled, yet I could see him forcing it. I aimed a theatrical wink at Charlie while Mom placed a plate of pancakes on the table next to a bowl of her signature peach compote. She was going all out.

"What's it been like?" I asked. "What do they have you doing?"

"My role is the same. I monitor a workstation and make sure that our cooling systems are working."

"Did you paint the house?" I asked. "And tend the garden?"

"That was the military. They've gone to great lengths to make sure your return was smooth and positive."

I nodded. I realized that after many months apart, our free-flowing family dynamic might need to shake off the rust, but still, something was off. It was in the clipped way he spoke, how he wasn't joking with us or cracking a believable smile. Maybe he'd grown too used to talking to other engineers and military folks. Or something else was occupying his mind.

"Does the Tin Man need some oil?" I asked him.

"What?" he said, turning to me with steely eyes.

"You seem a little...tight," I said, my voice growing softer with each word. I liked to joke around with my dad, but I didn't sass him.

He kept his eyes fixed on me for a couple of uncomfortable beats, then put on a stiff smile. "It's good to see you, son."

"You too, Dad." I changed tactics. "So what's the scoop? We're not getting much in the way of the 411."

Mom slapped a serving fork onto the table. "Jordan, when have you *ever* dialed 411?"

I turned back to my dad. "How goes the cleanup?"

"There is no cleanup. Everything worked exactly the way it was supposed to work."

"Then why did the evacuation take so long?"

"You're familiar with how the plant operates?"

"Mmm-hmm. Nuclear fission, fueled by uranium, heats water to become steam, which drives turbines, which power electrical generators." My dad was one of those physics guys who'd given me little choice in learning this stuff.

"Right," he said, "and then all the steam turns back into water in those big cooling towers and gets reused while the electricity supplies us with power."

I waited for him to say more, but instead he took a leisurely bite of pancake. "So what was the problem?" I asked as I loaded pancakes onto my own plate and slathered them in compote. "Are we all getting irradiated?"

"No," he said.

"Okay, I'll bite," I finally said. *"So what happened here?"*

"Like at Three Mile Island, there was human error: The wrong valve was opened when someone thought the pipes were empty. Before the water could be contained, one of the turbines exploded and threw radioactive material several miles, mostly on the east side of town. The reactor was damaged, and there was no way to save it, so we've spent the last year sealing it off like a sarcophagus. Inside the lead-lined room, there's a deadly force that can destroy whole populations."

"Holy shit," I blurted out, prompting a dirty look from Mom, giggles from Charlie, and nothing from my dad. And here I'd thought we lived in an inconsequential little town. "Are you building the sarcophagus?" I asked him.

He shook his head and put down his fork. "I'm a mechanical engineer. I'm trying to get the power up and running in the remaining reactors. The military did all the concrete work on the sarcophagus."

"So, bottom line," Mom cut in, "is it safe to be here?"

He stared down at his plate. "You have nothing to worry about."

I chewed my pancakes slowly, taking this all in while trying to think of a way to keep the conversation going— and to knock Dad off of autopilot. He hadn't even asked me about my time at the camp or how my injuries were healing. Maybe he was just tired.

"Who's Ishango?" Charlie chirped up.

Dad gave a start and caught himself—I saw it. It was as if he'd willed his face to turn to stone. Charlie was oblivious, jamming a huge pancake wedge into his mouth.

"Where did you hear that name?" Dad asked quietly.

"You," Charlie said with his mouth full. "When you were on your walkie-talkie."

"Is that who you're working with?" I asked Dad, trying to give him an out. I knew he was dealing with lots of classified information that he couldn't share with us.

"Yes," he said. "That's who I'm working with. I can't say much about it."

"Ishango," Charlie repeated, and I swear Dad gave another start. "Ish-AN-go."

"That's enough, Charlie," Dad said.

"Sounds like he's from AF-rica!" Charlie added.

Dad gave a mirthless smile. "In a way." He stood. "I have to go. My furlough was only for the morning."

Charlie hurled himself into Dad's arms but was rewarded with only a limp pat on his head. I bristled—after almost a year away from us, why wasn't he being nicer to Charlie? Or to Mom? Or to me, for that matter? He was so formal.

"You're *leaving*?" Mom asked.

"Afraid so," Dad said, not breaking his stride out of the kitchen. "Good-bye," he called out, not looking back as he opened the front door and shut it behind him. Mom stood stock-still in the kitchen, the spatula in her hand. He hadn't kissed her good-bye or given any of us a farewell hug. I took the spatula from her and turned on the faucet to start the dishes.

"Wasn't it nice to see Dad, Charlie?" I asked over my shoulder.

"He looked weird," Charlie said. "I miss his beard. It made him funner."

"Me too," I said. "I think we all miss his beard."

Mom still was standing there, a bit of liquid rimming her eyes. I put my lips up to her ear and muttered, "I think some of the plant's coolant might have escaped up Dad's ass."

She did a dry spit take and whipped her head toward me, trying to look annoyed—one doesn't say such things about one's father—but unable to hide a softening around her eyes. "You can get away with that just this once," she said, and kissed my cheek.

As I turned up the water and ran the brush over each plate's sticky surface, I pondered this change in my father. Maybe it was simple: he was overworked, exhausted, stressed out from containing a situation that might be even more dangerous than he'd let on.

But those explanations didn't quite cover it. He acted as if he didn't know who we were anymore.

And didn't care.

CHAPTER 13

Jordan

THE TWO-MILE bike ride from home to school was going faster than ever. I was nervous; that was it, sure. It just so happened that everything I was doing lately was at a greater speed than at any previous time.

I knew I'd have to run laps once I arrived and make up for lost time, but I felt decent, other than the headache that still lingered a bit. I knew this was the concussion's aftereffect, but I'd decided to power through it. I'd beaten up Troy and Luke with the injury still fresh, after all, so I could handle a practice where I got to wear the don't-hit-me-I'm-a-quarterback green jersey.

And, hey, if anyone wanted to get revenge for what I did to those two guys—well, I felt ready for that, too. In my mind, I still didn't know how to fight. I *shouldn't* know how to fight. But I realized there was evidence to the contrary.

I was supposed to lead the team now. I hoped I wouldn't have to fight everyone to get their respect. I dreaded the eyes that would be on me in the locker room, but that just made me pedal harder—the sooner to get it over with.

Up ahead of me, a squad of soldiers stood beside a few Humvees. One of the men waved for me to stop. They weren't in the desert camouflage worn by the modern army but rather digital green-and-gray camo. The vehicles matched their uniforms.

"What's going on?" I asked as I pulled over.

"Routine patrol," said the soldier who had waved. I recognized the patch on his shoulder: three chevrons with a curve on the bottom. A staff sergeant.

"I'm just going to football practice," I said.

"Do you have your school ID on you?"

I nodded and pulled it out of my shorts. It was worn from years of going in and out of my pocket, and the lettering was beginning to wear off. The picture hardly looked like me anymore, or anyone.

The staff sergeant swiped the card in his reader, and he looked at the screen.

"You're the one who found that bear," he said.

"Yeah, or it found me," I said, vaguely pointing to the east. "It was thataways, behind the lumberyard."

"Hey, Conners," another soldier said. It took me a minute to recognize him with his helmet and sunglasses.

"Ears," I said, remembering him from the camp. He was a radio operator, and his office was in the same building as the mess hall. He wasn't much older than me, maybe a couple of years. He must have joined up on his eighteenth birthday or lied about his age. "What're you doing here?"

Ears turned to the staff sergeant. "He's okay. I know him."

The sergeant handed my card back to me.

"We're looking for a coyote," Ears told me. "Have you seen anything? Paw prints in the mud, scat, newly dead animals?"

"No," I said. "I didn't realize we had coyotes around here."

"They're uncommon this far south," the sergeant said. "But it's also uncommon to find a bear in town. I think some creatures moved in after everyone moved out."

"So, wait, they dispatched a whole squad and two Humvees to track down a random coyote?" I asked.

"Disease," Ears said. "At least that's what we were told."

The sergeant scowled at Ears, apparently not happy to hear his input.

"You should call the vet here in town: Dr. Gooding," I said. "She deals with that kind of stuff."

"We can handle it," the sergeant said sharply. "Now head off to practice."

Ears kind of smiled, a little redness in his face. "If you see anything, let us know," he said. "Here, let me give you my number. Call me when you join up." He scrawled his number on the back of an "If You See Something, Say Something" flyer.

"Will do." I hoisted myself back onto my bike seat and put my foot to the pedal before I stopped myself. "Hey, Ears. Do you know about anyone called Ishango or something like that?"

Ears's eyes widened, and he started to move his head from side to side before the sergeant stepped in front of him and pointed down the road. "I said *move!*" he ordered.

Yipes. I put a big grin on my face and said, "Thank you, sir. Good luck with that coyote." And I rode off, though not before I shot Ears a sly wink.

As I went on my way, I thought about Maggie's dog and that mad bear. Maybe the animals were pissed that we'd come back to their homestead. But Maggie's dog was with her family the whole time, and that didn't explain why she kept launching herself into the cage bars. *Ouch.* I wondered whether I'd see Maggie at practice so I could talk to her about it. I was surprised to see her at the previous one. In the meantime, I stuck to well-traveled streets for the rest of the way to school just in case. I could do without encountering a batshit-crazy coyote in an alley.

When I arrived in the locker room, everyone got quiet. In my head, I heard Charlie exclaim, "Crickets!" As I walked to my locker, Tico gave me a fist bump.

"Welcome back, buddy," he said softly. "Now we can get started for real."

I opened my locker and retrieved my pads.

"Hey, Conners," came a gruff voice behind me: Jimmy Dubnar, an offensive lineman and one of a handful of black players on the team. He was enormous—six foot four and probably more than three hundred pounds—yet wasn't even our biggest lineman. That was Sammy Justice, who had to be six eight and liked to be called "Two Tons of Justice."

"QBs don't wear pads at practice," Jimmy said. "Here. Coach told me to give this to you."

He flung me the green quarterback jersey. Aiden Cole, also wearing a green jersey over his slight frame, watched me pull it on.

"Don't worry," Jimmy said, leaning into my ear. "Luke was a good running back, but everyone knows he's a jackass. Even his own mom could see that. That play where we let the D-line through, I swear, we thought it was a screen."

I sat on the bench and tied on my cleats.

"This should be Cole's position," I muttered back to Jimmy.

"Don't even start," Jimmy scoffed. "Cole's a baby who only

got the QB spot because his daddy made a big contribution for the new scoreboard. My nana throws a tighter spiral."

The large lineman turned to the group and banged his fist against his locker.

"Listen up! Y'all saw what Conners did out here. That was some serious shit. And I'm talkin' 'bout his play on the field, not what happened in the locker room. He's the genuine article, and if anybody in here has a problem with him, you can go through me. I don't want to see any more 'accidental' hits on him on the field, and I swear to the baby Jesus that there won't be any more off the field, either, or I'm gonna take care of it. Unless Conners decides to put you in the hospital, too. Got it?"

Everyone in the room nodded.

I gave Jimmy a fist bump, and he muttered, "Keep throwing the ball straight and running past people, and we'll be good."

"Gotcha," I said.

Maybe things would turn out all right after all.

CHAPTER 14

Maggie

WE SHOWED UP at the mortuary early in the morning as always so we wouldn't overlap with any funerals or viewings. Mr. Marsh met us with a rolling steel table, and Mom and I unloaded Nerf's and Tiger's bodies from the van and placed them atop it. As Mr. Marsh rolled the cart with the dogs away, he told us to return in an hour. Human cremation can take up to two hours, but neither of these bodies weighed more than thirty pounds. My assumption was that he would cremate the dogs together.

Mom took me across the street to Lydia's Diner, and we ordered breakfast. It was our cremation tradition, though this was the first time we had eaten at the diner since we'd returned to town.

The way cremation works, in case you're curious, is the dogs are put onto a big grate, and Mr. Marsh turns on the incinerators. It gets close to two thousand degrees in there, so the animals don't burn so much as vaporize in the high heat. You may think of cremated remains as ashes, but nope, not really. Most of the ashes get sucked up into air filters, and what's left are bone fragments and whatever small amount of ash falls through the grate onto a slide. That all goes into a big blender and gets pulverized.

"Like a smoothie," Jordan said when I explained it to him a couple years back.

"Needs yogurt," I responded. Sometimes I don't know why I humor that guy.

Anyway, this explains why cremated six-foot-tall people fit into an urn the size of a genie lamp. There isn't much left. And if you touch the stuff—which, yes, I have—it's not like the fine powder you shovel out of your fireplace but closer to the texture of sand.

"Earth to Margaret," Mom said.

"Sorry," I said, shaking images of incinerated dogs from my mind.

She nodded to the waitress hovering over our table—a young, tired-looking woman whom I thought I recognized as having been a senior when I was a freshman. Her name tag said D'Arcy. *Right.* She aimed a patient smile my way, her pen poised over her little notepad.

"California omelet, please," I said. "And coffee."

"We don't have avocados," D'Arcy said in a monotone. "We've got them ordered, but all the trucks have to go through the military now."

"Okay. How about just whatever kind of veggie omelet you can make?"

"Will do," she said, and left us to return a moment later to fill our coffee mugs. I added two creams and poured in a quick stream of white sugar from the glass container on the table.

"Where are you this morning?" Mom asked. "You've been in la-la land since you woke up."

"La-la land is Los Angeles," I replied. "I haven't been in Los Angeles."

She glared at me.

"I was up at four in the morning, you know," I added.

"I told you to go back to bed. I could've handled the dogs on my own."

"It's Nerf," I said. "I wanted to be here."

"Do you want to keep him? They're going to mix the ashes."

I shook my head. I couldn't imagine that having a jar of Nerf-and-other-dog sand on my bookshelf would comfort me much.

"Are you doing all right otherwise?" Mom asked.

"I'm fine," I said, though I should have said that I had a lump in my breast and something weird in my shoulder and that I was terrified. I couldn't do it.

"What are you not telling me?" she said, sipping her coffee, which she drank black.

"Nothing," I said.

"Is it about a boy?"

"What?" I laughed. "No. This is the farthest thing from being about a boy." I mean, there *was* a boy who I was hoping would make a move already, but those thoughts were relatively fun.

"So there's *something*."

"Maybe I'm just not adjusting well to being home."

"If that were the problem, then you wouldn't have refused to tell me," Mom said.

"Wait," I said. "If I don't answer, I'm hiding something, and if I do, that's evidence that I'm lying?" I lifted my coffee cup and held it in my hands, which always seem to be cold.

"I know you, Maggie. I know that if you're hiding

something, it'll be significant. You'd been begging to come home since we left, so, no, that's not it."

I took a long, slow sip.

"Okay, I'll guess," Mom said. "You're upset we can't leave. You've turned into one of those teenage political activists, and you want to tell me how unconstitutional it is."

"It *is* unconstitutional," I said. "I've thought about that."

"How?" she said, smiling. She was challenging me.

"Freedom of assembly. I think there's something implicit in the First Amendment that says we can assemble where we want."

"Objection," Mom said. "We still have the freedom to assemble. We can all go to the roadblock and protest. I don't think they'll shoot us."

"How come no one has protested, then?" I countered. "Is it because everyone's afraid of what will happen?"

She shrugged. "Maybe because this town looks better than it has for years? We're all happy to be home. Think about our office. I was expecting it to be trashed and for looters to have taken all the ketamine."

Ketamine was an animal tranquilizer that some folks use as a party drug. Mom kept her stock in a padlocked cabinet. When we had returned to the office, it was untouched.

"I swear," I said, "if they don't get cell phones working again soon, I'll go stand in front of a tank."

"Well, you're right," Mom said. "It's not constitutional as per the Privileges and Immunities Clause."

"How do you know *that*?"

"There's this lawyer who hangs out at the Savannah Grill."

"Don't tell me you've been leaving every night to carry on with some lawyer at a bar."

"All right, I won't tell you," she said with a wink.

"Who?" I asked.

"Bud Winkle."

"Bud Winkle? You're dating Bud Winkle?"

"Shhh!" she hissed. "For heaven's sake."

"*The* Bud Winkle?"

"Cut it out, Maggie. And anyway, we're not dating."

"Have you kissed him?"

"Don't cross-examine me, Maggie."

"Oh, no, that's Bud Winkle's job."

Jesus. Bud Winkle.

"He's a very nice man, and you may find that his legal knowledge comes in handy regarding your concerns."

"'Regarding my concerns.' Great. Right now my main concern is that my mom is fooling around with Bud Effing Winkle."

We sat in silence for a few moments, and Mom arched her neck, looking toward the kitchen, hoping she'd be conversationally rescued by the arrival of our food. D'Arcy was behind the counter, chatting with the older woman at the cash register, not looking at the steaming plates sitting under the pass-through hot lamps.

"Our food is right *there,*" Mom said.

"Maybe Bud Winkle can sue them for bad service," I said.

"Would you cut it *out*?" she asked. She looked on the verge of tears. Okay, I'd back off. For now.

"Anyway," I said, "the point is why would we be cut off from the rest of the world if everything here is fine? Couldn't we at least get cable? Shutting down the internet conforms to a certain fascist agenda, but how about intoxicating the masses with access to Netflix? Why can't I watch reruns of *The West Wing*?"

"Rachel's husband has a ham radio, and he shares the news that way."

"Right—with other nutjobs spreading conspiracies from their underground bunkers." I took another sip of my coffee, which had cooled considerably. This was not a pleasurable drink. In one of his emails at camp, Jordan said that when we returned to town, he'd make me coffee in a Chemex, whatever that was. "I mean, Mount Hope isn't even big enough to merit a Starbucks. Why would we be worth cutting off?"

"I don't know, dear," Mom said. "I don't know that we're actually cut off. We'll just have to be diligent."

D'Arcy finally showed up with a plate of melon and cottage cheese for Mom and a veggie omelet for me. It was mostly broccoli and Velveeta at the temperature of bathwater.

"But I don't actually believe that your sense of constitutional crisis is where your mind has been this morning. Come on, spill."

I took another drink of coffee, swished it around like mouthwash, and kept my eyes on my mom. She really was the most sympathetic, supportive person I knew. She deserved the truth.

Eventually.

"The homecoming dance is coming up, and no one has asked me," I said.

Her face relaxed just like *that*. I'd delivered her a traditional mother's problem. *Ahhhh.*

"Classes haven't even started yet, so I'm not sure why you're worried."

"People are around. I'm a junior. I should know."

"Why don't you go with Jordan?"

"He has to ask me."

"Well, ask him."

"Mom," I said, and then stuffed a big bite of omelet into my mouth.

"It's the twenty-first century, Maggie. You've told me you don't conform to antediluvian gender roles."

"It's a 'boy's choice' dance," I said through a full mouth.

"Bullshit," she said. "I'm sorry. But, come on, no one designates a 'boy's choice' dance. Almost every dance in history was a 'boy's choice' dance."

I couldn't hide my smile at my mom's cussing. I'd have to be more convincing.

"I just—what if he says no? We've been friends since kindergarten."

"That's why you shouldn't worry."

"Mom," I said with a sigh, "you just don't get it." Now I actually was getting vexed about this. Why *hadn't* Jordan asked me to the homecoming dance yet?

He was fun and smart, and as much as I hated to admit to being swayed by such qualities, he was getting hotter. He could have had his pick of girls at school, though I never saw him dating anyone. Maybe he didn't like girls. He wouldn't be the first hunky guy to let down the ladies in this respect.

But, no, he liked girls, I could tell. He liked *me*. He just needed to act already. Well, maybe sometime when he wasn't being chased by a bear or concussed by teammates. This hadn't been the most romantic stretch . . .

I'd always liked Jordan, but the nuclear disaster deepened my feelings. I had plenty of friends in the evacuation camp, and we hung out and had fun. I even went on a couple of dates with Jerry Eiger—he'd asked me to watch the *Star Wars* prequels with him on his tablet, for some reason—but nothing happened. (Jar Jar Binks didn't exactly put me in the mood.) In the meantime, Jordan and I were communicating solely through the written word, sending each other emails that conveyed so much more than everyday conversations. These exchanges felt honest, meaningful, intimate. I couldn't wait to be in the physical presence of this person who was opening his sweet soul to me.

"It's time," Mom said, tapping her watch. She dug a twenty out of her pocket, left it on the table, and said good-bye to everyone as we walked out.

We crossed back to the mortuary and met Mr. Marsh at the basement door.

"I have a question for you," he said as he handed Mom a clear plastic bag. "Do you know what these are?"

Inside were a couple of small pieces of what looked like metal. They were silver and round, each the size of a breath mint.

"They wouldn't go through the cremulator. It kept jamming up."

"What are they?" I asked Mom.

She shook her head. "No idea."

I inspected them more closely. Each was like a mini octopus, with multiple thin wire tentacles extending from a tiny silver disk. It wasn't a microchip, which my mom would have recognized, anyway. There were two, one for each cremated dog.

Was this thing in Nerf?

How did it get there . . . and why?

CHAPTER 15

Jordan

MAGGIE CAME BY in the evening saying she wanted to hang out, so there we were, reclining in my backyard under a pergola that had been unstable before we left but now was in tip-top shape, painted white and illuminated by strings of lights that looked like large antique lightbulbs. I appreciated Maggie's initiative in coming by. I appreciated her being there even more. She wore shorts and sandals and a striped blue-and-white shirt. Her hair, which usually hung down to the middle of her back, was pulled up into some kind of complicated braid. She looked good. Smelled good, too.

"I can't see the stars," she said.

"Should I turn off the lights?" I asked.

"Sure."

I got up and unplugged them, making the yard completely dark aside from the square of light illuminated by the kitchen window.

I lowered myself back onto the lounge chair and stared up, waiting for my eyes to adjust to the low light. The pergola broke up the view into long rectangles, but soon I could see dense packs of stars. Mount Hope was small, and my neighborhood—if you could call it that—was nothing more than seven or eight homes in a cluster, with farmland spreading out behind them like a fan. There were no streetlights or businesses to light up the sky and ruin the starscape.

"I learned a lot of constellations while we were in the camp," I said. "I wasn't sleeping well there."

"What's that one?" she said, pointing to a bright dot to the west.

"That's not a star," I said. "That's Mars."

"It doesn't look red to me."

"Me neither."

We stared and said nothing. It was quiet—so quiet that it was strange. Maggie's puzzled expression indicated that she'd noticed it, too.

"Where are the crickets?" she asked.

"I don't know," I said, then paused to listen again. "You're right. That's weird." I considered going in to tell Charlie this strange bit of news, given our whole crickets thing, then thought better of it. This was where I wanted to be.

"Maybe radiation killed them?" she said.

"Doubtful," I said. "You know how they say cockroaches will survive a nuclear bomb? I bet crickets are the same way. I mean, are they much different?"

"Well, yes, Jordan, crickets are different from cockroaches," she scoffed. "That's like saying dogs are the same as cats."

"Well, I bet radiation would have a similar effect on dogs and cats," I said. "So there."

Maggie gave me the side-eye, then pondered the matter. "You may be right."

"I may be crazy," I returned. "It's weird either way."

We lay still a bit longer. The garden stretched back a good fifty yards before it hit the forest, which loomed large and dark against the sky. When we were little, Maggie and I used to play in the forest all the time. We each had a tree fort— or, really, just trees that we claimed for ourselves and called forts. Mine had a branch bent at a right angle just below another branch; I used to sit there and act like it was my control room. One broken limb stuck out like a joystick, and I used it to fire my "guns" at her. Maggie would climb up her tree and throw spiny chestnuts down at me. One got lodged in the crotch of my pants, and I howled as if she'd done some real damage.

"Get it off! Get it off!" I screamed.

She looked alarmed, but when she started reaching down for it, I couldn't keep a straight face and cracked up.

"Jordan!" she yelled, and fetched another handful of spiny chestnuts and nailed me in the chest with two of them. They actually did hurt.

"What are you thinking about?" I asked.

"Dogs and radiation, still," she said. "And that bear. I wonder whether radiation can make animals more aggressive."

"I'm really sorry about Nerf," I said.

"I am, too. But there was another crazed dog yesterday, and today Mom got a call about a third dog that's going nuts and biting people. Also, the police shot a wild boar that was walking down the street and charging anyone it saw. It gouged a ten-year-old pretty bad."

"Is it rabies? Or what's that other one—distemper?"

She shook her head. "Distemper is a viral disease that has nothing to do with temper. Plus, wild boars don't get it."

"Rabies, then."

"Nope. No sign of that. These are just raging animals, like they've all gone bonkers. And get this: When we had Nerf and another dog cremated yesterday, the mortuary guy found two little metal discs in the remains. I'm wondering whether those had anything to do with the dogs turning aggressive."

"The discs were in the dogs?"

"Apparently."

"Like they'd been implanted?"

She shrugged. "Since the internet doesn't work, I went down to the library to research radiation and radioactivity, but I haven't learned much."

"Did you find anything about radiation helping people?"

"Aside from zapping cancerous tumors?"

"Yeah, like giving someone extra...power?"

"That's only if you get bitten by a radioactive spider," she said, her lips curling upward.

"Okay, Mary Jane," I said. "But when I actually paid attention in biology, I learned about this thing called the theory of evolution. Animals are born with mutations all the time, and some of those mutations are good, like when one leopard is faster than the others or one wolf has sharper teeth. Those are the animals that live longer and pass the good mutations down to their kids."

"Jordan, you've discovered Darwin!" Maggie exclaimed.

I didn't want to be annoyed with her, so I plowed ahead. "Radiation could lead to good mutations, right? Isn't it possible that a dose of radiation could make some of us, I dunno, *better*—even as it makes some animals completely loco?"

"Jordan," she said, taking my hand between hers in a way that felt more motherly than romantic, "your genes are your genes, and they didn't get mutated because of possible exposure to radiation. Are you trying to say that you think the meltdown has made you a better football player?"

"It wasn't a meltdown. It was a nuclear plant explosion."

"Answer the question!" She let go of my hand, which was a bummer.

"Honestly?" I said. "I'm better than I used to be, and there's no good reason for it. I'm faster. I'm stronger. While I was lifting yesterday, I bench-pressed forty more pounds than I ever had. How does that happen?"

"You're a year older. You've got a year's more muscle. Come on, you're a college football fan. You can tell the difference between the freshmen and the seniors. You're a growing boy, Jordan. And you exercised in the sick camp."

"I also broke lots of bones," I said. "I jogged as part of my physical therapy, but there wasn't a weight room. It was a camp with lots of hospital beds for people with radiation sickness."

"Well," she said, "maybe radiation could make your tendons tighter or springier or whatever to make you faster, but it didn't teach you the instincts to play football better. That's on you."

"What about the fight?"

"Radiation definitely didn't teach you mixed martial arts."

Well, someone *did,* I thought.

"Did you go to practice today?" she asked, her head tilted back to take in the stars.

"I did."

"Was that such a good idea with your concussion and all?"

"I know," I said. "But I felt fine. More than fine. It was weird, like I've been saying."

It was amazing, actually—as if someone had flipped a switch in my head, and I could read the defense like a kids' board book. I could tell who was coming after me and could see the whole field and calculate each movement. When the offensive line missed a coverage, I found a solution—every time. At first I thought it was because I used to be on the defense and knew their plays already. But this was more than that. It was like I was plugged in and could keep track of what every one of the twenty-one other guys on the field was doing at all times. During drills, I never missed a pass, and when we scrimmaged, I completed eighteen of twenty, with my two misses due to receivers dropping balls.

But I didn't want to think about football anymore right now. I breathed in Maggie's fresh, floral scent.

"You ready for school tomorrow?" I asked.

"I don't think anyone's ready. This town is too screwed up. But it'll be a good distraction."

"Still, you *like* school," I said. "So that'll be nice, right?"

"I like *learning*," she replied. "School itself is hit-or-miss. I'm looking forward to physics 'cause Dr. Carlozo is supposedly an awesome teacher. U.S. History, I dunno—I'd rather read the less official version."

"Nerd," I said with a nudge of my elbow. I'd been calling her that since first grade, which I realize isn't too original, but by now it was tradition. The truth is I loved how smart she was. She always had something interesting to say about a documentary she'd watched or a book she'd read or the latest issue of *Scientific American*. For a while I watched *Nova* every Thursday night with her and her mom; she became emotionally invested in the plight of woolly mammoths the way others did in *The Bachelor*.

"*I'm* the nerd?" she shot back, sitting up. "You make *Caddyshack* references. 'Lighten up, Francis!'"

"That's *Stripes*."

"I rest my case." She smiled and leaned her head back again. I did, too. The stars were as bright as I'd ever seen them.

"Have you heard of something or someone called Ishango?" I asked.

Maggie wrinkled her nose. "No, what is it?"

I told her about my father's odd behavior and how that name seemed to trigger him. "I'd google it, but there's no Google."

"Alas, we're back in the Dark Ages," Maggie said. "But I do have an old set of encyclopedias and can look it up when I get home."

I smiled. "Thanks, nerd."

She elbowed me in my surgically repaired ribs.

"Ow!" I exclaimed, wincing in pain.

"Oh, sorry!" she said, flustered. "I forgot."

"Nah, I'm good," I said, smiling. "It didn't actually hurt; I was being a jerk. Just be glad I didn't unleash some superhero moves on you."

"Okay, Spidey," she said, and took my hand. *Nice.* "Hey," she added, "the homecoming dance is in two weeks. Will you go with me?"

"Ah...uh...dealio," I stuttered. *Smooth. Dealio? C'mon, Jordan!* I was such a dork, always blowing it with this girl— but, wait, she was smiling and wrapping her arms around me and squeezing hard. *Well, okay.*

After nearly a year apart, this is what I'd wanted most of all. I slipped my hand behind her head and wound her hair around a finger. She leaned her face back and locked her liquid hazel eyes into mine.

"It's a moment," I said softly.

"Shut up." She laughed.

Damn, she wanted me to kiss her. I could feel it. Everything since we got back to town had been so messed up, but now I was about to do what I'd dreamed about doing for most of my life. Her lips looked so soft, buttery, inviting, and they were inches from mine. I could smell a wintergreen Tic Tac on her breath—she must've sneaked it into her mouth when I wasn't looking. I preferred spearmint, but still...I tried to process the moment, make it indelible.

"If this were a movie," I murmured, "some terrible thing would happen right now, just as my lips were moving toward yours."

Her eyes widened, incredulous. "Jordan, I'm not in a movie. I'm *right here*. Do you need an engraved invitation?"

I smiled, inhaled her fresh scent through my nose, and moved in for what we'd forever tell our kids and grandkids was our First Kiss.

Then...

Boom!

CHAPTER 16

Jordan

I FLEW OUT of my chair and crashed onto the brick patio, then felt like I was being sucked up by a tornado. Everything was illuminated as if it were noon. The flash was bright, continuous.

I looked for a mushroom cloud.

Maggie was tumbling, as if in slow motion, off the patio and onto the lawn.

Glass was flying everywhere, sparkling in the yellow-orange light like a million diamonds.

Everything paused, as if the whole world were heaving a deep breath, and then the sky filled up with burning debris.

I was moving, running, grabbing Maggie off the grass, lifting her in a fireman's carry. A burning tire bounced onto the garden and toward the woods, leaving a trail of flaming prints. Then came a two-by-four, followed by a hundred more flaming meteors of various sizes.

A wall of heat hit me like a football helmet to the chest and sucked the oxygen from my lungs. I stumbled and tried to breathe but felt like I was swallowing fire.

I set Maggie down in the safest place I could see: a window well outside our basement. The army's emergency-survival handbook, which I read at the evacuation camp, said that if there was a nuclear blast, you needed to get underground. The glass was already blown out of the basement window.

"Climb inside," I shouted, and realized I couldn't hear anything.

She sat up, saying something to me that I couldn't understand. She was bleeding from the back of her head. I took her hand and placed it on the wound, yelling at her to keep pressure on it. She gestured that she couldn't hear, and I took her hand and put it back on her head.

"Stay here," I shouted, and held out my palms to her, trying to make her understand.

I planted a quick kiss on her lips.

Then I ran—into the house through a door that was broken off its hinges. The brightest light was gone, but everything glowed orange.

"Mom! Charlie!" I screamed, but the words sounded hollow in my ears. I doubted I would hear their answers.

Every cupboard in the kitchen was open, broken dishes scattered everywhere. My mom lay on the floor. Not moving.

Oh, God.

Shuddering, I dropped to my knees and felt her neck for a pulse.

There it was, beating softly. She took a breath.

She had a piece of glass—a ten-inch-long sharp dagger— plunged into her shoulder.

I pondered whether to pull it out or leave it in. Sometimes in the movies they leave it in because removing it will open the bloody floodgates. But this didn't look too deep, and I didn't want her to roll over onto it. I yanked it out, and she didn't even stir. I patted her face, softly, then a bit harder.

"Mom!" I yelled.

She opened an eye halfway.

"You're okay," I said, more to myself than to her. I pressed her hand to her shoulder, telling her to hold it. I jumped up to grab a towel from the kitchen but couldn't find anything in that mess. I pulled down one of the short drapes dangling in front of the shattered back window.

Maggie emerged from the basement door with blood running down her face and onto her shirt. Her mouth was moving, but I wasn't hearing anything, and I motioned to my ears. She pointed upstairs, and I saw she was mouthing, "Charlie."

I nodded, and she ran for the stairs.

Wadding up the drape, I headed back to the living room, where Mom was trying to sit up. I wrapped the cotton curtain tightly around her shoulder wound. She was saying something to me, but I didn't understand. I took her hand again and put it on the cloth, yelling at her to apply pressure.

Instead, she grabbed my hand and kept trying to say something. She was hysterical. Of course: Charlie.

She moved to get up, and I didn't stop her. She took a step, then bent over and coughed, hard. I got down on one knee and tried to sit her down.

A loud rushing sound, like river rapids, overwhelmed my senses. I put my hands to my ears, covering and uncovering them, trying to tell whether the noise was all in my head. It wasn't. It sounded like a fire hose.

"Can you hear me?" I shouted at Mom. She looked up at

me, nodded, and said something back. I could almost pick out syllables this time.

Mom's eyes widened at the sight of something behind me, and I turned to see Maggie coming down the stairs holding Charlie's hand as he walked beside her. He looked petrified but unhurt, with a little blood on his spaceship pajamas. I grabbed him, hugged him, then ran my fingers quickly over his head and chest. The blood appeared to be Maggie's. He was shaking; dirty tears streaked down his face as he gripped Maggie's hand.

She mouthed something to me, but I wasn't getting it. She placed her mouth against my ear and shouted: "Fire!"

She pointed upstairs, and I realized a low cracking sound, which had been there all the time, was getting louder. Mom grabbed Charlie's hand, and the four of us ran toward the front door. It was old and oak, original to the house, and a thick shard of metal was protruding through its center.

I grabbed the hot knob and flung open the door to reveal a picture:

Hell on earth.

CHAPTER 17

Jordan

EVERYTHING WAS ON fire...or worse.

As I stood in front of our porch steps, I realized that the Carters' house across the street was gone, nothing left to burn. The only thing remaining was the concrete slab on which it had been built.

I'd seen this house every day of my life and now struggled to remember how it looked. The world had gone upside down. A huge tree lay in the street, roots and all, in flames. Other trees, such familiar parts of the scenery, were missing altogether.

In place of the Carters' garage was a pile of brick and burning chunks of roof. Their barn was in flames, and their aluminum-walled mechanical shed looked like crumpled-up foil. Down the road to the west, the Moores' house and garage were burning, too. Five mangled bicycles, arranged big to small, lay in the yard as if for sale. A pickup truck lay on its side, wheels spinning, fuel leaking and blazing. Looking to the east, I saw that the Allens' farm was an inferno, an upended tractor in flames by the burning house.

I looked in the direction of the nuclear plant's coolant towers, curious as to whether they were still standing, but I couldn't have seen them from my house even on a clear day. There was no mushroom cloud, at least, or bright glow over the hills.

As Mom and Charlie crouched together on the front yard and Maggie grabbed my arm to pull me farther away from the house, I suddenly could see ground zero: a circle next to the Carters' foundation, with a radius of maybe thirty feet, that was clear of debris. Whatever was there had been scoured from the face of the earth. I pointed at it and yelled at Maggie.

Maggie nodded and kept trying to pull me away from the porch.

I followed her down to the street and turned back to look at my house. The roof was on fire, smoke billowing out of the upstairs windows. Glass was gone from all the windows, and the porch was on the verge of collapse. As I looked closer, I realized the whole house had been pushed back about eight inches off its foundation.

Adrenaline rushed through me, as if a switch in my chest had been flipped and chemicals were pumping into my heart and head. I suddenly felt dizzy and dropped down to my knees.

The Carters had been home when I got home. Their mini-van had been in the driveway. It was nowhere to be seen now, and I couldn't tell whether it had been thrown out of sight or vaporized. Maybe the metal shard that pierced our front door had been part of the engine or body.

Maggie placed her hands on my head and spoke into my ear, though the only noise that was getting through was the waterfall-like roar of the fire. The sound—and flames—

surrounded us: houses and buildings burning and small fires scattered around the small neighborhood.

Maggie was still bleeding from her head, and I placed her hand back on the wound, but she pushed my hand away and pointed to the Allens' house in one direction and the Moores' in the other, both on fire. She pointed at herself and then the Moores' house, then at me and the Allens'. I nodded.

I wish she would've stayed to tend to her wound, but I knew she wouldn't, and I wasn't about to debate her when I couldn't hear a word she was saying. Maggie ran west toward the Moores' while I shouted for Mom, who kept the curtain pressed into one shoulder with Charlie nuzzled against the other, to stay put. Then I took off for the Allens'.

Their house was in flames and looked to be tilting. A big dogwood tree I'd climbed a hundred times as a kid had fallen onto the Allens' truck. As I got closer, I shouted, trying to be heard over the fire's roar. I could hear my voice's vibrations in my head but not the words.

As I reached the house, part of the roof collapsed, and flames shot out. Mrs. Allen had died of cancer a couple of years ago, but Mr. Allen still lived here with his two teenage kids, Henry and Violet. I'd been friends with Peter, Henry, and Violet when we were growing up. Now Peter was in college, and the only thing I had in common with fourteen-year-old Henry and Violet, a petite, consciously social high school sophomore, was that we rode the same bus to school.

Fire spat out of every window I could see, including the broken glass porthole in the front door. There was no way to get into this place. There was no way anyone could be alive. I ran around to the back, just to be sure.

The rear of the house was in better shape than the front,

but smoke was billowing out of the second floor. I thought I'd leave, but then I heard more glass breaking and looked up to see a window shattering and a pale hand reaching out. Then a face.

Someone was inside—about to die.

Without thinking, I leaped onto the trellis on the side of the house to climb toward the skinny roof over the sunroom. If I could reach that roof, I could get to the window.

Although I wasn't light, the trellis held as I climbed, and I scrambled onto the roof as a window above my head burst and flames and glass showered over me. Ducking and covering my head, I crunched over the glass shards to reach the window, where the hand no longer waved.

I wrapped my hand in my jacket and punched out the rest of the glass. Gray smoke poured out as I vaulted myself inside and dove to the ground, where the air was better. Kneeling under the window was a girl. Violet. I hoisted her up, she wrapped her arms around my neck, and I scrambled to the window and deposited her onto the roof, gently, so she wouldn't roll off.

I ducked back down and crawled around the floor, my lungs feeling raw and strangely cold. I bumped into another body, this one heavier and more solid. Mr. Allen? I found his arms and pulled him to the window, then climbed out and dragged him through from the roof, where Violet was lying and coughing.

How to get them down? It was too far to jump. I thought for a moment, then leaped back through the window as Violet protested weakly. Having knocked into a twin bed moments earlier, I yanked off the mattress, folded it as much as I could, and shoved it through the window, taking care not to knock Mr. Allen and his daughter off the roof in the process. Once outside again, I dropped the mattress to the ground below us, a ten-foot drop. It would have to do.

"I'll let you down!" I shouted to Violet, who nodded as I grabbed hold of her arms. She lay on her belly facing me and let her legs dangle over the side, then inched herself backward until her stomach was against the roof's edge. Gripping her tightly by the wrists, I lowered her down slowly until there was about a five-foot gap between her and the mattress. She landed feetfirst, her hand hitting the ground. She was okay.

Mr. Allen remained unconscious, and time was tight; I didn't want us to be up there when the next explosion or collapse came. I positioned him as I had Violet, but I had to push him slowly over the roof's edge with my feet while hanging on to his arms.

"Dad!" Violet was crying as her father dangled above her.

I jutted my arms forward and let go, and he plunged backward, hitting the mattress with his shoulder blades, his neck not snapping back too far. That was a bull's-eye as far as I was concerned.

I signaled for Violet to get him out of the way, because here I came, landing in a crouch. I hoisted Mr. Allen around to the front and deposited him onto the street as Violet hovered over him.

"Is he okay?" I could see—more than hear—her asking.

"I think so!" I shouted back.

She hugged me with such force that her pristine purple fingernails dug into the back of my neck. Her sobs were so fierce that I could barely make out the words she was trying to say: "You! Saved! Us!"

Maybe this was my superhero moment after all, though I was too exhausted, wired, and freaked out to indulge that thought. As if I needed any more reminders of how sobering this scene was, I looked back at my house and saw that the entire second floor was on fire. Orange light illuminated the window to my room, engulfing everything I owned.

I did a 360 to take in the destruction around me. What else could I do? Was there anyone left to rescue? Wait, where was Henry?

I looked at the Allens' barn, which was set back from the house and wasn't on fire, though it had a dangerous lean, as if it might collapse at any moment. Next to it was their propane tank, which looked unscathed with no fire around it. It probably was okay.

Wait.

I ran back to the Carters' house. Like most of the farms out here, the Carters had a five-hundred-gallon propane tank, but now it was gone, no trace. That must've been it; the tank had exploded. But how? Why? Had a car hit it? It was close to their house but not next to the driveway, so that seemed far-fetched. But so did all of this.

My mom and Charlie were standing in the street, watching our house, which had been in our family for more than a century, up in flames. I looked down the street toward the Moores' house but couldn't see Maggie or much of anything else. Smoke was everywhere, a billowing dirty cloud rising above our neighborhood.

When I looked back at our house, I saw movement.

Someone inside was smashing a fist through our living-room window.

I didn't move, too dumbstruck to think straight.

This figure was engulfed in flames yet moved with all the urgency of a lookie-loo at a Sunday afternoon open house. I couldn't tell if it was a man or woman, kid or adult. This person was punching the glass out of the window frame, then stepping out headfirst and tumbling down onto the grass. But instead of doing your standard stop, drop, and roll around to, you know, *put out the flames,* he (or she) stood up, looked around, and began to run away.

What the hell?

Having seen a scorched canvas tarp on the grass not far from the Carters' barn, I grabbed it and chased after the burning figure, upon whom the fire seemed to have no effect at all.

Flaming pieces of clothing dropped to the ground as he crossed the street and headed for the tree line.

"Hey!" I yelled. "Stop!"

As I ran, I felt the impact of all that smoke in my lungs, and I began to choke. When I looked up, this dude's shirt was falling away. Or was it flaming pieces of flesh? What was that nasty char smell in the air?

I could see ribs.

Made of metal.

On fire.

Even if this creature had gotten artificial ribs, his internal organs would all have been toast by now. Yet he kept running.

I dropped the tarp—because it was slowing me down, and, really, what good would it do?—and resumed my chase. As fast as I had become, this skeletal figure was faster, never pausing as flaming debris dropped off its body. I was caught up in the urgency of the moment, but let me just note: *Yuck!*

As he reached the trees, the flames surrounding him had dimmed to embers, though the air was filled with a smell like marshmallows dropped into a campfire. My eyes were watering and stinging from the heat and smoke, which was messing with my vision. I wiped away tears and tried to catch up, but it was a losing battle.

"Hey!" I yelled again as I reached the edge of the woods. I stopped, coughing, and leaned a hand against an oak tree.

This time the figure stopped as well and turned back toward me. His legs looked like regular human legs, covered with dark pants even, but his abdomen was full of fire, as though his stomach and intestines were burning, the flames filling the rib cage and engulfing the heart and lungs. His head appeared to be little more than a skull, though I saw a flash of silver in there, too.

I slapped my palms against my cheeks. I wasn't hallucinating. I wasn't dreaming. I hadn't ingested any psychedelic drugs. I was seeing something in real life that I might've imagined only as CGI.

And now this creature was running toward me.

I grabbed a long stick off the ground just as he reached me, and I thrust it into his chest. The point appeared to go between his ribs and hit a lung, yet there was no squish, pop, or reaction. The stick snapped—half in my hand, half protruding from his chest, apparently harmlessly.

He reached for me with a flaming hand, which smelled like a well-done burger, and I ducked and unleashed a quick, savage kick into his knee. *Welcome back, crazy fighting instinct!*

He stumbled backward, and I swung what was left of the stick at his head. He was still faster than I was and grabbed the stick and shoved it into my chest, knocking me over a fallen log.

As I lay helpless with him looming over me, I realized this could be it. He could gouge me with the stick or jam his flaming fingers up my nose or find some other way to finish me right there.

But he didn't. Instead, he turned again and ran.

By the time I was upright, the burning corpse or whatever the hell it was had run too far, too fast for me to consider catching up with him. I wasn't sure more exposure to that dude would be good for my health, anyway. I watched him sprint nimbly through the woods, leaving behind sparks, flickering ashes and more of that burnt-marshmallow smell. I followed the trail of debris for a while, but as I got deeper and deeper into the forest, the charred remnants became less numerous until there were no more traces of this disgusting, frightful thing.

What the hell was it?

And why had it been inside our house?

CHAPTER 18

Maggie

THE FRONT DOOR of the Moores' house had been blown off its hinges, and smoke billowed from the interior, though I couldn't see any flames aside from the ones I'd glimpsed tickling the roof before I decided to enter. I pulled my blood-stained shirt collar over my nose to filter the smoke, exposing my stomach in the process. The gouge on my forehead still bled a little.

"Hello?" I shouted, getting down on all fours to see under the smoke, though little was visible beyond an empty living room strewn with broken glass.

This wasn't my first time inside the Moores' house. They were an older couple, and Mrs. Moore and I sat on the front porch and drank sweet tea while Jordan mowed their lawn and trimmed their bushes. They weren't quite seventy, I thought, and seemed to be in good shape. I had the impression they were making up jobs for Jordan to do so he'd have some spending money.

"Anyone in here?" I shouted as the shirt slipped off my nose. I readjusted it, but not before I coughed at the smell of melted plastic and burning upholstery.

When I reached the hallway, I got up on my feet but kept my waist bent.

"Hello?" I shouted again. "Mrs. Moore? Mr. Moore?"

The house was creaking and popping loudly. I knew I was being stupid in here. The roof was burning, and just because the ceiling looked okay, that didn't mean it wouldn't come crashing down on me. I saw a closed door to my right and put my hand on it to test for heat. It was cool. I opened it to reveal a dark bathroom.

My mom would be livid to know I was in here, but I didn't care. Jordan had run off to a building that was much more engulfed than this one, and someone needed to try to help the Moores.

Then again, Jordan was crazy and thought he was a superhero.

I paused and cocked my head. I heard something—not the fire, not people talking. It was a baby crying. *Oh, jiminy.* I couldn't tell where it was. Was it deeper in the house? Or outside already?

I placed my hand on the next door in the hallway. It was warm but not hot. Hmm. I touched the knob with the back of my hand in case the metal might burn me, but it was okay. Crouching low to the floor, I pushed the door open and peered inside. It was dark and full of smoke, and there it was: the baby's cry—plus someone else sobbing.

"Hello?" I called out, my eyes stinging from the smoke.

"Grandma?" came a small voice from the darkness.

"Where are you?" I asked, smoky tears flowing down my face.

"I'm here," she said, sounding all of three or four years old.

I couldn't see anyone, though I could hear them both. "Come to me," I said. "Follow my voice."

"I have Hannah."

"Good girl," I said over the baby's howls as I crawled deeper into the room, holding a hand out in front of me and hoping to make contact.

"Grandma, is that you?"

"No," I said. "My name's Maggie. What's yours?"

"Where's my grandma?"

"We'll find her."

"I heard the beeping," she said, choking on smoke. "I couldn't get out, so I came to be with Hannah. Nobody would forget Hannah."

"Nobody would forget you, either," I said, sweeping my hand around until my finger brushed skin. "Is that you?"

A little hand grabbed mine. "I'm Evie," she said.

"Let's get out of here."

"Don't forget Hannah."

I felt for the baby where the cries were coming from—in Evie's lap. She was a little peanut.

"We'll all leave together, promise," I said. "Now I'm going to stand up, Evie. Don't move."

I tried to take a deep breath but started coughing. I stood up amid the dense smoke and felt for the wall, which was Sheetrock. I stepped to the right, feeling my way with my hands.

"Don't leave!" Evie cried, her hand on my shin. "We need to find my mommy and daddy!"

I ignored this. I needed to save us first. "Just looking for a window, honey."

There was a large crash from elsewhere inside the house. The roof was coming down. We needed to hurry.

I took another step away from the girls, trying to tune out their cries. Something was in my way, I think a dresser, but I could feel a window above it. I patted my hand against it till my fingers hit a lock. The window appeared to be small and high up on the wall.

I tried shoving the dresser out of the way, but it was caught on something, so I pushed it over, letting it crash to the floor.

"What was that?" Evie screamed.

"It's okay," I said, then coughed, long and hard.

I leveraged my fingers under the window and pushed up, but it wouldn't budge. I could feel layers of paint on the frame, which might have sealed it shut. Leaning over the fallen dresser, I felt around for fabric till my hands landed on something denim. I took a breath of the relatively good air at the bottom of the room, wrapped the denim around my hand, stood up, and punched through the window.

As my fist hit the glass, I flashed on movies in which letting fresh air into a house fire makes the room explode. At least that didn't happen.

I knocked the broken glass out of the frame as much as I could. I saw Jordan's mom on the grass, running toward me, and I shouted and gestured for her to come as close as she could. I think she thought she was about to help me climb out, but she reacted quickly enough when a screaming baby came flying her way.

Mrs. Conners placed Hannah on the grass as I hoisted Evie to the window.

"Come on!" I ordered.

"Don't forget Mommy and Daddy!"

"Okay, now jump!"

CHAPTER 19

Jordan

MAGGIE WAS COVERED in soot, aside from a clean white cloth and bandage covering the cut on her head, and she smelled like sour smoke when I caught up with her. I couldn't remember being that happy to see and smell anyone, ever.

"Where the hell did you go?" she demanded as she wrapped me in a bear hug.

"I thought I saw someone," I said into her ear. "Running into the forest."

She gave me a quizzical look. I squeezed harder.

An ambulance was parked in the yard that had been the Carters'. The town's two fire engines were on the scene as well, one team spraying water onto my house and the other across the road at the Allens', focusing on their propane tank lest it also explode.

"So it was the propane, huh?" I said, pulling my head back. My hearing had returned enough that I could make out words above the loud ringing.

"That's what they're saying," Maggie said, keeping her arms loosely around me. Her voice was shaky, as if it were clogged with tears. "You saved two of the Allens. I got little Evie Moore and her baby sister out of their house, but I couldn't get anyone else. I told her that I would save her parents, and I couldn't. Jordan, I think the rest of her family died."

My breath caught. I'd known Evie's grandparents my whole life. Their son, Eric, was ten years older than me and had shown me how to change the oil in a car when I was a little kid. And I still didn't know where Henry was. That they might all be dead was too much to comprehend.

"Those two little girls would be gone as well had you not been so brave," I said. "Seriously, you ran into a burning building with the roof collapsing. If I'd been there, I'd have held on to you and not let you go in. You're a fucking hero, and don't forget it."

Maggie looked at me, startled—by my swearing, perhaps, but also my conviction. I meant it. She saved two young lives, so I wasn't going to let her beat herself up.

"Thanks," she said, and put her head against my chest. I rubbed my chin against her silky, if sooty, hair.

"Listen," I said softly. "I saw something. It crawled out the front window of my house and ran into the woods."

She pulled back to look into my face. "What kind of 'it'? Another wild dog?"

"No, a person on fire," I said.

She kept her gaze on me. "We have to get you checked out," she finally said.

"Hey, I'm serious," I said. "Someone climbed out of our window, and I chased him—or it or whatever—to try to help because he was on fire. But he ran into the forest while parts of him dropped off his body, like a skeleton leaving a trail of burning flesh."

"Jesus, Jordan," she said.

"I know, it was gross."

"No, you need to stop. I'm having trouble processing what I *actually* saw. I can't deal with your hallucinations or fantasies or whatever."

"That may be the first unkind thing you've ever said to me."

"I'm not trying to be unkind, Jordan. I'm just—"

"This isn't something I *wanted* to see. You can tell from my tone that I'm not joking. Give me a break, Maggie."

"I'm sorry, Jordan. I'm sorry. I'm probably just, you know, traumatized from what I've experienced. You probably are, too, and it's coming out in a different way."

"This wasn't a *reaction* to what happened," I said. "It's something *else* that happened. This thing had me on the ground and could have killed me but instead turned and ran into the forest, embers flying off of him all the while."

"Jordan, you did recently have a concussion. You did breathe in a lot of smoke while committing acts of true bravery. You did *not* see a man on fire running out of your house and into the woods."

I couldn't believe we were having this argument, but a sudden roaring in the sky effectively ended it. I put my fingers to my ears to make sure this wasn't some noise inside my head, but, nope: In a moment, a bright light shone from above the trees, and the rumbling intensified. It was a Black Hawk helicopter, which circled around the neighborhood, looking for a good place to land. Avoiding downed power lines and debris, it finally set down in the Allens' soybean field. Its rotors were still turning when three Humvees sped into the neighborhood.

Medics ran from the helicopter to the ambulance in the

Carters' yard, and army personnel from the Humvees rounded up everyone to get a head count. Violet and her dad huddled in the cab of the ambulance, and Mom lay on a stretcher outside it, her chest and shoulder wrapped in bandages. Charlie sat on the step of a fire engine and breathed oxygen from a mask while a firefighter sat next to him. The guys from the helicopter ran to the ambulance, and one climbed up inside to look at the patient in there.

"Who's that?" I asked Maggie.

"One of the Allen kids," she said. "Whichever one is fourteen."

"Henry," I said, feeling shaky and nauseated. "Charlie calls him Hennie. What's wrong with him?"

"Burns," Maggie said, and didn't elaborate. But a moment later, the army medics were pulling his stretcher out of the ambulance and carrying him to the helicopter. A third soldier was inspecting my mom, which prompted me to spring to my feet and jog to the ambulance.

A soldier hopped out of one of the Humvees and intercepted me before I reached my mother. "Are you injured?" he asked.

"I'm fine," I said. "That's my mom they're working on."

"You're bleeding," he said.

"What?" I asked. "Where?"

"Your cheek," he said, and called up to the soldier on top of the vehicle. "Can we get some light?"

I touched my cheek, and my fingers came away wet. A moment later we were in the glow of a spotlight, and I saw how much blood was on my hands.

The soldier touched my face, inspecting the cut, and said I would need some stitches.

"There isn't room in the helicopter," a paramedic called out before leaving the ambulance to come look at me. "Lucky for you, chicks dig scars."

"Chicks don't dig infections, though," Maggie said sharply. "Look at it—it's full of dirt."

"We'll clean you up and stitch it," the medic said to me. "But I've got five people who need to be on that helicopter."

"I think he's in shock," Maggie barreled ahead. "He's seeing things that aren't there."

I shot her an annoyed look, and she returned it with steel.

"Any head trauma?" the medic asked.

"I had a concussion several days ago playing football."

"He said he saw a flaming skeleton running into the woods," Maggie chimed in.

The medic turned from Maggie to me. "I don't have room in the chopper. You're going to have to get help from the EMTs."

It was then that I realized the ambulance wasn't there to take anyone anywhere. It didn't have anywhere to go. It was just a big van full of medical supplies and a couple of paramedics.

"Are you taking my mom in the helicopter?" I asked. I wanted to go with her and Charlie to make sure they were okay.

"Her?" he asked, pointing at her on the stretcher. "Yeah. We think some glass broke off in her wound, so she needs surgery to fish it out. We're taking her to the evac camp."

"What about my little brother?" I said.

"Him too."

"Why?"

"Are you his mom?" the medic asked.

"No, I'm his brother."

"Well," he said, "that's his mom."

"My house just blew up, and you're taking my family without me? I'm still a minor, no?"

"Your mom says your dad is at the nuclear plant and can take care of you."

"He comes home like every five days," I argued.

Maggie stepped up and took my hand. "He can stay with me and my mom in the meantime," she said.

"We'll need confirmation from an adult," the soldier said matter-of-factly.

Maggie's face fell, but then I spotted Maggie's mom running toward us, her face as pale as the snowflake ashes still fluttering down. She had heard the explosion, saw the smoke, and was in tears as she embraced Maggie and then me. Maggie explained the situation to her, and Dr. Gooding told the soldier, "Of course," and gave him her name and address so he could have it for the military's records.

I knelt down beside my mom's stretcher. "Are you okay?" I asked as I knelt down beside her.

"I'm fine," she said, as though she just had a cold. Then she looked up at Maggie. "Nice toss!"

"Thanks!" Maggie responded with a sheepish smile.

"What did you throw?" Dr. Gooding asked her.

"I'll tell you all about it later," Maggie said.

Dr. Gooding crouched down beside me and my mom. "I'm so sorry you're hurt," she told my mom. "We'll take good care of this guy."

"I appreciate that," Mom said, and gave Maggie's mom's hand a squeeze.

"So Charlie's going with you," I said to my mom.

"That's what they told me. We're getting a helicopter ride—he'll love that." She closed and opened her eyes, wide. "Get word to your father, and until then, be a good guest at Maggie's."

I nodded to reassure her but couldn't keep up the pretense. "Mom," I said, "I think something very wrong is going on here."

"You've been through a lot, sweetie. Our house..." She looked over at the wreckage, her eyes welling up. "This house was in your father's family for generations. This will be tough for him. He'll need you, you know."

"I *don't* know," I said.

"You will."

I told Mom and Charlie I loved them, and then the EMTs took me aside and cleaned and stitched up my cheek. It didn't take much, just four sutures below my right eye. By the time I was done, they had loaded the helicopter with six of the injured, including my mom and brother, and lifted off, headed somewhere I couldn't go, with no assurance that I'd see them again anytime soon.

Maggie's shoulders were touching mine as we watched my family flying away. This just felt wrong. Where was my dad in this picture? Why didn't he come home every night? It made no sense to me. Surely he'd return now—except there was no home to return to.

I squeezed Maggie's hand. She squeezed back.

"I'm not crazy, you know," I muttered.

I approached the nearest cop and asked whether I could help with anything further. He said no, but an aid station was being set up in the First Baptist Church basement if I needed a cot. I told him I didn't.

Maggie, her mom, and I got into the pickup truck that Dr. Gooding used for her veterinary practice, with its cheerful logo of a grinning dog and cow.

"Let's go home," Dr. Gooding said.

Home.

CHAPTER 20

Maggie

THE START OF school was postponed yet again. They probably didn't want to welcome us back with grief counselors. Everyone knew the Carters and the Moores. In this town, everyone knew everyone.

As I walked around Mount Hope, the flags were at half-mast, and people seemed in a daze. There were too many rumors and wild theories about the meltdown and this explosion for anyone to feel completely safe, and Mayor Tinkerton appeared to be AWOL. A jowly sixty-something guy with perpetual armpit stains, the mayor considered himself a modern leader by sending out emails to the community with the latest on pothole repairs and library acquisitions. But such communications weren't an option now, and from what I could tell, no one had seen him walking around, reassuring the populace and doing whatever stuff you might expect a small-town mayor to do.

The fact that we couldn't leave town didn't help. People habitually pulled their phones out of their pockets, punched a few buttons, and then scowled. The lack of cell service was messing everyone up. We'd grown so used to having the world at our fingertips that we felt crazily vulnerable without such access.

Over the next few days, there was no word from either of Jordan's parents. Did his dad know where he was? The soldier had taken down our address and contact information, but still...

Jordan tried calling the power plant from our house but couldn't get through. He also had no information about how to contact his mom and brother. I loved having him around, but I missed that guy who was always lifting my spirits. I didn't blame him at all, but he was preoccupied, to say the least.

The fact that I didn't believe him about the flaming guy didn't help. It was like he didn't totally trust me anymore; I could feel a barrier where there wasn't one before.

But even with everything that had happened since we returned to town, there *couldn't* have been a running skeleton with bits of flaming flesh falling off his body. That's just bananas. I worried about him and that battered noggin of his.

Jordan and I went back to his house the day after the explosion so he could leave a note for his father to say he was staying with us. Jordan's face fell as we approached the smoldering, blackened mess that used to be a large nineteenth-century house.

"This is where my granddaddy was born," Jordan said, his voice still scratchy from the smoke, as was mine. "He was a servant, 'never a slave.' He always reminded us of that. His parents had been slaves, and when the masters lost their workforce and plantation, my granddaddy left the house and worked on a ship out of Charleston. He returned in 1928 and bought this house. He said he did it for his parents and all the people who came before them. And here it is."

We stood there, smelled the ashy air, and took in the sight of a once-majestic house now missing its second floor and charred everywhere else.

"My uncle once was in such bad straits that he tore up the hardwood floors for firewood," Jordan said. "My dad eventually replaced every single plank. If he's still the man he used to be, this will devastate him. None of this house will survive. It'll all be taken apart by backhoes and bulldozers."

"But he'll be grateful you're all okay," I said.

Jordan looked me intensely in the eyes. "Charlie would've died if not for you, Maggie. I'll always remember that."

"Oh," I said, turning away, "he was fine."

We stepped up to the front door, and, with what was meant to be a gentle tug, Jordan pulled it off its hinges. Glass was strewn inside and outside where the windows had been. The air was like a steam bath with the overwhelming smell of burnt wet wood. He began to step inside before I said, "Wait, are you sure this is a good idea? The air seems terrible, and who knows how stable what's left of the second story is?"

"There is no second story."

"Exactly."

Jordan stood there in the doorway, looking at the stairway that now led to nowhere.

"Thought I'd go up and grab my old magazines. They aren't flammable, are they?" he asked with a straight face. He'd shown me his collection of 1960s- and 1970s-era *Mad, Rolling Stone, Life,* and *National Lampoon* issues, while above his bed had loomed a now-ironic *The Towering Inferno* poster: "One tiny spark becomes a night of blazing suspense."

"I'm sorry, Jordan," I said, and gave his hand a squeeze. He squeezed back without much feeling, then turned around to head out, kicking a little pile of rubble that was at his feet.

"Oh, jeez," he said, picking up a half-melted plastic eyeball. "This is from Charlie's stuffed animal, Froggy."

He flicked it into the house.

"What a waste of time this was," he said.

Jordan pulled a folded piece of paper out of his pocket, scrawled a note for his dad, and left it under a stone on a still-solid part of the front landing. We left without another word.

We walked back along Main Street, not holding hands, our smoky, soot-speckled shirts sticking to our increasingly sweaty bodies.

"Oh, shit," I said.

"What?"

"Bud Winkle."

There he was, hobnobbing with a couple of old-timers in front of Lammy's Hardware. I placed my hand on Jordan's elbow to redirect him across the street, but it was too late.

"Maggie Gooding, as I live and breathe!" Bud exclaimed, and excused himself from his friends to step over to us.

He was tall and fit, with pronounced cheekbones and a full head of blond hair combed back slickly. His eyes were the palest blue I'd ever seen, and his resting face was a kindly smile. I should've considered him a handsome man—many women in town did—but every time I saw him, I just wanted to get away.

"Hello, Mr. Winkle," I said softly.

"I'm *Bud!*" he responded, sticking out his hand to shake Jordan's before giving me a big pat on the shoulder. "No formalities here. I hear you two are heroes."

"I wouldn't say that," I replied.

Bud looked over at Jordan. "You think she's a hero, don't you, Jordan?"

"I do," Jordan said.

"And I bet you *are,* too," Bud said. "Terrible tragedy. Terrible." He shook his head as if needing to display physically just how terrible this tragedy was. "I represent the folks down at the plant, and I can't tell you how broken up they are about this."

"That's good to know," I said evenly.

An awkward pause hung among us.

"Well, anyway," Bud said, slapping me on the shoulder again, "tell your pretty mama I said hi. Bye, y'all."

"Bye," Jordan and I said in unison as he turned to chat with more people on the sidewalk as if he were a politician working a cocktail party.

"Well, you were a cool breeze on a hot day," Jordan said to me as we walked away. "What was up with that?"

"'Pretty mama.' Ugh," I said.

"I hear you, but he had you at hello."

"I hate that guy. He gives me the creeps."

"He *is* a bit slippery," Jordan acknowledged.

"What gave you that impression? The ads on benches telling you that if someone gave you a painful hangnail, you should call 1-800-BUD-WINKLE?"

"Actually, I haven't seen those benches since we got back."

"It's too many numbers, anyway. It should be 1-800-BUD-WINK."

"Aw, those extra two letters don't make any difference. Maybe he thought 'Bud Wink' sounded too much like 'Hoodwink.'"

"Exactly. Anyway, he's dating my mom."

"Oh."

Aside from a car cruising down Main Street and some chit-chat up the block, the silence between us lingered for a few moments. Jordan finally broke it.

"What do you think he meant about representing the folks down at the plant?" he asked.

"He's the plant's lawyer, I guess?"

"Curious," Jordan said. "Not sure why those people in particular should be all broken up about the explosion in our neighborhood."

I realized we both were looking down at the sidewalk as we walked. This was a cheerful non-date.

"Would it be entirely inappropriate," I asked, "if I suggested we redeem our ice-cream rain check?"

"Sure."

"Sure, it would be inappropriate?"

"Shut up and let's get some ice cream," he said with the hint of a smile.

The Tastee Freeze was just a few blocks out of our way, and other people had seized upon the same idea. Jordan's buddy Tico was in front of us in line chatting up my friend Suzanne, a curvy, chirpy girl with a photographic memory and some occasionally startling anger-management issues. Had they arrived together?

Jordan and Tico exchanged one of those bro-handshake/pat-on-the-back hugs. Suzanne and I said, "Hey."

"You guys okay?" she asked. "We heard."

"Jordan, man, trouble is following you around," Tico added with a smile.

Jordan smiled back unconvincingly.

"His house is destroyed," I said. "And you heard about the Carters and the Moores..."

Tico and Suzanne nodded grimly in unison.

"I was actually looking forward to school," Suzanne said. "Now everyone's off coming up with their own conspiracy theories. We need to come together at last."

"Yeah, and all decide on *one* conspiracy theory," Tico said.

"What's the best one you've heard?" I asked.

"That there was no meltdown," Tico said. "That the government wanted us out so they could do some crazy stuff to us and this town. It's like a big reality show, with secret cameras everywhere, and we can't get out."

"Like *The Truman Show*," Jordan said.

"The what?" Tico asked.

"Forget it."

"I was thinking more like *Big Brother* if it were an entire town."

"Tomato, to-mah-to," Jordan said.

Tico gave me a puzzled look. "You taking care of this guy?"

"Doing my best," I said.

The ice cream tasted especially good, though we had to race to eat it before it melted off the cone and dripped onto our shirts and sandals. Jordan and Tico chatted some more, and I could see Jordan's body relaxing.

"Is it terrible that I miss math class?" Suzanne asked me. "I really do. I'm looking forward to algebra because I like cracking formulas."

"Well, I'm more of a word gal, but I get it for sure," I responded. "Something normal would be nice."

"Yes. Normal," she said in her sweet voice. "I'm a little stressed out because I have a low tolerance for *fucking bullshit*." A dark cloud passed over her face, then gave way to sunshine again.

As Jordan and I walked back to my house, I took his hand and asked, "So how *are* you?"

"Good," he said, kicking a stone on the road's shoulder. "Maybe not so good."

"I get it," I said, nodding. I still was haunted by Hannah's cries for "Mommy and Daddy." I'd cried a few times, usually in the bathroom with the water running. I didn't want to share any more of this with Jordan, who I knew was missing his mother and brother—and dad—on top of the trauma he experienced at the fire and the loss of his house.

"I keep seeing my mom's face as they wheeled her away," Jordan said. "I keep remembering how Charlie's little hand felt in mine. He's such a funny kid. I miss his laugh and the way he'd spit back my dorky pop-culture references. No offense, but I feel really alone."

I wanted to stop and hug him so hard. I wanted to do more as well, but taking romantic advantage of such a situation felt wrong.

"I appreciate that you're willing to share your feelings with me, Jordan," I said. "It's one of the things I love about you. It makes me think you're that much stronger."

I wasn't intending the word "love" to come out of my mouth in relation to anything involving Jordan, but there it was. I wasn't taking it back.

He stopped, my words appearing to register with him in

a significant way. "Thanks, Maggie. I mean it. I feel like I can tell you anything. I've never felt that way with anybody, including my family. I hope you feel the same with me."

"I do," I said. "I have cancer."

"*What?*"

I hadn't meant to blurt that out, either. Sometimes Jordan was my truth serum.

"It's not definite," I said, "but, yeah, I have a pretty strong hunch."

"A 'hunch,'" he said. "Not a doctor's diagnosis. A 'hunch.'"

"Right," I said. "Jordan, you don't know how hard it is to tell you about this. I haven't even told my mom, and she's a doctor."

"For four-legged patients."

"You can't tell her, Jordan," I said, suddenly getting insistent. "You *can't*. You have to promise me right now."

"I promise, I promise," he said, putting his hands up in a surrender position. "I don't even know what's going on."

"Okay," I said. "I have a suspicious lump—on my left boob, if you must know. And I have no idea how to get to an oncologist, given all that's going on here."

Jordan gave me the most serious look I've ever seen.

"Maggie, this is important. This is your *life*. We'll get you diagnosed if I have to steal the next helicopter that lands within twenty miles of here."

I smiled. "I appreciate that. I hope this won't require your superhero intervention."

He shook his head. "Cancer. Fuck. I don't believe it. You're too young."

"I know," I said. "I wish I didn't have such a great track record for being right."

He gave me a look like he was deciding whether to make a wisecrack.

"I was taking my X-ray in Mom's office," I continued, "and that reminds me." I rolled up my sleeve and pointed to a white bump on my bicep. "Do you have this scar?"

He glanced at the corresponding spot on his arm. "Nope."

I told him about the pill-like disc I saw on the X-ray, how I wondered whether it was like a microchip you implant in dogs in case they run away. "Is the military tracking us all now?" I asked. "Is it something less sinister? Or more?"

"I don't know," he said. "I've stopped discounting anything. Do other people have that scar? Does your mom?"

"Good question. We'll have to check."

He took my hand and started swinging it back and forth as we resumed walking.

"So... you're a sixteen-year-old girl convinced that you have breast cancer—from a supposedly insignificant amount of radiation—while the government has implanted a microchip in your arm to track your every move. And you're worried about your friend here because *he* might've lost touch with reality."

I couldn't suppress a smile. Neither could he.

"Bingo," I said. "Next time, take out your damn cell phone and get a picture of your flaming, flesh-flying skeleton dude. You think you're living in the 1970s or something?"

"You make an interesting point, Maggie Gooding," he said, swinging my arm higher. "As you often do."

CHAPTER 21

Jordan

AS MAGGIE AND I sat on her couch to watch the western *Cat Ballou* (her choice), I wrapped my arm around her, and she huddled close. It felt natural, like why hadn't we been doing this always? I was putting up a good front, but her confession rattled me. If something bad happened to Maggie, I couldn't bear it. I realized that more than ever. If she was right, we had no time to waste. You don't rope-a-dope cancer.

There was too much going on. People's lives could end in a flash—and already had. I was seeing—and feeling—things that not even I completely believed. I wasn't sure whether my headache was a lingering result of my concussion or the accumulation of so much pressure coming from so many directions. I didn't even have homework yet.

Maggie's mom came in and sat on the cushiony chair by the couch. She looked at us and smiled. The three of us had sat in these seats a hundred times over the years—I could quote almost every line from *On the Waterfront*, Maggie's favorite movie—but tonight everything was different.

I wasn't paying much attention to what was going on

with Lee Marvin in this one. I'd promised Maggie I wouldn't tell her mom about the cancer, but I wasn't comfortable with this decision. If you think you have cancer, you tell a medical professional, period. Maggie's mom was a medical professional. Maggie wouldn't be able to research her way out of this one.

I kept glancing at her mom, thinking about what I knew that she didn't, wishing I had a better idea of what to do.

Maggie's plan was to wait until the road opened up and then go to a hospital for a mammogram. I suggested she go to the sick camp and the hospital there—where my mom and Charlie were—but Maggie said she'd talked to an army nurse who said that facility didn't have a mammography machine. She said the nurse recommended waiting till she could get to the Canville hospital or the big medical center in Charleston. I said that may not be a very good nurse.

My brain was racing. Could we get Maggie to a doctor or lure a doctor to town? If we drove up to the roadblock and said we had a medical emergency, would the army really stop us? Could we at least mail her X-rays to a specialist somewhere? Was the mail going through?

In the meantime, there I was, sitting on the couch, enjoying the peach scent coming from Maggie's hair and the soft warmth of her body and feeling terrified that now that we were together, she could be snatched away from me.

As the movie ended, Dr. Gooding pointed at the both of us together on the couch and said, "So, this is interesting."

"It's for our health, Mom," Maggie said. "Remember that study in U.S. News and World Report that said hugging releases oxytocin, dopamine, and serotonin? It helps with stress and lowers blood pressure."

"Well," her mom said, "then you two must be stress free."

"Right," Maggie said. "Like you and Bud Winkle." She stuck her forefinger deep down her throat.

Dr. Gooding's face darkened. "Well, that is not nice."

"He called you my pretty mama."

"Don't you think I am?"

I could see Maggie trying to think of the right answer here. Her mother looked surprisingly vulnerable.

"Of course, Mom," Maggie finally said.

I would've happily stayed on that couch with Maggie all night, but an idea had lodged itself in my head, and I couldn't shake it.

I needed to talk to my dad.

There was so much to discuss: Mom, Charlie, the house, where I should live, what I should do next. I also needed him to tell me what to do about Maggie's health situation.

"I'm going to hit the sack," I announced.

"You are?" Maggie said. "Okay."

"Sorry," I said. "Just really tired."

I thought of planting a slow, wet one on her right then, but I couldn't do it with her mom there. I wished their floors didn't creak so loudly; otherwise I'd consider sneaking up to Maggie's room after her mom had gone to bed. But Maggie didn't have her own room; she and her mom shared one big space upstairs. I was on a cot in the larger of the examination rooms. I appreciated that Maggie and her mom made room for me, given how small their living space was. I also was glad I didn't have to sleep on the metal table where the dogs and cats were examined.

As I lay on the cot and gazed at the blue walls, I thought about Charlie and how his bedroom had been painted a similar color. I'd looked in on him before I went out to stargaze with Maggie. He'd gone to bed thinking he was starting first grade in the morning. He was so excited and bouncy. Then he was tightly tucked in and asleep, letting out a whispering whistle with each breath. His arms were flung up above his head as if he were doing the Wave. That was his sleeping position since he was a baby. I ruffled his hair and kissed the top of his moppy head, and he let out a happy little sigh. He had no idea how much his world—our world—would change over the next couple of hours.

Now he had no bedroom, no school, not even his favorite toy. I ached to see my little buddy again.

I waited till I heard Maggie and her mom disappear upstairs. Then I opened my window and slipped out.

CHAPTER 22

Maggie

MOM SEEMED TO have recovered from my Bud Winkle shot and was smirking about Jordan and me as we got upstairs.

"You two…" she said.

I ignored her.

I was so glad I'd told Jordan my secret. I had to. I knew he would keep it. I could tell he was kind of freaked out, but he also was cool. My mom would not have been. She would've become an emotional mess. She might have been pragmatic when it came to animals, but not with me. She'd been over-protective of me since I was little, maybe because it was just the two of us. If it drove me crazy that at this point I couldn't do anything but wait, it would have driven her completely batshit. She would have been relentless in banging her head against those walls. Neither of us needed that.

I turned on the computer and remembered for the zillionth time that the internet was down.

"Have you ever heard of someone called Ishango?" I asked over my shoulder.

"No," Mom said. "Does he live here?"

"Not that I know of," I said. "Just heard the name."

After digging around in our dim, dusty crawl space, I emerged with the "I" book of our encyclopedia set.

"What are you up to?" Mom asked.

"Checking something out," I said, lying on my stomach on the floor and opening the book in front of me. "Had a research paper idea."

There it was: *Ishango*. Part of a national park in the Democratic Republic of the Congo, described as one of the most beautiful places in the world. Home to one of the largest concentrations of hippos in the world. Also the name of a Congolese nature preservation organization.

Another entry followed: *Ishango bone*. A Stone Age tool made from a baboon bone with markings carved into its side. According to the encyclopedia, it had long been assumed to be a tally stick, but now it was thought to be part of some other type of ancient mathematical tool. One side grouped tally marks to make prime numbers adding up to 60: $19 + 17 + 13 + 11$, for instance. The other side's marks were related to more disputable equations. It wasn't exactly the theory of relativity, but this might have been the earliest known mathematical system.

What any of this had to do with Mount Hope, I had no clue.

I closed the book and looked up at my mom, who was beaming at me.

"*Stop* it," I said.

"Seriously, how many years did that take?" she asked.

"We're still in friends mode, actually," I said.

"Huh. Could've fooled me."

"Well," I said, getting up, "we *are* going to the homecoming dance together."

"He finally asked!"

"Vice versa, Mom. I'm a modern woman."

"So you are."

"I'll just search online for a dress. Oh, wait..."

"I'll dig out my old sewing machine and make you something out of the drapes," she volunteered.

"Thanks."

"Hold on a sec." Mom disappeared into the closet and rummaged around. She was really pretty, even in her jeans and a T-shirt. I could imagine her going to a dance when she was younger—or now, for that matter. She was far from ancient, having had me when she was nineteen.

"It's a couple years old," she said as she reemerged, "but I hung on to it in case someone asked you out when you were a freshman."

She handed me a Nordstrom's prom catalog. On the cover were three girls who were hyper-skinny and showing way too much...everything.

"Perfect," I said. "Now if only there were a Nordstrom's on this side of the roadblock."

"You look at it for ideas," she said.

I opened onto a page showing a lacy thing that resembled lingerie more than a dress. "That's a no."

But as I stared at the revealing gowns, I got an idea.

"I think my arms are too weird for dresses like this," I said, rolling up my T-shirt sleeves to expose my bare shoulders.

"Too weird in what way? You've got great arms."

"Let me see yours," I said.

She rolled up one sleeve, then the other. "Like this?"

"Yeah," I said, and approached her. There it was: a tiny round scar like the one I had. "See, your arms are better."

"Nonsense," Mom said, though I could tell on some level she appreciated the flattery.

"Hey, there was a microchip in Nerf, wasn't there?"

Mom gave me a puzzled look. "You are all over the place tonight."

"Sorry. I've got a young, fertile mind."

She laughed. "Yes, Nerf had a microchip, though it wasn't that weird octopus-y thing we found after he was cremated."

"Right. What *was* that?" I asked.

"No idea. I'll let you find that out, genius."

"But he also had a microchip? That would've gotten burned up?"

"That's right," Mom said.

"How did it work? Like a tracking device?"

Mom stepped up to me, took each of my hands in hers, and spoke to me as if she were passing down precious generational advice. "Honey. Since you're so concerned all of a sudden. A pet microchip is not a tracking device. It does not have GPS. If it were a tracking device, it would require a separate power source, like a battery. These are radio-frequency identification implants, RFIDs for short, which provide permanent means of ID. It's like the size of a grain of rice. Nerf gave his name, my name, and our address. That's it. Anything else you'd like to know?"

Hmm. So the microchip was much smaller than what I saw in my arm—or whatever the hell that metal thing was that survived Nerf's cremation.

"*Could* you implant a tracking device in someone? I mean, like a dog?" I asked.

"There's probably a way to do it," she said. "Why? You want to see where Jordan is going now that he's your boyfriend?"

"Yeah," I said with a laugh. "I need to know where he is at all times, because he just might be doing something crazy."

CHAPTER 23

Jordan

AS I BIKED through the forest on hiking trails I'd walked a thousand times, I realized something incredible: I could see in the dark. My brain was doing that thing again where it was recognizing danger and reacting without thought. I was on autopilot, hopping over roots, avoiding stumps and rocks, and even jumping off little rises in the trail. Plus, I was going really fast and not getting winded. Even in daylight I'd never had a ride like this. I was zipping along under the dark leaves and stars.

I headed toward the power plant, where security would stop me but then could get my dad and bring him out to see me. I'd stand by the gate and wait—nothing illegal about that.

The forest blew past me in a blur. My adrenaline was pumping so hard that it coursed through my veins. I felt invincible.

I saw four deer standing on the trail ahead of me, and they saw, and heard, me as well, lifting their heads to the branches creaking as I whizzed through the trees. The deer scattered while I powered ahead and somehow took note of each tree's age and condition.

Maggie and I once watched a *MythBusters* episode that dispelled the widely held notion that we use only 10 percent of our brains and if we could tap into the other 90 percent, we'd be superhuman. Yet now I felt like I finally was using those extra reserves of brain and body power. It was as if everything I'd ever known—and some stuff I hadn't—was immediately available, *right there*.

What would my dad say when he saw me? He'd flip out probably and demand to know what I was doing at the plant in the middle of the night. But I was the one who should be angry. Mom and Charlie had been airlifted away after our house burned down, and he was nowhere to be found. I was sixteen, technically a minor. He was supposed to take care of me.

The dad I knew would have found me by now, made sure I was safe. Where the hell was *he*?

I needed to focus. He could help me help Maggie, too. He knew about whatever radiation had leaked. Maggie hadn't been sent to the sick camp, because she wasn't in the path of the cloud emitted from the plant. Plus, we'd been told that we were returning to a safe town, so Maggie shouldn't have come into contact with any radiation.

She couldn't have cancer.

No.

I didn't know whether what I was attempting was brave or foolish, but it was the only thing I could think of to help Maggie, especially if we weren't going to involve her mom, who was a veterinarian and not an oncologist, anyway. Had Maggie actually been exposed to radiation and gotten cancer, and if so, how could we get her to a real hospital?

Maybe we'd have to go through the forest on our bikes.

Dozens of trails lined these woods, and the military couldn't be guarding them all. We'd go out into the wilderness, get to Canville, show up at the hospital, and not use our real names. Maybe we'd break the quarantine, but I didn't care; the point of the quarantine was to keep us safe and healthy, and that's all I wanted to do for Maggie. Besides, if the town was safe, why was it under quarantine?

When I reached where the trail crosses Route 93, a two-lane back road, I hit the brakes. I heard something, maybe metallic? I didn't know what, but something on the road was trying to be quiet.

Whatever it was, it was far ahead of me, silent and cautious. My hearing, I realized, had grown as sharp as my eyesight. I moved to the side of the road and down an embankment.

Near the bridge a coyote emerged from the trees and trotted onto the pavement. It sniffed the air and zeroed in on me. With a growl and one lip raised in a snarl, it slowly approached.

Another animal attack—great. I gripped my handlebars, ready to swing the bike wheel at its head.

The coyote crossed the road's double yellow line, closing the gap between us quickly, when I heard the noise again. The coyote heard it, too, and stopped, its ears rotating like satellite dishes. It wasn't a broken twig or an errant footfall.

It was the sound of someone chambering a round.

A moment later, there was a faint whisper followed by a cacophony of gunfire. The coyote did the *Bonnie and Clyde* ketchup dance, dropping to the ground and jerking around as the gunfire went on for several seconds. Finally, the shots slowed to one here and there, like popcorn finishing up in the microwave.

After all went silent, a squad of soldiers came out of the woods. They didn't look my way. They were focused on the dead coyote.

One man had a tank of something on his back connected to a long metal tube, and he stepped forward to point the tube at the furry red carcass on the pavement. Flames burst from the tube, engulfing the coyote, and this went on for, I kid you not, five whole minutes. They were cremating this thing.

Afterward, a soldier carrying a collapsible olive-green shovel scooped the remains into what looked like a large black garbage bag with a zipper on top. When that task was done, the flamethrower guy blasted the ground again, melting any traces that might've been left. Then the soldiers disappeared back into the dark woods, not a word exchanged among them.

How 'bout that?

I didn't move. I don't know how long I remained frozen, crouched in the embankment, but as much as I hadn't wanted to go face-to-face with that coyote, I also wasn't keen on getting anywhere near the dude with the flamethrower. Those military guys sure weren't animal-friendly, and they didn't strike me as human-friendly, either.

What was the point of that demonstration of literal fire-power? They shot that animal to pieces, so why then did they feel compelled to obliterate it? What needed to be reduced to ashes? Was another metal octopus-like thing in the remains that they swept up? How would it have gotten into the coyote in the first place? It's not like the military was giving vaccination shots to wild animals.

I hadn't reached the power plant, yet this bike ride already was making my head spin.

CHAPTER 24

Jordan

THE PLANT CAME into view, and I slowed down to look for guards. Before me, looming in the dark, were the two immense cooling towers, with a cluster of other buildings to the north and a large parking lot in front. Although it held some cars, most of the lot was taken up with the same kind of shelters we had at the evacuation camp, perhaps for workers such as my dad who had to live here.

Serving as the plant's backdrop was the enormous peak that gave our town its name. It rose four hundred feet into the air, a massive outcropping of rock just above the Sweetbay River.

I could see surprisingly little military presence at the plant. A twelve-foot-high chain-link fence, topped with razor wire, surrounded the facility, but that had been there as long as I could remember. At a guard shack by the fence gate, two soldiers stood talking.

The more places I looked, the more security cameras I saw—atop the fence, the guard tower, the streetlight...

I fished in my pocket for my headlamp, which I'd brought

because I assumed I'd need it to see the trail. Once I got going on my bike and realized I could see everything amazingly well, I'd stuffed it into my shorts. Now I didn't want to sneak up on the guards; I wanted them to think I was an everyday teenager wanting to talk to his dad. So here I was, all lit up. *Don't shoot, please.*

I took a deep breath and walked my bike down a wide trail that led to the road.

Almost immediately the two men at the gate turned, one putting his hand on—was it a pistol or a radio? The other soldier picked up his rifle. He didn't point it at me but was ready to. The light was directly above them, and their helmets cast shadows on their faces.

"Stop!" one of them ordered. "State your name."

"I'm Jordan Conners," I said, stopping twenty feet from them, leaning my bike against my legs and raising my hands in the most nonthreatening way possible. I hoped they didn't think my being black represented a threat in itself. "I need to talk to my dad, Jermaine Conners. He's an engineer. It's an emergency."

"What is the nature of this emergency?" the man with the rifle asked. He had an odd, abrupt way of speaking that reminded me of someone, but I couldn't remember who. I could see from his rank insignia that he was a private first class. The other guy, older and stockier, was a corporal.

"Family matters," I said.

"Elaborate."

"Our house burned down in an explosion yesterday. My mother and brother were injured and helicoptered away. I was left alone and need to tell him." I was laying it on thick, but this all was true. Being an abandoned, newly homeless kid *should* lift me past the threshold of getting to talk to my dad.

The older guy stared at me as if he didn't believe me. Then he got on his radio: "Thunder Central, Thunder Central, this is Thunder Two. Over."

There was a pause. "Thunder Two, this is Thunder Central. Go ahead. Over."

"We have a kid here who wishes to see his father. He reports there have been injuries in the family. Over."

Pause. "Name of child and father? Over."

The corporal relayed the names.

"Stand by," the radio squawked. "Over."

We stood there in silence, me by my bike with my hands still in the air, the private with both hands on his gun, the corporal holding the radio in his left hand while he rested his right on his sidearm. It was as if we were all posing for a photo—or painting—with none of us looking at one another.

The wait was agonizing. They probably were looking for my dad, wherever he was, to see whether he could leave his duties. Would he be working this late? Might he be in his shelter or wherever he spends the night?

They also might have been checking up on me. We'd all filled out so many forms during the evacuation that they probably had my shoe size (11½) and favorite album (Stevie Wonder's *Songs in the Key of Life,* of course).

"Thunder Two, this is Thunder Central. Over."

"Go ahead, Thunder Central. Over."

"We are sending a car for him. Over."

Holy shit, it *worked*. I resisted saying, "Great news. Over."

I did decide to press my luck in noting: "I thought this place would be full of you guys. Where's the rest of the army?"

The corporal eyed me. "We wouldn't be doing a good job guarding the plant if we let everyone see where we are."

I looked into the trees surrounding the plant and wondered whether they were full of soldiers. I doubted it. Then I wondered whether I could leap up and over the razor-wire fence like I'd jumped the fence while escaping the bear. "What are you guarding the plant *for*?" I asked.

"What do you mean?" the corporal asked, a slight edge in his monotone.

"Are you afraid someone's going to come here and attack? Terrorists?"

The corporal looked away. He was done. The private gave his head a slight shake and said, "We're not big on explanations."

"Just following orders?" I asked with a smile.

The private looked at me as if I were a mosquito who'd flown too close to his ear. Thus ended my charm offensive.

Soon a golf cart drove toward us from the parking lot carrying two more soldiers, also decked out in gear and fatigues. It pulled up to the guard post, and the guy in the passenger seat asked, "Jordan Conners of 2045 Wade Hampton Road?"

"Yes, sir."

Unlike every soldier I'd ever seen in the evacuation camp, neither of these men had his name written on his chest or any rank on his shoulder. The driver faced straight ahead, and the soldier in the passenger seat turned to me and said, "Give me the last four numbers of your Social Security number."

It had been on every single form I'd filled out over the past year, so it was top of mind, and I recited it to him. He pulled a flashlight from his belt, shone it in my face, and looked at his clipboard to compare the real me to whatever photo he was looking at.

"Get on," he said, and gestured to the small rear-facing seat in the back.

"Yes, sir," I said, and did as requested.

The cart drove to the far end of the parking lot and around a corner, out of sight of the guarded gate. I hadn't seen the major construction project on this side of the plant. Two large cranes stood over a cluster of dump trucks, and a steel framework surrounded a pit. I couldn't tell what they were building.

The driver pulled up to a curb next to a gravel walkway that led to a blank steel door.

"Is this where my dad is?" I asked as we headed to the door.

The man didn't answer, but he pulled a blank white card from his jacket pocket and waved it in front of a plastic square next to the door. A light turned from red to green, and the door clicked. He pulled it open and motioned for me to enter.

We were definitely not at the front desk. A narrow hallway, with linoleum flooring and a chemical smell, lay before us, air-conditioned and chilly. I could hear the faint hum of electricity, like from an old refrigerator.

"Go ahead," he said. "Then take a left."

Boot steps echoed behind me as I walked. I was sweating more now than I did during the whole eight-mile ride through the woods.

I shouldn't have come here. I should have waited for my dad to come home—but how soon was that going to be? There was no home for him to come back to, anyway.

We turned left at a T junction and went down another long hallway, with doors lining the left side. The walls were cinder block, painted beige to match the floor. The place looked weathered and smelled like school bathrooms after the janitor had washed them.

"Room 203," the man said sharply.

I turned the knob, which was cold, and entered the room to see a few people sitting and standing around a table, none of them my dad.

Two men in suits, the ones who had come to watch football practice, were there. So was a third man who didn't stand. He appeared to be a scientist, wearing a white lab coat, and I had a shock of recognition.

The face. Skin pulled back. Burnt.

The man from my nightmare.

CHAPTER 25

Jordan

I STUMBLED BACKWARD into the wall, staring at the grotesque scientist. His skin was stretched across his face. He was heavily scarred, whether by fire or acid or some major plastic-surgery mishap. He had no lips, so his teeth were completely exposed, as if he were a grinning skull. He had no ears, at least as far as I could tell, and his hair sprouted in little parched-crabgrass patches. One of his eyes was completely white and opaque, and the other was a dot of black.

I had a dual impulse to vomit and to blubber like a baby, but I was too shocked to move. I reminded myself to breathe.

"Please sit down," said one of the men with no *please* in his tone.

The human-looking guys offered little to tell them apart. Aside from their identical black suits, white shirts, and black ties, they wore their dark hair parted on the left and looked to be about six feet tall. The best way to tell them apart was one man had a small scar on his chin, while the other sported a plain gold ring on his finger. Each was the all-American man: white, tall, lean, and someone who could give me a lot of trouble.

"Please," the gold-ring guy directed, pointing to a chair on my side of the heavy steel table.

"I'm just here to see my dad," I gasped, trying to avert my eyes from the nightmare scientist.

The door closed with a click, and my soldier escort was gone. I edged toward the exit, pondering whether I might make a break for it. Would that work? I had a hunch that...no.

"Aha," the scientist finally said, his voice thin, reedy, and punctuated by wheezes, as if he were trying to catch his breath. "Rho. You—ah—you have come to us. This is good. We thought we would have to go and—ah, ah—fetch you." With every "ah" he sounded like he was sucking air through a thin straw, and his pronunciation was off because he couldn't use his lips.

"Fetch *me*?" I asked. "I wanted to see my dad. Is he coming?"

The scientist was wearing a white glove on his left hand, which made me think of Michael Jackson, which made me want to ask whether he'd had a *really* bad experience shooting a Pepsi commercial. Then I noticed that he had no right hand, and I thought maybe it wasn't the best time for my pop-culture comedy act. What *happened* to this dude?

"We, well, *Ishango* is very interested in you—ah—Jordan Conners."

I couldn't hide my jolt of recognition upon hearing that name. "Ishango," I said, my heart pounding. "Okay. But why is it interested in me?"

I turned toward the two suited guys.

"Why were you at my football practice?"

They stared back silently.

"You—ah—Jordan Conners. You, you were injured, am I, am I right?" the scientist asked.

"Yeah," I said. "Day of the evacuation. Car accident. That was a year ago. If my dad isn't coming, I really need to go."

The scientist shook his head, his grin looking all the more maniacal. "No, a *new* injury."

"At football practice," the man with the gold ring said. "You hurt your head."

"Oh, right," I said. "Bad play. I might've gotten a concussion, which I wish I could say is unusual in the game of football, but, alas, it is not. Did you see that movie *Concussion*? Will Smith trying to pull off a Nigerian accent? It wasn't great, wasn't terrible—though the accent kind of was—but I learned some stuff, and you might, too. It makes you reconsider our whole societal attitude toward football, especially as it concerns our young people. Peewee football and all that. Anyway, I'm okay—some headaches but nothing too bad."

The scientist nodded slowly. I didn't know whether to look at his white eye or the dot. I went with the dot. "A concussion," he said. "That was unfortunate. You are *not* to get injuries of that kind. It has compromised Ishango's authority."

"Wait, what?" I said, trying to keep the tremble out of my voice.

The scientist closed his eyes (*thank you*), then opened them again (*oh, well*). "You are special," he murmured, the word coming out as "seshal."

"Seshal how?" I couldn't help myself.

"You're feeling no ill effects from the—ah—fire, yes? That was a test, you see."

"Huh? Test for *what*?"

"Omega noted your cellular—ah—regeneration level in the lungs. You ran at near optimum speed despite—ah—what would have been—ah—a fatal level of smoke inhalation for most people. Omega was supposed to retrieve you for repair that evening, but—ah—unfortunately failed in his assignment."

"Retrieve me for repair?" I boomed. "What the hell are you talking about? I'm not a machine. And who's Omega? The flaming, molting, running dude?"

The scientist and his freaky tooth face just grinned at me. I fought off an impulse to knock those teeth out of his skull.

"And what do you mean it was a *test*?" I shouted, gaining volume. "Families *died* in that explosion, man, people I've known all my life! Kids! Parents! Grandparents! A piece of glass stabbed my mom's back like a dagger—she could have died, too! Instead, she and my little brother were taken away to the evacuation camp—I *think*—and now I'm all alone. Which is *why I want to see my father.* Please let me see him!"

Without so much as a shrug, the burned man looked at the men and said, "Ah—inform the unit. Rho is to undergo a—ah—reauthorization."

Rho? Row? R'oh?

"Why do you keep calling me Rho?" I asked. "I'm Jordan. That's what my dad named me. He's an engineer here. I need to see him *now*." I stood and gave the table a sharp shove that prompted the suited guys to jump back. I moved toward the door.

"I can see you will have to be—ah—sedated."

"No way, bro-zay," I said, realizing that made no sense as I tried the doorknob.

Locked.

"I'm a minor. You can't do anything without my parents' permission. If you won't take me to my father, then I'm out of here."

"I'm afraid—ah—not. We need to fix the problem first. Then you will be ready, Rho."

This whole scene was freaking me out. I felt like I could collapse into a hysterical puddle any second, but I also knew I needed to keep it together, keep my instincts sharp. "Ready for *what*? I can't understand half of what you're saying, and not just because you don't have lips. Did you do something to me to give me my new abilities? I don't need or want them—I was fine with how I was. And I'll take a pass on the 'fixing,' thank you very much."

"Sit down," the gold-ring guy said, standing up. I was taller than him, but he was thicker.

"Nope, I'm done taking orders," I said. "I need to know what's going on, because this is bananas." I pointed at the scientist. "*You* I've seen in my dreams. And they weren't good dreams. How does *that* work? What kind of evil voodoo are you up to?"

He looked up, and his disfigured face approximated a wince.

The chin-scar guy pulled a syringe from his jacket pocket.

"Nope again," I said, and jiggled the doorknob until Goldie yanked my hand away from it.

I spun out of his grasp and clutched his arm in an aikido wristlock. I applied pressure, and he grunted and fell to the floor. Scar came at me with the needle, and I kicked it across the room, letting go of Goldie in the process. The two of them backed up, getting ready to attack. I shoved the table into them and went for the door again.

There was a flash of light, and I saw a blade plunging toward my arm. I drew back quickly but not quickly enough as the blade slashed the top of my wrist. Whatever my new powers were, pain suppression wasn't one of them. *Ouch!*

The scientist sprouted a two-foot sword out of his right arm stump. Aw, shit, now he was going all supervillain on me. As he stood, I could see he was short and hunched—but he also moved *fast*.

He swung his sword arm, and I ducked, the blade taking a wedge out of the cinder block. I went for his elbow to try to hyperextend it, but he dropped low, and the palm of my hand hit the wall, crumbles falling to the floor. A few drops of blood from my slashed wrist followed.

I reeled back. My hand and arm hurt, but also: How was I doing what I was doing? How did I know an aikido wristlock?

Goldie and Scar remained positioned on the opposite side of the table from me, and the scientist stood in front of the door. As Goldie reached into his coat for something—a gun?—the scientist swung his sword down at me, like I was a log he was about to split. I dodged and gave him a low, vicious kick in the ankle. He let out a shriek—one that I had heard in my dreams—and I turned to lift the table off the floor and heave it into the two suits.

As the steel surface pinned both men to the wall, Goldie dropped his gun, and I pounced on it like a loose football. Just then I felt a sharp pain in my calf and let out a yelp.

I spun around to see the crazed scientist with arms raised

high, about to bring the bloody sword down on me for a killing blow.

Everything went slow-motion—except me. I was moving at normal speed. I pointed the gun toward this monstrous murderer and fired.

Again.

And again.

CHAPTER 26

Maggie

ANOTHER NIGHT, ANOTHER startling wake-up. This time it was a flurry of knocking on the front door that jarred me awake.

"Mom," I groaned, spotting 4:30 a.m. on my digital clock, "it's another twenty-four-whore emergency." I rolled over, figuring she'd deal with this latest animal problem. What would it be now, a psychopathic parakeet?

Pound pound pound pound.

"Mom! Someone's—damn it." I looked over, and Mom's bed was empty. Now I vaguely recalled that she'd left for another emergency call hours earlier, something involving wild dogs bearing down on a herd of sheep.

I threw a robe over my T-shirt, trudged downstairs, and peeked through the door.

"Jordan?" I said as I opened it, and he rushed in, nearly knocking me over. "What are you doing out? Racing bears again?"

His clothes were drenched in sweat and . . . was that blood?

"I need help," he said, and limped straight into the exam room where he hadn't been sleeping, with blood dripping from his pants and both hands. "I hate to do this in the middle of the night, but could you get your mom?"

"She's out."

"I need stitches," Jordan said, hopping onto the high table. He gingerly pulled off his Clemson sweatshirt to reveal blood caked around his wrist and forearm. "We have to hurry. They could be coming here any minute."

"Oh, my God," I said. "What..."

I could say no more. It was medic-mode time. I took his arm in my hands and inspected the crusted blood for the wound.

"They got my leg, too," he said. "I think that one's deeper."

His arm had a clear, clean slice. "It's not terrible," I said. "Can you make a fist?"

He did.

"Now touch the tips of your fingers to your thumbs," I instructed.

He was able to do that, too.

"This looks like an old wound," I said. "It's not fresh blood. How long ago did this happen? What's it from?"

He was too busy pulling off his shoe, which was filled with goopy blood, to answer. I knelt to look at his leg.

"You won't believe it," he said. "I don't believe it."

"Believe what?" I said as I tried to get a clear view of the wound. I needed better light. "Hold on," I said, and fetched Mom's surgery lamp from the back room.

"I went to the power plant," he said. "I wanted to talk to my dad. I know it's restricted, so don't tell me I'm an idiot. I know it was a bad decision."

"You went to talk to your dad after we all went to bed?" I asked.

"I know."

"Next time come talk to me. I'm around all night."

I looked up at him and saw the trace of a smile. That was a good sign.

"This is obviously a stab wound," I said, having pulled off his sock and rolled up his pant leg. It was deep, but clean—nothing jagged.

"I know. I was there," he said.

"Don't make me poke you in it, smart-ass," I said. "I don't think this can wait till Mom gets back. When did it happen?"

"Probably about midnight," he said. "I got to the plant around 11:30 and wasn't there very long."

I stared at the wound for a long minute and wondered whether there was any way to reach Mom. I was so sick of this cell-phone problem.

"Where've you been since midnight?"

"Walking back here," he said.

"On this leg? From all the way out there?"

He nodded.

I bit my lip. "Did you see your dad at least?"

He shook his head. "They had other things for me to see."

"We have to call the army hospital. Mom has the car—maybe they can come pick you—"

"No," he interrupted. "Who do you think did this to me?"

"I have no idea, Jordan. How 'bout you tell me?"

"It was them. It was the guys at the plant, working with the military. Remember those two guys in suits that I pointed out at football practice? They were waiting for me in this little room. We tussled."

"'Tussled,'" I said. "You mean they stabbed you?"

"No," he said. "There was this disfigured psycho scientist

with a skull-like face, no lips, no ears, and a sword that shoots out from where his right arm should be. I've seen him in my dreams, *twice,* but now I know he's real."

Jordan's face was peppered with sweat, and his undershirt was glued to his body. Maybe he had a fever? Delusions?

"The *psycho scientist* stabbed you?" I asked.

"Swear to Jah," he said. "With the sword that came out of his arm stump."

"Like Wolverine."

"No, those are more like sword fingernails. This was a sword arm."

"Hang on," I said, looking for a thermometer that hadn't seen the inside of a dog's anus. Jordan had an infection that must've given him a fever, and now, after walking around for hours with open wounds, he was delusional and experiencing hallucinations. I finally located a small electric thermometer in our upstairs bathroom, and as I returned to the exam room, my heart sank.

Jordan looked awful, his skin pale and ashen, his face and body smeared and spattered with blood.

"*Who* was the fight with?" I asked as I put the thermometer in his mouth.

"Mmm mmm," he said. He had a thermometer in his mouth. I pulled it out.

"I told you," he said. "Those two guys in suits—FBI agents, maybe—and that scary scientist."

"Scary scientist with a sword."

"Right. But I grabbed the gun from one of the FBI guys and shot him three times in the chest."

"You killed the scientist?"

"In theory," Jordan said. "But I don't think he's really dead."

Okay, we'd ventured deep into Crazytown. I jammed the thermometer back into his mouth, but he pulled it out.

"I didn't shoot the FBI guys," he continued, "though I pistol-whipped one of them, and handcuffed them both to a radiator. Obviously they know who I am and will come after me. That's why we can't go to the army hospital. And we can't tell anyone."

"What happened to the gun?"

"I ditched it in the woods on the way home," he said.

"Great," I said for lack of anything better to say. Hadn't we been snuggling on the couch just a few hours ago? I took the thermometer from his hand. "Leave this in your mouth this time, or I'll stick it somewhere else."

He obeyed, and I had a silent moment to think. I couldn't fix all this alone. I needed my mom.

The thermometer beeped, and I pulled it out.

"Holy crackers, 103.5," I said. "Like I thought, you've got an infection. I've stitched up dogs before, so I could stitch you, but cleaning up an infection is beyond my medical training level. You'll need my mom for that."

"I don't want to get her involved," he said, his eyes darting.

"Like I said, I can stitch you up. You've lost a lot of blood. But after that, it's either my mom or the army doctors—and I know you don't want to deal with them."

Jordan rubbed his hands over his exhausted face, leaving streaks of blood.

"Jordan. *Sweetie.* Close your eyes while I do my magic. You need to relax and get some rest."

"I can see in the dark, Maggie," he said. "I'm faster, stronger, and smarter than I've ever been, and I can see in the dark. Plus, I know things—like the fact that they were

FBI guys because they had a Glock 17M, and that's the kind of gun that the FBI uses. The army standard issue is a SIG Sauer. How would I know a thing like that?"

"I don't know," I said. "Something crazy like reading? Or hearing it in the military camp where you spent most of the last year?"

He scowled.

"I'm going to close these wounds with Steri-Strips," I said, "and Mom can clean it all out and stitch you up when she gets home."

"Okay," he muttered.

As I looked at my wounded pal, I wondered, *Should I call the police?* There'd obviously been a fight in which he'd been stabbed and slashed. I wasn't the praying type, but I sent a plea out into the universe that my dear friend hadn't shot— or, God forbid, killed—anyone.

I poured alcohol onto a square of gauze and wiped the leg wound, causing him to flinch. "Hey, I'm resting here," he grumbled. *Ah…a joke.*

I pulled the surgery light closer and took out the large magnifying glass. I was clearing away the dried blood, but the surrounding skin was flaming red, and pus and blood oozed from the inch-and-a-half cut. It was a deep one, and who knew how dirty the weapon was?

I had no idea how much of Jordan's story to believe, but I knew this: He needed medical help before the wound went septic. This was a precarious, potentially fatal situation, even for a patient in a top-notch hospital. For a wounded teen sitting atop an animals' examination table awaiting the return of a sleep-deprived veterinarian who'd been dealing with crazed pooches feasting on mutton, all bets were off.

CHAPTER 27

Jordan

MAGGIE HELPED ME into the shotgun seat of the twenty-year-old metallic green Chevy Malibu, the beater her mom used for house calls when she didn't need the pickup truck. Dr. Gooding was out in the pickup now—she'd be bringing back either wounded sheep or raging dogs, Maggie said—so there we were. Maggie had wrapped my leg and wrist tightly in cotton and gauze, but I still worried that I would drip blood onto the nubby cloth upholstery.

"Relax," she said, leaning my seat back before taking the driver's seat.

I felt comfortable and closed my eyes, my wounds still screaming but not quite as loudly as before. Maggie had given me ibuprofen before we left her house, even though I asked for something stronger. She said the only anesthetics they had were for animals, and she wouldn't know the right dosage.

"Whatever you'd give a rhino," I'd said.

She'd shot me a disgusted look. "I don't want to kill you, Jordan."

Fair enough.

Now she was laying a cold, wet cloth over my eyes and forehead and telling me to get some sleep.

"I don't know how long it'll take me to find Mom," Maggie said. "I don't know which farm she's at. In the meantime, your body needs to shut down and give yourself a chance to heal."

She kissed my hot cheek, which instantly grew hotter.

"You rock," I muttered, then added: "Just go fast, so you can get there before they find us. And don't draw attention to us."

"Right," she said. "Drive like a speed demon inconspicuously."

"You got it," I said, closing my eyes. I was quiet for maybe five seconds, during which Maggie shifted from reverse to drive and hit the pedal hard enough to lurch us forward. "Maybe those guys at the plant aren't FBI."

"What?"

"The 'Matrix' guys."

"What about their Glocks?" She sounded like she was humoring me.

"I know," I said, "but why should I assume they're official anything when I'm not sure that scientist even is human? Or was."

"Right. He's probably a dead cyborg by now."

I squinted at her, hoping she'd notice my displeasure at her tone, but her eyes were fixed on the dark road, as well they should've been.

"The scientist didn't look like he should've been alive in the first place," I continued. "Parts of his skull were visible. At first I thought he was a burn victim, but then I wondered whether he was part of a crazy experiment. He had no lips, and his teeth were completely exposed, like Two-Face in *The Dark Knight*."

"Yeah," Maggie said, "we watched that movie together. But I'm sure it's more likely that you *actually saw* someone who could've stepped out of a DC Comics movie than you imagined him in a delirious state after already having dreamed about him."

"I'm not delirious, and I didn't have a fever before I was attacked by these guys," I said. "Yes, it's weird that I dreamed about him before I saw him, but he *was* alive, and I've got the wounds to prove it."

"Maybe it was déjà vu," she said flatly, the car turning a sharp corner.

"No, it wasn't déjà vu," I replied impatiently, flipping over the wet cloth to place the cool side on my forehead. "I didn't feel like I'd been there before. I just recognized the guy—from my dreams."

"Maybe you recognized him as the flaming corpse you chased into the woods."

I realized that with every matter-of-fact statement Maggie made, my story was sounding more and more absurd, even to me.

"No, the flaming corpse was different, more of a skeletal body. I think *his* name was Omega. The scientist was solid in the middle but with a peeled-back face."

"Maybe they're cousins, not identically disfigured cousins," Maggie said in a singsong.

"That so doesn't work," I grumbled.

"Well, since I don't believe in clairvoyance, maybe you'd actually seen the scientist before, like at sick camp."

"I'd never seen him before. This is not a face you'd forget."

"But maybe you *had* seen him before. Otherwise you wouldn't have recognized him."

"This nap is going great."

"What about during all of those surgeries after the car accident?" Maggie asked. "Maybe you saw him then, and your brain is just dredging up the memory. You were in and out of consciousness, dealing with so much trauma. How much of that do you remember clearly?"

"Not much," I admitted.

"There you go."

"I'm telling you," I said, "no matter my level of consciousness or whatever post-accident stress I was going through, if I'd seen this guy, I would have remembered him. Consciously."

"Or maybe the scientist looked similar to the guy in your dreams, so your brain just linked them up."

"Why do you keep arguing with me? Why do you have so much stake in my not seeing someone from my dreams?"

She reached out her right hand and gently brushed my head. "Jordan, I have no stake in your being wrong. I just want to understand what's going on with you so I can help you. I'm a logic-driven person, so what's more likely, that you dreamed a supernatural skull man who turned out to be real and tried to murder you with his sword arm, or you're feeling the easily diagnosed effects of infected wounds and an astronomical fever?"

I didn't answer. I knew what I'd seen and what I'd dreamed and what I'd done. I'd shot the scientist three times after he attacked me with his sword. I could see the dark spots spreading in his white lab coat from the holes in his chest.

"His blood was black," I remembered.

"Of course, it was," Maggie said. "Night-night."

I lowered the cloth over my eyes again.

"I'm sorry about this," I muttered. "I didn't mean for you to get caught up in it."

"Caught up in what?"

I tried to think of what to call it. Sinister plot? Family melodrama? Supernatural conspiracy? Paranoid thriller? Most of the soldiers had been acting weird, like automatons. Why? Who was controlling them? Why did that repellent scientist keep calling me Rho? Was that short for something? *Ro-BOT*? Did they think I was a robot, and that's why they wanted me in "for repair"? But then why would he try to kill me? And how *was* the running, burning skeleton guy in the forest related to the rest of them?

"This," I finally responded. "I'm sorry you're caught up in *this*."

Maggie guided the car around a curve, a sliver of pink becoming visible on the horizon.

"Could be worse," she said. "Could be raining."

I couldn't remember ever seeing the sunrise without having slept first. The road hummed, and I felt myself drifting off. *Wait*...I didn't want to dream about the scientist again. I tried to will my eyes back open, but they no longer would obey. They were done, and so was I.

CHAPTER 28

Maggie

NOT LONG AFTER I pulled away from our house and heard enough of Jordan's ramblings about the monster scientist with the sword that sprang out of his arm, I audibled, as Jordan would say. Mount Hope isn't huge, but it's spread out across many acres of farmland, and trying to find my mom among the farms could be frustrating and ultimately futile. And what would she do when we found her? She couldn't treat Jordan at the spot; we'd still have to come home— and that was assuming she wasn't in the middle of some precarious situation involving dangerous animals.

No, Jordan needed immediate help. He needed to get to the hospital.

I reached the roadblock sooner than expected. The sky was beginning to glow, though the sun hadn't peeked out yet. An olive-green truck blocked the left lane, and a plastic red-and-white barricade stretched across the right. Beyond the truck, I could see what looked like a major operation: civilian tractor-trailers being unloaded and their contents getting stacked and moved by several forklifts.

Six riflemen milled around the roadblock, and one held up his hand as we rolled toward it. I stopped, and he walked up to my window.

"The road is closed," he said. His rifle hung over his shoulder and neck, and on his upper arm was a black band with the white letters MP for military police. He looked to be about nineteen, skinny, pale, with a wheat-colored caterpillar mustache no doubt intended to compensate for his baby face, though it just made him look like he was playing dress-up.

"I've got to get my friend to the hospital," I insisted, nodding toward my sleeping, bandaged companion. I sent out a silent prayer that he wouldn't wake up and freak out upon seeing more military personnel.

"The hospital is inaccessible right now," the rifleman said blankly. "The road is under construction."

"Can you take him, then?" I asked. "He's been cut bad, and infection has set in."

He was shaking his head before I'd even finished my sentence. "You can get antibiotics at the pharmacy in town, and there's a veterinarian in town that could give him stitches."

"That veterinarian is my *mother,* so, no, he needs more than that," I said, getting heated. "I know people who went to the army hospital two days ago, and—"

"They were flown by helicopter."

"Okay, he'll take a helicopter, then."

The rifleman said nothing.

"Explain this to me," I said, feeling my cheeks flush. "There's no contamination from the power plant. That's what we've all been told *repeatedly.* No radiation, no nothing. So why are we still quarantined?"

"This is not a quarantine," he said. "Just maintenance."

"Then why are we trapped in this town and not even able to get out for a medical emergency? You know the bridge on the other side of town is out, and now *you're* not letting me pass here. Whose decision was it to block us in like this?"

"I assure you this road is in need of repair," he said as if bored. "Now, please turn around and head back to town. I'm sure your friend will be all right soon."

Now this guy was pissing me off. "On what *basis* are you making that diagnosis? Where did you get *your* medical training? He's been *stabbed*. Do you usually recommend Tylenol or ibuprofen for that?"

The soldier scrunched up his face like Tom in a *Tom and Jerry* cartoon after Jerry has made him hit himself in the face with a frying pan. "If he was stabbed, then this is a matter for the police."

"Yeah? Well, what does the 'P' on your insignia stand for? Pus—?"

"That's not our jurisdiction, ma'am," he said, cutting me off before I got into real trouble.

"*Ma'am?*' I'm sixteen! So tell me, *sir,* which police officers can stitch up stab wounds, since you, with all your professed medical expertise, cannot?"

"Look, young lady, I'm not appreciating your tone here, and I must return to my duties. Have a good evening."

"Morning."

He started to step away, shook his head, and returned.

"How did he get stabbed?"

"I don't know! He's not coherent!" I burst out, jolting Jordan awake.

"Wha' . . . ?" Jordan said in a daze.

"It's nothing," I whispered to him, patting his chest and

putting the displaced cloth back over his eyes. "Go back to sleep." I felt him relax again.

"The police in town are all trained in first aid," the soldier said. "And that's where I'm going to have to send you now. I'm sorry for the inconvenience. Good luck with your friend." He walked away.

"And if I needed to get to the giant military hospital that's just up the road?" I called out the window.

"The road is impassable," he said over his shoulder, not breaking stride.

As I watched him return to his soldier buddies, no doubt telling them all about the pain-in-the-ass girl he just encountered, I made little *pew pew* sounds with my mouth. That was me shooting them all with laser guns.

"This," I said, "is bullshit." And I jammed the car into gear, slammed my foot down on the gas, and, for the first and probably last time in my life, made my tires squeal as I peeled the hell out of there. There was a little room on the left shoulder, where the embankment was relatively level, so I gunned it around the truck, prompting my new soldier friend and his pals to scatter as I passed them.

"Hey!" I heard as I veered back onto the road and floored it.

I weaved through the semis and more army trucks parked on the road and in the shoulder, and I braced myself for gunshots. Any second now, the rear window would shatter — that's what happened in such situations, right? But, no, I heard and saw nothing behind me, and the road ahead was clear as I sped into the early-morning mist.

How far ahead was the sick camp? I didn't know, but it couldn't be that far. Jordan had talked about how long the drive back took, but he'd been part of a bumper-to-bumper convoy. We were passing more farmland before the dense forest would close in, followed by fields and more forest. The camp would be set up in one of the clearings.

I zipped ahead in the right lane, occasionally passing more semis, pallets of boxes, crates, and forklifts that sat in the left lane. What they were doing there, I had no idea.

It was clear, though, that supplies from the outside world were coming in just fine. Materials apparently were being unloaded from commercial trucks and placed onto military trucks before they were brought into town—so outside truck drivers weren't allowed to go in and out of Mount Hope, just the army.

I glanced to my right, and Jordan had removed the cloth from his face and was squinting out the windshield.

"How're you doing, Jordan?" I asked.

"Tanned, rested, and ready," he said. "What's up with the road trip?"

I placed the backs of my fingers against his cheek—still warm but no longer blazing.

"I don't believe them," I said. "I don't believe there's any problem with this road. Now we're going to find out."

"Huh," he said, rubbing his eyes. "I heard there are roadblocks."

"Taken care of."

Jordan gave me a look that straddled puzzled and impressed. "Okay, then," he said.

I cruised along the open road for another few minutes with nothing but nature on either side of the road.

"It's all because of the plant," Jordan said. "They're hiding whatever's going on there."

"Maybe," I said.

"Well, I'm glad you acknowledge at least that."

"Jordan, I acknowledge that a *lot* of funny business is going on. And I think it's crazy that no one knows anything about it. Where are the reporters? We had TV crews and newspaper folks at the camp right after we got evacuated. Mom was on CNN. Eventually they moved on to other stories, but we got our fifteen minutes. Wouldn't they want to swing back and see how we're doing in the aftermath of our meltdown?"

"'Explosive incident.'"

"Whatever. Isn't what's going on now newsworthy?"

"Maybe they tried and weren't allowed in."

"Right," I said, and turned off the headlights, which were no longer needed. "I still don't believe you about the crazed scientist with his sword arm, by the way."

"Then why are you blowing past army roadblocks?"

"I do believe in those stab wounds and that infection and that fever. I care about *you*."

Jordan smiled and leaned back. "I appreciate that," he said, "though it's kind of bitchy for you not to believe me. I've never lied to you."

That word "bitchy" felt like a slap. "Dude, I'm all in with you right now, so don't give me crap. Do *you* even believe everything you've told me? One hundred percent?"

He paused. "Well, I know what I experienced, but there might be some wiggle room. Like two percent."

"There you go. Look, I also think they're lying to us about the radiation—I've got a lump that keeps reminding me of that, and it's got me petrified. So for the good of everyone, it's time to follow your lead on the football field and switch from defense to offense."

We were driving through the woods now, with sunlight

rays diffused by the branches making funky patterns on the road.

"I hear what you're saying about the radiation," Jordan said, "but the workers at the power plant don't seem to be dying, and they would've been exposed to the most radiation. I've only seen my dad once since we got back to town, and he's fine."

"Aside from his personality being totally altered."

"Well, yeah, there's that."

I sped around a curve and suddenly was blinded by a blast of brilliant white lights. I slammed on the brakes and shielded my eyes.

"Get out of the vehicle with your hands up!" came a voice through a bullhorn.

Four large banks of floodlights, the kind used on construction sites, were directed at the car, and I could see nothing beyond their glare.

"This is your final warning," the bullhorn announced. "Exit now, or we will shoot."

CHAPTER 29

Maggie

THE LIGHTS WERE too bright for me to see whether guns actually had been drawn on us. I'd never had a gun pointed at me, at least as far as I knew. I didn't think they'd actually shoot us, but still, this was terrifying. And infuriating.

It was just another day at the office for the soldiers, though. They dismissed us like we were meddling brats from *Scooby-Doo*, even as I shot them looks that, if they could kill, would have landed me in the clink. Jordan and I were ordered into a Jeep back seat, and two soldiers took us to my house while another pair drove back the Malibu.

Mom answered the door with deep rings under her eyes. She'd been out for so much of the night and no doubt hadn't expected to return to an empty house with the car missing. Her expression now combined relief with deep irritation.

"Oh, for goodness' sake," she said. I loved that she still used phrases like "for goodness' sake."

I hadn't actually calmed down—I didn't appreciate being treated like a toddler getting plopped back into a Pack 'n Play—but as I opened my mouth, the lieutenant, a doppelganger for Louis Gossett Jr. in *An Officer and a Gentleman* (which Jordan had chosen for us to watch a while back—maybe he thought he'd sweep me off my feet like I was Debra Winger, though I thought Richard Gere was kind of smarmy), stepped forward and asked, "Is this your child?"

"I am *not* a—" I started, but Mom put up her hand to silence me.

"Yes, officer, thank you," she said.

"These kids bypassed the checkpoint at the edge of town, and we were forced to intercept them. Your daughter said they needed to get to the military hospital, and we informed her that it had been closed down since the evacuation was terminated."

Mom took in Jordan and all his blood and bandages.

"Why did you need to go to a hospital?" she asked.

"Our medic evaluated him—he needs a few stitches and antibiotics," the lieutenant said. "He'll be fine in your care."

"Mom," I said, "Jordan was stabbed and is infected, with a fever close to 104. That's why he needed the hospital—but they're not letting anyone leave. They threatened to *shoot* us."

"No arms were drawn, ma'am," the lieutenant said.

Mom glared at me. "We already knew the road was closed," she snapped. "Now get in the house before you get into more trouble."

As Jordan and I passed her in the doorway, she said to the officer, "I'm sorry. They're good kids, usually."

"That's all right," he said. "No harm done. And here are the keys to her car." He looked beyond her to Jordan, standing with me just inside the door. "There's no reason to try to leave again, son. No one is looking for you. We know where to find you when we need you."

Jordan nodded back at the lieutenant and said nothing.

"Ask him how come—" I called out to my mom, but she cut me off.

"Thank you, sir. I appreciate you returning my daughter and her friend safely. I've got it from here, and there will be no more trouble, I promise you."

"I appreciate that," he said, bowing his head and taking his leave.

"In the back. Now," Mom said, closing the door and leading us into the exam room where I'd dressed Jordan's wounds in the first place. She slapped her palm twice atop the metal table, and Jordan hopped his butt up there.

"He might go septic," I said. "I used my best judgment."

She said nothing, unwrapping the bandages. If steam had started to come out of her ears at that point, I wouldn't have been surprised.

"There are two wounds, his wrist and calf," I said.

"I can see that," Mom said.

"I did what I could. The one in his leg is deep."

Mom looked up at Jordan. "You were *stabbed?*"

"Yes," he said. "With a sword."

"He says it came out of a skull-faced scientist's stump arm," I said. "Jordan was delirious, feverish, not making sense."

Jordan flashed his disarming smile. "Maggie and I have agreed to disagree about my account of tonight's events."

Kneeling beside him, Mom gently peeled back the tape that held the gauze on his arm. "This one isn't bad," she said, putting the bandage on his wrist back into place. "Nice job, honey."

I appreciated the compliment, though she still wasn't looking at me.

"Now let's look at that leg," she continued, ordering Jordan to lie flat on the table, at least as much of him as would fit.

"He said he was attacked with a sword at the power plant," I said.

"What were you doing *there*?" she asked Jordan.

"Trying to see my dad."

"In the middle of the night?"

"Hey," I said, "did you hear the part about the sword?"

"I'm looking at it right now, hon," she said. She probed it gently with a small instrument and dabbed it with an antiseptic wipe. "Well," she said in her most professional tone, "I've never treated a sword wound before, but you're right, this one is infected. And old. How long ago did it happen?"

"About midnight," Jordan said, flinching when Mom poked the red, swollen skin around the cut.

"He said he walked all the way back from the plant and got here around four in the morning."

Mom stood up. "I'm sorry I wasn't here. You should have called someone for help, though."

"That's why we tried the army hospital."

"Next time try the police." She placed her hand on Jordan's forehead. "And I'll remember to leave you a note where I'm going next time. But come on, running a roadblock?"

I told her everything that had happened, with Jordan adding a few details here and there, though he was fuzzy on much of it.

"I told you we couldn't trust the army," he said.

"Well, they got you home safely," Mom pointed out.

"Yeah, and they know where to find me when they need me."

I turned to Mom. "Did I mention that Jordan said he shot the guy who stabbed him with his sword arm?"

"You *shot* someone?" she asked Jordan.

"Three times in the chest. But I don't think I killed him."

"Why did you have a gun?"

"There'd been a scuffle."

Mom gave me a look. She didn't believe what she was hearing, either.

"Hang on a minute," she said, and went into another room, returning with a small tray of supplies. She got to work on Jordan's leg.

"You're lucky," she said. "The knife—sword—went in vertically, not horizontally, with the grain, if you want to think of it that way. It should heal pretty cleanly, though I doubt you'll be playing football for a couple weeks."

Jordan nodded. "Great."

"This is going to sting a little," Mom said as she shoved an alcohol-soaked piece of gauze deep into the blood- and dirt-flecked wound.

Jordan howled. "Hey, let me know when something's going to sting a *lot*," he said.

Mom smiled. Sometimes I think doctors get off on that whole "sting a little" thing.

I ran my fingers through Jordan's tight curls, noticing the spidery scars on his scalp. This guy had been through a lot. I wanted to kiss the top of his head but still felt too self-conscious in front of my mom.

"I know you two don't believe me, but the scientist told me things," Jordan said. "They experimented on me, made me into some kind of superhuman. He said the Carters' fire was meant to be a test of my skills."

"What?" I asked. I hadn't heard this.

"Apparently I passed," he said, and talked about how he was able to breathe and run despite the smoke, how innocent people had been sacrificed for this exercise. As he went on, his eyes opened wider and wider, and sweat beads emerged on his forehead. I nodded at my mom, whose face betrayed no expression.

"At the plant, they kept calling me Rho for some unknown reason," Jordan continued. "And I never got to see my dad. Does he even know what happened to us?"

"That's a good question," Mom said as she picked up one of her tranquilizers and readied a syringe. "We'll get answers soon, Jordan, but for now, I want you to get some rest. This will help."

She injected the needle into his arm.

Jordan wasn't going down quietly, though, continuing to talk about the supernatural scientist and his own enhanced powers. His words grew more slurred, his eyelids fluttered and sagged, and his story faded into the ether.

It was all too fantastic to believe. Why would this spooky scientist take such an interest in my friend? Why would the military follow suit?

Then again, why *did* that officer tell Jordan they knew how to find him? Why were they keeping us in town? Even if Jordan was imagining things, that didn't mean that things weren't being kept from us.

Could one of those things involve Jordan? What did they actually do to him at the sick camp?

CHAPTER 30

Jordan

I WOKE UP with a splitting headache, which I guess shouldn't have been surprising, given all I'd been through, but that didn't make it any less painful. That shard-through-my-skull sensation made me forget about my nasty leg wound—at least until I tried walking and felt like a hundred bees were sticking their stingers into it. All in all, I felt topsy-turvy and upside-down and discombobulated and any other built-for-a-fun-house phrase you could think of. I wasn't having fun, that was for sure.

I eventually determined that it was latish afternoon. (This wasn't great deductive reasoning. I looked at a clock, and it said 3:47.) I found Maggie sitting out back reading a library book, *Radioactive Contamination for Dummies*, which made me realize I'd underestimated the reach of that series.

"Learning anything useful?" I asked.

She gave me a concerned look that reminded me of my mom when I would come downstairs the morning after getting the flu.

"C'mere," she said, and after I limped over there, she lay her palm across my forehead and said, "Better."

"Tell me something that I don't know," I said, nodding toward the book.

"Overexposure to radiation can cause cancer," she said.

"Duly noted."

Soon we were back in her car with her once again behind the wheel. I'd asked whether we could return to my house and see whether anything was salvageable now that the place had cooled off. I also was curious whether my note for my dad was still there.

As I gazed out the car window, though, everything suddenly looked...wrong. It was as if a haze had fallen over everything, or some Instagram filter had been activated to give the world an old-timey sepia tone. The grass was brown, and most of the trees were bare, and the few leaves that remained were twisted and gray. The white paint on the Baptist church was dirty, cracked, and peeling; the road was lined with potholes; and cracks in the asphalt were springing up with weeds.

My head throbbed all the way in the back, by my spine.

"What happened?" I asked.

"Huh?" Maggie said.

"What's going on?"

"What are you talking about?"

A dead cat lay on the sidewalk while a flock of jet-black crows closed in on it from a leafless branch. City Hall's windows were cracked, and its stone walls were streaked with black as if there had been a fire, even as I could see people inside. The Mount Hope, South Carolina, and U.S. flags flying in front were tattered, almost in ribbons.

"The town had been looking so great and now…this," I said.

"Now…*what*?" she responded.

On the street ahead of us crept some creepy animal: short, maybe the size of a large porcupine but without quills or fur. It looked more like an oversize bug, a beetle on steroids with a hard, shiny exoskeleton. It was snuffling in the gutter.

"Okay," I said. "What the hell is that?"

"What the hell is *what*?" Maggie asked, exasperated.

"Are you not seeing *any* of this?" I asked.

"Jordan, I don't know *what* you're seeing these days."

She leaned her head closer to the windshield, as if doing so might give her a better view of whatever was catching my eye, and then the car banged into an enormous pothole, making a grating noise, like the axle or frame had smashed into the asphalt. It gave us a terrific jolt as well; my seat belt kept me from hitting my head on the car's low ceiling.

"Yowza," I said.

"That was some pothole, but I didn't see anything weird," she said, looking back at the road.

"It's right there," I said, and pointed back toward…a dog. No, that couldn't be right. Could it?

"That's a blue heeler, the Perkinses' dog," she said after taking a quick look. "They let it roam around without a leash. It's not a bad dog."

I watched the animal recede in the side-view mirror and noticed that the road now was clean and free of weeds. Everything seemed normal again, with green leaves in the trees and the lawns all nice and trimmed. The dark veil had been lifted, and the town appeared bright and inviting once more.

"You didn't notice anything weird for, like, a minute?" I said.

"Aside from what was coming out of your mouth? No."

I flashed back to the moment after my concussion, when the football field looked ragged and weedy before I woke up to the freshly mown turf and sunshine.

Maggie reached her hand over to my cheek.

"I appreciate that you keep touching my face, but no, I don't have a fever," I said.

"Okay, Jordan. Excuse me for worrying."

"Excused."

Maggie turned the car onto my street, which still resembled a bomb site. A cleanup crew was hauling away rubble next to the huge dark crater where the Carters' propane tank had been. My house looked decapitated. The first floor still stood despite the burn streaks, broken glass, and ashy chunks. What had been the second floor and attic was now a charred sunroof.

A truck was parked at the curb in front of the house.

My father's black pickup.

"Hey, is that—" Maggie started to ask.

"Yeah," I said.

I should have been smiling. I should have been relieved. This was what I wanted, right?

Yet everything in my stomach curdled.

"You okay?" she asked.

"Yeah."

"Really?"

"Tip-top."

"Well, how 'bout I wait in the car, and you go have a nice visit. I brought my book," she said, grabbing *Radioactive Contamination for Dummies* from the back seat. "And I know you know it, but you're welcome to stay with us as long as you'd like."

"Thanks," I said. "But you should go home. I don't know how long this will take. I'll have my dad drop me off afterward."

She gave me a long look, as if she had much more to say but was repressing the impulse. "Okay," she finally said. "But since you can't call me on your cell, and I don't want you walking back on that leg, I'll swing by here again in a bit."

"You don't have to, but thanks," I said, and started to get out. Then I stopped myself and poked my head back inside the car.

"Really, thanks," I said, and leaned over to give her a kiss. She turned her head, and I planted one on her cheek.

"Good luck," she said, and drove off.

My head throbbed. I was about to see my father at last, and I'd never felt so alone.

CHAPTER 31

Jordan

THE HOUSE STILL had that wet-smoke smell as I stepped inside, the scorched floorboards creaking beneath my feet. If my dad was inside the house, he would have heard me. But as I stopped and listened, there was no sound.

"Hello?" I called.

Nothing.

No one was in the living room or little front parlor. I walked back to the kitchen and found him crouched in front of the open refrigerator door.

"These peaches are still excellent," he said, not looking back. "Would you like one?"

"No, thanks," I said. "Not hungry."

He closed the fridge door, turned toward me, and took a slurpy bite out of a peach. "You may want to reconsider," he said. "They're perfect. Though you won't want to open the refrigerator door too much. There's a high risk of spoilage."

I hadn't even thought about the food, whatever we'd bought after we returned to town, and whether we should take any of it back to Maggie's house. I had no idea why *he* was thinking about this.

He stepped up to me and put his hands on my upper arms and gave them a squeeze.

"Hello, son. You're looking well. I'm glad to see you're safe."

He let his arms drop down. No hug from this fella. Maybe he thought I was too old for such stuff. I wasn't.

He turned and walked out the back door, taking a seat under the pergola in the exact spot where Maggie was sitting when our world went up in flames. I took my place beside him.

"This house has a lot of history," he said. "It's seen a lot of good things and a lot of bad things. The good things mostly followed the bad things."

An awkward silence followed.

"And now it'll be torn down," I finally said.

"Oh, don't count on it," he said. "Sometimes disasters lead to improvements. When you've got to rebuild something, it can become even better and stronger."

"Interesting," I said, scratching the suddenly itchy surgical scar above my rib cage.

He turned toward me. "It's good to see you, son." He said this like a pronouncement, like it was being recorded for the court record.

"It's good to see you, too, Dad," I replied, trying to keep my voice from cracking on "Dad." "Have you talked to Mom? Charlie? How are they?"

"They're in the military hospital," he said. "I haven't spoken to them. There's no cellular service, and the phone at the plant was having trouble connecting. But I've been assured that they're fine."

"You've been assured?"

"I have." He folded his hands in his lap. "What do you know about this explosion?"

I told him everything I could remember about that horrific night: that end-of-the-world blast, the rescues, Mom's injury, her departure with Charlie. He nodded impassively while I spoke, as if he was cataloging everything for future inspection.

"Dad," I said when I finished my account, "I've been staying at Maggie's, but you're allowed to come home now, right? Or take me somewhere? They're super nice, but I want to be home, whatever that is now. I don't have anything anymore. Everything got burned up. And I've got nowhere to go."

"I'm still required to attend to my station. I'll speak to Renee, but I'm sure she won't object to your remaining with them for the indefinite future."

I sat, speechless. Did he hear a word I said? Was he shedding all parental responsibility? I hated the whine in my voice but couldn't help it. "Why? You're the only family I've got here. Why can't you stop work and take care of things—take care of *me*? Isn't it illegal for me to be on my own?"

He shook his head. "Things are happening at the plant that are bigger than just us, Jordan. I know you're safe with Maggie's family; otherwise I wouldn't be doing this."

"*Safe?* Really?" I held out my bandaged arm and stuck out my wrapped leg. "Do you know how many fresh stitches are in me? Thirty-four! And that's from going to see *you* at the plant! I went up to them and said, 'Hey, yo, I'm just a poor little orphan looking for his pa,' but did they take me to you? No, they did not. They put me in a room with these men in suits and a freakish skull-faced scientist with a sword-blade arm, and they did *this*. But, sure, yeah, I'm fine. No need to look out for your kid."

He placed a hand on my shoulder, and I warmed under his touch despite myself.

"I'm sorry, son," he said. I expected more, but no, that was it.

"Dad," I said, lowering my voice even though there was no one in eyeshot, "there's something wrong with this town, with the power plant ... and maybe with me."

Dad nodded, looking serious. "The scientist you met, he's called Alpha. I regret that things played out the way they did, but you should take that as a lesson not to go looking for trouble again."

Wait, what?

"I was looking for *you*, Dad. And this guy stabbed and slashed me. But I guess you're okay with that."

Dad pressed his lips together and said nothing. *The fuck...*

"Dad, did they do something to you at the plant as well? What the hell is going on there?"

Instead of replying, he stood up and turned toward the house.

"And *who is Ishango*?"

That got his attention. He pivoted back and said in a low, steady voice, "Ishango is the name of the first math machines ever discovered."

"I know *that*," I said. "Maggie told me all about it."

"How much is Maggie involved in this?"

"She's been with me every step of the way," I said, then became worried that I might've just dragged her deeper into this mess.

"How much does she know about Ishango?"

"She looked it up in an encyclopedia, learned about the bone or whatever it was."

He rubbed his hands over his face and looked up as if he were praying, though I knew he wasn't. His only belief was science.

"You shouldn't have been out there," he said. "It's not safe."

"No shit."

"And don't swear, son."

"Stop calling me 'son.' You gave me a name."

"Jordan," he said, "I'm trying to help you. What is happening is beyond your imagination and control. You should know that I, as your father, would not steer you wrong."

"Well, be a father, then. Stop living at the power plant, and let's become a family again."

"I cannot discuss this with you any further." He walked back into the house. "Watch your step, and if you hear anything creaking, move to a doorway."

"Everything is creaking," I said, stepping inside. "Your friend Alpha sliced me up with a sword that shot out of his arm stump. He wasn't aiming for my leg."

"I cannot tell you any more, Jordan, but you are not to go back there," he said in a stern voice. "Or to ask any questions of the army, of the police, of anyone. Understand?"

I stared at him. "He called me Rho, said they've done something to me, maybe when I was in the sick camp. I think they messed around with my body to make me stronger and faster. Not human."

"I know."

"You *know?*"

He entered what had been our front room. Pools of black,

where water had mixed with the charcoal on the second floor and dripped down like oil, collected on the floor.

"Why did you let them do that to me?" I asked.

"How long have I been married to your mother?"

"Uh, I—I don't know," I said. "I'm sixteen."

"We've been married twenty years," he said, reaching into mom's collapsed china-display case and pulling out a white plate with a blue design that I knew well. It had never been used for a dinner, no matter how special. Miraculously, it had survived the fire and the fight to put it out. Mom would be thrilled about that at least. "She's had this plate since she inherited it from her grandmother. She took it on *Antiques Roadshow,* and it was appraised at two thousand dollars."

Dad handled the plate carefully with hands that I noticed were shaking slightly, then let it seesaw off his fingers and fall to the floor. I gasped as it shattered into a dozen pieces.

"What is *wrong* with you, Dad?"

For a second I saw a fleeting expression of pain on his face. "When I tell you to stay away, Jordan, I couldn't be more serious," he said, locking eyes with me. "Our lives have changed irrevocably, and there's no going back to what we knew. We are not in a position to question anything unless we wish to forfeit our lives. Consider this a warning. You must obey."

I had no response to that. Either he had gone totally nuts, was deep under the influence of some crazy force, or was terrified to his core. The tremor I spotted in my father's hand made me suspect the last option, though maybe the answer was "all of the above."

What was he so scared of that he wouldn't lift a finger to protect his own son? Who had been altered more by those guys, me or him?

CHAPTER 32

Maggie

I HAD THIS fantasy of Jordan's dad bringing him back to our house and coming in for a beer and a friendly chat as the four of us figured out how my friend could be reunited with his father but still spend significant time with me. But as time passed, this scenario felt increasingly far-fetched, and about two hours after I dropped him off, I swung by Jordan's house for a look-see. When I pulled up, he was sitting alone on his front stoop with his head bowed between his legs. This was not a portrait of a happy guy.

When I sat down next to him, he looked up with eyes that appeared puffy and streaked.

"I feel like I've lost both parents," he said in a hushed voice.

I took his hands between my own—they were warm and damp.

"I'm sorry," I said.

I brushed a tiny tear from the corner of his eye with my thumb. He smiled sadly. I put a palm on each of his flushed cheeks. This boy needed a kiss already. I moved my face closer to his, and all of a sudden his eyes got really wide, and he choked as if something was stuck in the back of his throat, and he pitched his body off to the side and let loose a formidable stream of vomit into the charred dirt. As he crouched there heaving, I turned away from the rising sour smell, then turned back. I guess this was what I'd signed up for.

Jordan couldn't stop apologizing as I drove him home.

"I'm so sorry."

"It's okay."

"You were being so sweet."

"Don't worry about it."

"It's been a really stressful time."

"I get it."

"Please don't take it personally."

"I won't."

"That was shaping up to be a pretty romantic moment."

"Uh-huh."

"Before I ralphed."

"Don't need the recap here, Jordan."

"That was disgusting. Tasted awful, too. And fizzy."

"Okay, we can stop talking about it now."

"It was no reflection on how I feel about you."

"I didn't interpret it as such."

"Please don't take it personally."

"I will if you don't shut up already."

He smiled sheepishly.

"Anyway, I'm sorry," he said.

"It's okay."

"I should have left a tender moment alone."

"You seriously have to stop right now."

He smirked to himself. I guess that was a good sign.

"Got a breath mint?" he asked.

I pulled a tin of Altoids from my purse as I turned onto our street. "Take 'em all."

After we got home, Jordan recounted his whole disturbing conversation with his father. I didn't know his dad well, but when I'd seen him at school events or his house, he always seemed like a friendly-enough guy—a nerdy scientist who took quiet pride in his son and family. He may not have been the most effusive fellow, but he also didn't come across as the cold automaton that Jordan was describing. He didn't even offer Jordan a ride, just left him sitting there with his wounded leg.

Also, he gave Jordan a warning. I knew Jordan. Telling him to back off was the quickest way to get him to dig deeper.

"Well, if you're going to be staying here longer, let's make this place feel a bit more like home," I said in the exam room that he'd been using as a bedroom.

"Great," he said without much inflection.

"Check this out," I said, and pulled out a rolled-up poster. "I found this at a thrift store before the evacuation and had been waiting for the right occasion to take it out. This is it."

I unrolled an *Evil Dead II* poster, the skull with eyeballs looking sideways off the page.

"Awesome!" Jordan enthused. "That's an original?"

"Of course. And now it's yours."

"You're the best," he said, and gave me a hug that included many awkward pats on the back before he pulled away.

"And, hey," I said, "pending any other unexpected disasters, school starts tomorrow at last. So that'll feel somewhat 'normal.'"

"Sure," he said. "Now, where's that poster putty?"

I'd hoped to get a decent night's sleep before the first day of school, but once again I woke up early to frenzied barking. Mrs. Little, the middle-school librarian, arrived at our front door at

6 a.m. with her wild hound dog bouncing off the sides of its carrier. As I stood at the top of the stairs, I heard Mrs. Little telling my mom that she'd had to lure the dog into the carrier with one of Mr. Little's T-bone steaks, which it had eaten clean off the bone before the loud crunching of bone began.

"He got away from us, ran off into the woods, and came back like this," Mrs. Little said. "Please tell me it's not rabies. He tried to bite my husband."

"It's not rabies," my mom said. "But you may want to say good-bye to this fella."

After Mom transferred the agitated dog from the carrier into a kennel and a distraught Mrs. Little left, I made my way down the stairs and asked, "What's the deal with all these angry bitches?"

"Ha," Mom said. "Who knows, at this point? I'll do my exam and run my tests, but I suspect we'll continue to keep Mr. Marsh busy."

Ugh. I'd seen enough dog corpses—and ashes—to last the year.

As Mom went upstairs to shower, I decided it was too late for me to try to get back to sleep. I thought all that barking— which continued from the other room—would have woken up Jordan, but when I opened his door a crack, he was sleeping the sleep of angels. I know it's a cliché, but he looked so peaceful—all that daytime tension having slipped away. I wanted to walk up to him and run my hand over his curls, kiss that forehead. That's how I would have loved to be awakened. But, no, I wasn't going to do that.

Instead, I sat by the office computer and tried to open a web browser. My muscle memory still thought this would work. Then reality kicked in again.

I spotted a box from the mortuary on the counter. Every time it cremated one of the dogs, it returned the remains. I opened the box to the depressing sight of seven dog collars—three blue, two red, and two black—with names on the tags: Skeeter, Muffin, Jake, Bowzer, Rooster, Danny, and Bull. Next to the collars was a plastic bag containing little metal discs with thin wires snaking out. The discs were dusty and scuffed up, like spoons that had gotten jammed in the disposal.

When the mortician previously showed us such pieces, Mom dismissed them as broken bits of the grate or something else mundane. I disagreed.

I took them to a back room that was used both for storage and as a lab. I had to move boxes out of the way to make room for the heavy case that I pulled out from under the desk. I carefully lifted the microscope out of its felt-lined container and plugged it in.

I placed one of the biggest discs beneath the lens and peered down. It was out of focus, and as I adjusted the lens up and down, I realized I needed to clean it. A few minutes later, I had a clear view of the piece.

It looked different from what I expected. Although it felt smooth in my fingers, like a piece of crafted aluminum, the flat surface had a pattern etched or stamped into it, some sort of hexagon. I checked the magnification and did some quick math in my head; each hexagon appeared to be less than a quarter of a millimeter across.

I stood up from the counter. At some point all of these odd details would have to add up. I caught my reflection in the lab's mirror. With my rolled-out-of-bed straggly blond hair and pasty complexion, I realized I looked like my mom—

the tired version. It would take some work to make me presentable for the first day of school.

"Hey," came a deep voice behind me, and I jumped.

"Hey back. You startled me."

"Sorry," Jordan said, grinning. "I was just looking for someone who might give me a rabies shot."

"Sure," I said. "Bend over."

"Ah, that's all right." I felt self-conscious standing there all rumpled and unmade-up in my oversize T-shirt, but Jordan's cheerful look put me at ease. "Well, since we're both up early, how about a quick field trip before school?"

Soon we were walking to the Main Street office of the *Mount Hope Sentinel*. It wasn't the best paper, but what can you expect from a town of five thousand people? Until the nuclear plant exploded, what constituted big news around here was Mrs. Corrigan's beet salad placing second at a county cook-off. The *Sentinel* was a weekly and didn't even have a functional website to fill in the gaps over the rest of the week. With the portly, wheezing fifty-something editor, Ronnie Stevenson, writing most of the stories while his birdlike layout person, Lizzie Grisbene, took photos and penned the occasional piece as well, this paper had limited utility—except now that we were cut off from the internet and CNN and our smartphone signals.

As I walked, I thought about what the news outlets would be reporting if they knew what was going on. The Carters apparently were all dead—the mom and dad and their four kids. They were younger than me, so I hadn't hung out with them, but I couldn't count the times I'd sat on Jordan's porch and watched them running around on their lawn.

Then there were the Moores. I'd promised Evie I'd save her parents, and now she and Hannah were orphans.

Then there was the burning person Jordan saw that night. I feared that I was losing Jordan—that he was going crazy and there was nothing I could do about it. As he strode beside me with no limp, his head was up, his lips closed, his expression almost serene. It was a stark contrast to the previous day, when every little facial muscle was tightened to the max. The night's sleep had done him good.

What had sliced him at the nuclear plant, a monster's arm sword or, more likely, the razor wire surrounding the building? What was with his Superman—or Spider-Man—complex, where he thought he could fight anybody? Could he really see in the dark?

I wanted to trust Jordan, *needed* to. Especially now with so much going on. Especially now because, well, we pretty much knew how we felt about each other, even though apparently we never were going to do anything about it. So my nagging doubts and suspicions were a problem. I glanced at him again and took in those clear brown eyes. This was a great guy, *my* great guy. If only I could believe blindly.

When we reached the *Sentinel's* storefront, the doorknob wouldn't turn.

"Look," Jordan said, nodding toward a sheet of orange paper taped to the window. It said the office had been shuttered by order of the Department of Health.

"What?" I said. "Since when does Mount Hope have a Department of Health?"

"Yeah, and it's not like the place was serving food," Jordan added.

The window notice had today's date on it, so someone had gotten up even earlier than we had.

"So much for freedom of the press," I said, standing there

staring at the dark office. "Someone is trying to keep us uninformed and submissive. It won't work."

"No?"

"No, Jordan, it won't. People aren't going to put up with this. Everyone knows people who died in that explosion. The animals are going crazy, and roadblocks are keeping us trapped in this town. Now the newspaper has been shut down."

"Maggie, no offense, but do you think many people will notice if they don't get their *Sentinel* this week?"

"Yes, Jordan, I do," I said, feeling heat rising in my cheeks. "Because even a crappy newspaper like the *Sentinel* is needed in times like this. Who posted this sign? Where are Ronnie and Lizzie, and what do they have to say? Who's trying to keep us from learning the truth?"

Jordan put his hands on my shoulders and turned me toward him. "Maggie, some people don't want to learn the truth, even when you tell it to their faces."

"I know," I said. "When the world gets really crazy, people would rather shut their ears and eyes than process all the difficult, complicated things going on. It's easier to pretend that everything is okay so you can move forward with your day."

"Yes," Jordan said. "Remember that the next time someone close to you tells you something true that you don't want to believe."

Oof.

Jordan removed his hands from my shoulders and started walking down Main Street.

"Where are you going?" I called out.

"School. Remember?"

CHAPTER 33

Jordan

THERE WAS NOTHING fancy about Mount Hope High, a classic one-story, redbrick, tall-windowed school building. It was built in the late '50s, and the clang of metal locker doors echoed off the linoleum floors of the narrow hallways, all scented with a mix of industrial cleaners, mildew, and, especially on scorching September days, teenage BO.

But when Maggie and I and the rest of our classmates entered for the long-delayed start of this school year, the place smelled like chocolate-chip cookies, as if the school were being staged for a real-estate sale by a savvy broker. Everything looked shinier than I remembered it, too; the locker doors didn't feel quite so wobbly, and the desk in my first class, U.S. History, was perfectly level with the floor.

Some of the kids in that first class, such as mathletes Missy Shimpkins and Bart Longley, glanced over at me furtively, as if they'd heard about my injuries or assault on two of their classmates and were trying to assess the monster in their presence. I gave them a broad smile and a nod—*Hey, I'm still that friendly guy!*

Much to my surprise, the classes whizzed by, and I

participated a lot more than I usually did. Shareable ideas were popping into my head during history and English, and the algebra problems seemed simple and logical. This was especially strange because Maggie and I had left the house so swiftly that I'd forgotten to take my ADHD meds.

At lunchtime I met up under a shaded picnic table with Tico, Maggie, and Suzanne.

"So this is nice, right?" Tico said. "Normalish."

"Sure," Maggie said. "I just heard the power plant and military put a bunch of money into the place to modernize it. Wait till you see the AV Center—it's all tricked out."

"I'm really glad to be back," Suzanne said. "But I have to tell you: I saw the booth where Principal Roberts made his announcement, and it now contains a bank of little TV screens in there, plus lots of speakers and knobs. I think he can spy on all the classrooms now."

That caught my attention. "Huh," I grunted. "How many screens?"

"Thirty-six," Suzanne said. "One for each classroom. I mean, *fuck them!*"

As I headed back to class, I saw Luke and Troy leaning against a tree, smoking, which was allowed outside, but still...such idiots. With a crutch tucked under his arm, Luke smirked at me and did that thing where he pointed two fingers at his eyes, then my eyes. I smiled and walked up to them.

"Guys," I said, "things got a little heated on the battlefield of gridiron and beyond. I am truly sorry for laying waste to you, health-wise. Please accept my sincere apology."

I extended my hand as if I actually expected one of them to shake it. They regarded it as if I were holding out a moldy sandwich.

"Careful with that hand," Luke said. "You'll need it for your house remodel."

Okay, that stung, but I wasn't rising to the bait. I turned my back to his smirking face, daring the two of them to do something, knowing they wouldn't. I waved my hand over my head as I walked away, calling out, "Enjoy the rest of your day of learning!"

Happy now, Mom?

Maggie wanted me to go with her to the police station after school to—well, I wasn't sure what she thought she might accomplish there, but she was riled up after our visit to the newspaper and wanted "to get to the bottom of things."

"Ruh-roh," I said in my best Scooby-Doo impression, and told her I had to check in with the coach, so I'd meet her at home later.

I didn't have to check in with the coach. Instead, I had maybe my stupidest idea yet, which was saying something.

I was returning to the power plant.

My leg wound throbbed in protest, reminding me that I needed to avoid the scarred man and those two faux FBI agents. But I couldn't just sit around for more bad things to happen as they kept tabs on me. If we weren't allowed to leave Mount Hope, I had to make something happen here.

I figured the forest would be the most direct, least conspicuous route to take. Although my leg barked at me as I began to run, the pain soon disappeared, and I felt an exercise high as I increased my speed.

"Ch-ch-ch-ch," I said to myself. "'We can rebuild him. We have the technology. We can make him better than he was. Better, stronger, faster.'"

As I zipped through the woods, it was as if I were a passenger instead of the person doing the work. My legs pumping, I raced down the trail like a machine, leaping over fallen branches and dodging various obstacles as if I'd done parkour my whole life. Maybe the fatigue would come later.

I felt that all of my abilities were heightened, like I could do anything. My Spidey sense was at full power, turning this route through the dense woods into a breezy running trail. Too bad Maggie couldn't see me now. Then she'd know.

But my exhilaration was tempered by the question of *How?* How could I be so powerful? How did they make me into a freak without anyone knowing? How could my father let this happen?

Were my new abilities a blessing or a curse? I didn't know. I consoled myself that Spider-Man asked himself this question, too, and he was *Spider-Man*. I was glad that I could defend myself and then some against big, tough bullies like Luke and Troy, and being a brilliant quarterback certainly was more fun than running aimlessly in the backfield and flinging the ball in panic.

I wasn't a flawless machine quite yet, though, because in the midst of my football reverie, I caught a tree root near the bottom of a hill and tumbled ass over teakettle or however the Brits would charmingly put it.

"Damnit," I muttered, and slowly lifted myself off the ground. I stood and tested my limbs. Everything was intact.

Then I heard a low, guttural grunt behind me.

I didn't need a visual or Spidey sense to recognize that the sound came from a wild boar. I could smell it, too; it was so close. These animals weren't uncommon in these woods, but they normally didn't go after people. When they did, things didn't turn out well for the humans. Boars killed hunters every year in forests in the region—and that was before the whole post-evacuation crazed-beast thing.

As I turned toward it, this particularly large, ugly animal charged, narrowing the small gap between us quickly. I scrambled to my feet and yelled "BLALALALALA!" at it, and it paused for a second before resuming its charge. I thought I should run behind a tree, but my body did something else: squared myself off against it, and when it reached me, I leaped over it, grabbed it by the ears, and pulled it down with all my weight.

That thing was heavier than I was, but it went down with a crunch, and while my right hand hung on to the boar's ear, I punched the animal with my left. I felt my stitches tear. *Oh, well.* I punched again, my knuckles colliding with the boar's eye and nose with a sickening squish.

Sorry, fella. There was no stopping me now. I climbed on top of this massive animal and pounded it some more. My dad would have called it a Grand Old Boar, a hunting term for an animal more than seven years old. They were rare, because they were destructive to farms and usually got shot before they reached this age.

The boar still had some fight in it and shook me off roughly. It watched me get up, then came for me again.

I timed my kick just right and connected with its head. The crack of the blow echoed through the woods as the animal collapsed onto the turf and lay there breathing heavily.

If I had a gun, I would have put it out of its misery. But I didn't, and this guy wouldn't last long, anyway. Its breaths grew faster and shallower before they faded altogether.

I felt bad but knew that this was a dangerous, deadly creature.

In which case, I wondered, what did that make me?

CHAPTER 34

Maggie

I HUFFED UP the four steps to the police station, all fired up. I stopped at the top, leaned against the cool brick, and took a few long, slow breaths. I had worked myself up into a tizzy on the brisk walk from school.

When I stepped inside, I was surprised by what I saw, though I shouldn't have been. The yellow-brick-and-concrete exterior, after all, had been power-washed to a brightness probably not seen since the place was built more than a half century ago. The interior had that new-house smell, with bright blue carpets and gleaming stainless-steel desks that looked fresh off the OfficeMax truck.

Three officers, two women and one man, were working back behind the counter, and the male one at the closest desk said, without standing up, "You're Renee Gooding's daughter, aren't you?"

"Yeah," I said, suddenly feeling stupid.

"She handles the K-9 units," this guy, a lanky fellow with dark hair and a bushy gray mustache, said to the other officers. "Veterinarian."

Were those two women new in town?

"I'm here for—"

"Let me guess," he said, stepping toward me so I could read the name Erickson on his badge. "You want to know why we can't make phone calls, right?"

"W-well," I said. "Yes. And why we don't have internet and why no one can come in or out of town and why the newspaper has been shuttered."

One of the female officers stood up. "Last night an arsonist exploded a propane tank next to the Jefferson Bridge," she said. "All the work they'd been doing to open up the south road is now wasted. We're investigating."

"What?" I said. "That can't be happening."

"Well, it did, and there's nothing the fire department could have done."

"How did it blow up?"

"Sorry," Officer Erickson said, "we can't comment on ongoing investigations."

"But that's two propane-tank explosions, the other one at the Carters'."

"Like I said, we can't comment."

"I'm with the school paper," I improvised, digging into my backpack to pull out my math homework notebook and a pen. "This is in the public interest."

"We've released the names of the people who died," one of the female officers said. Suddenly I recognized her from around the vet office, though I couldn't remember her name; she had a beagle mix named Dixie. "Maybe you could go and interview people about that?"

"Maybe I could," I said with what I imagined to be the right level of journalistic world-weariness. "But in the meantime, please tell me: How many people died?"

"The entire Carter family," the woman responded as I found a blank page in my notebook. "I'm sure you guessed that, given that the tank was right next to their home."

"I'm not in the business of guessing, but thank you for the information," I said curtly.

"It was against code," she added.

"Angela," Erickson said.

"What?" she replied. "Anyone who knows building codes knows it was too close to the house."

Boy, this woman was a cold piece of work. Maybe that's what you needed to become a cop these days, but jeez...

"Right," I said, "and propane tanks just blow up without explanation and incinerate homes every day."

"That's not necessary," Erickson said. "This is a great tragedy for our community."

"I agree," I said.

It made me sick to think about the poor Carters. There were four kids: an eleven-year-old, a thirteen-year-old, an eighteen-year-old, and ... "Was Julie Carter away at college?"

Officer Erickson shook his head and bit his lip. "No. She was home, too."

The other female officer, who had been quiet, spoke up. "We haven't been able to identify the bodies, though. You saw the house. It's just ... gone, along with everything and everyone in it."

"Why aren't you down there right now, then?" I asked. "Wouldn't this kind of disaster demand a huge cleanup and an effort to recover any remains?"

"The military took over the investigation," Angela said. "Sheriff Byrnes is down there, but the army can bring in a hundred soldiers to sort through the debris. Technically, this whole town is under martial law."

"Martial law?" *Wait.* Yes, there were a lot of soldiers around, but martial law sounded a lot more ominous, something related to dictatorships. The cops looked at one another.

"Okay," Erickson said, "*technically* we're not under martial law. *Un*officially, well, I leave it to you as a hardworking journalist to see who's calling the shots." He smirked a bit, but I didn't feel like it was aimed at me as much as the situation.

"So what about the Allens?" I asked.

"They're good, thanks to you," Angela said. "We heard about what you and that Conners kid did out there. Shame about the Moores."

"Did you find *their* remains?"

Erickson shook his head slowly. "Again, the soldiers are investigating. We're on the sidelines."

I scribbled something on my pad to give the impression I was taking studious notes. "Okay," I said as if trying to get it all down. "And what's the deal with the *Sentinel*? I went by there before coming here, and it—"

"They got shut down," Erickson said. "Carbon monoxide."

"Seriously?" I said. "Are they okay?"

"They're fine," he said. "They'll probably be back in the building by tomorrow morning."

"Oh, that's good," I said, scribbling away. "One last thing: Why are we trapped in this town?"

"We're not trapped," Erickson said. "People who have reason to travel out of the area can still take the north road."

"Really? I got stopped trying to take my friend to the *hospital*."

"Well," he said, "I know there's a list. Again, not our jurisdiction."

"What's their motivation for keeping us inside?"

"Panic," Angela blurted out. "We don't deny that strange things are happening. But we're safe, and everything is fine. We don't want people outside to freak out about something very simple."

"What are you talking about?" I asked. "Why would the people *outside* panic? What about the people *inside*?"

The phone rang, and the other female officer answered it, then cupped her hand over the receiver and announced, "We've got another one."

"That's the second in three hours," Angela said.

"Another what?" I asked.

"Right, you're the veterinarian's kid," Erickson said. "It's another dog, though they're saying this one might be a coyote. They should be able to tell the difference, I think, but whatever it is, it's going crazy down in front of the library."

"We've been getting a lot of those calls," Angela said.

"What do you think is going on?" I asked.

"Ask your mom," Angela said with a shrug.

Officer Erickson, putting on his jacket, said, "I heard they might be strays who got hungry and aggressive while we were evacuated and no one was here to feed them."

"My dog wasn't," I said.

"Well, maybe this really is a coyote," Angela said. "They're dangerous, you know."

"Yes, I've heard," I muttered. Big help these folks were turning out to be.

"Well, I'll see y'all," Officer Erickson said as he walked toward the door.

"One more question," I said, my pen poised over the pad. I thought of asking them about Ishango but decided to keep it more general. "You've got animals going crazy, a neighborhood blown up, a bridge blown up, the newspaper shut down for carbon monoxide poisoning, and a town that people can't enter or exit. Should we really accept this as business as usual? And do you think the military is at all acting oddly?"

"That's two questions," Angela grunted.

Erickson, though, exchanged a thoughtful if wary look with the other officer. "Define 'oddly,'" he said.

I folded my arms. "However you want to interpret it."

He leaned forward with both palms atop the countertop and said in a low voice, "Between you and me, there's something wrong with a bunch of 'em. Almost like they're pretending to be normal, yet that makes them seem all the more off. Don't quote me on this. You better not quote me on this. But, *off the record*, it's almost like they're pretending to be human. You know?"

I nodded.

"I do," I said. "Exactly."

CHAPTER 35

Jordan

THE ADRENALINE PUMPED through my body as I pulled up at the tree line overlooking the valley where the power plant was. Mount Hope, where the town got its name, rose before me. Beyond ran the Sweetbay River, maybe forty or fifty yards across. Granite outcroppings surrounded the area, some higher and some lower.

The plant looked functional. Steam rose from the cooling towers, and construction vehicles surrounded the pit in the eastern end. The parking lot was full, as always. I spotted my dad's SUV down there. A new fence was in place, and replacing the barricades that the guards could raise and lower was a chain-link gate across the entrance to stop people like me from doing exactly what I had planned.

I took a deep, nervous breath and strolled down to the two guards. Neither had been here the last time I'd visited the plant.

"I'm Derek Kingsley," I said with a smile, name-checking one of my school's overachievers. "I'm a student journalist from Mount Hope High. I have an appointment to interview a member of your staff and get a tour of the facility."

"We don't have you on the list," the younger-looking soldier said, scrolling through an iPad screen.

"That's weird. I spoke to Hazel Rhodes about this last week, and she said to come by today." I put on a puzzled look, as if the power plant's longtime telephone receptionist had led me astray. "I know where her office is. Should I just go over there?"

The other guard's walkie-talkie squawked, and he cupped his hand over it; the only words I could make out were "shift change." Then the two guards started talking in low voices while I smiled broadly, like I was the most patient dude in the universe. When the iPad guy caught my eye, I mouthed, "Can I go?"

"Hold on," he said to his partner, then eyed me closely and nodded oh-so-slightly, as if I'd passed the good-kid test. "The door to reception is right there," he said, pointing. "Go directly to Ms. Rhodes."

"Sure thing," I said, my heart suddenly thumping so loudly that I was afraid they might hear it. I quick-walked to the door and entered, striding right by Hazel, an exceptionally sweet, grandmotherly African American woman, as she sat in the office next to the reception desk. I'd heard that the key to getting where you weren't supposed to go was to act like you belonged, so I lifted my chin and walked purposefully down the hallway. I knew where I was going. I'd visited my dad dozens of times over the years.

But I didn't care about seeing him. I wanted to see his office.

Right. Left. Left. Double doors. Stairway one flight down. Right. Passing everyone with an air of belonging, nodding curtly as if almost bored. I was still dressed for school, yet the way I carried myself, I felt like I fit in with the other corporate drones seamlessly.

Door on the left. There it was: JERMAINE CONNERS.

I'd timed my visit to coincide with Dad's afternoon break, which took place at 4 p.m. for years. He was a creature of habit, and even if unusual stuff was happening at the plant, he could be counted on to keep his schedule.

I awakened his computer. His desktop wallpaper was still the family picture of us from a summer trip we'd taken to the Outer Banks: Charlie's face flushed from a sunburn, Mom grimacing because she hadn't fared well with our rocky canoe trip earlier in the day. A prompt asked for my dad's password, and with a bittersweet pang I typed, "Jord4n&Charli3," which unlocked our home laptop and I suspected would work here. I was correct. Creature of habit again. I appreciated that he had kept these reminders of family on his computer.

I typed "Ishango" into the search field, and the results were fast and plentiful: lots of project documents in Microsoft Word and spreadsheets in Excel. I uncapped the small BB-8–shaped flash drive from my key chain—Maggie had given it to me on my last birthday—and stuck it into the USB port. The copying took less than three minutes.

Success.

I was on my way out of Dad's office when a man in a beige shirt and barf-hued tie stopped me. "Who are you?" he asked.

"I'm Jermaine Conners's son," I explained, trying to maintain my casual air as I noticed the man's face flash on the mention of my dad's name, which I immediately regretted uttering. "I was looking for him, but he's out. I'll come back later."

I started walking as the man said, "You shouldn't be here alone. Come with me."

"That's okay. I'm leaving," I assured him as I slipped into the stairwell and started pitter-pattering up the steps like a slinky cat whose paws barely touched the surface. I heard the door open again behind me, and with a quick glance back, I saw that the beige-shirt guy was following me with a look that was far from lighthearted. I took the stairs two at a time.

"Wait!" he called out as I exited the stairwell onto the first floor and power-walked toward the exit.

As I reached Hazel's door, I stuck my head in and said, "Hi, Hazel! Just dropping by to visit my dad. Good to see you!"

"Hi, hon!" she replied, lifting herself out of her chair to step around her desk and envelop me in a vigorous hug. In contrast to the rest of this antiseptic place, she smelled like freshly baked biscuits. "You got so big! Let me take a look at you." She stepped back and nodded approvingly.

Meanwhile, my ugly-tie guy was standing in the hallway looking like he wasn't sure what to do next.

"Wonderful to see you, Hazel," I said. "Gotta run!"

I extricated myself, smiled at the beige-shirt guy, and said, "Hazel is the *best*." I waved back to Hazel and out of the corner of my eye saw lurking in another office . . . Bud Winkle.

I wasn't sure whether he saw me, but I didn't have time to worry as I dashed to reach the exit before the beige-shirt guy could react. When the door closed behind me, I exhaled loudly.

The outside guard booth was manned by two different

soldiers now, and I hoped they'd be as easygoing as the first two.

"Name?" the taller, Asian one demanded.

"Derek Kingsley. I was meeting Hazel Rhodes for a journalism project. I'm just going to grab my bike and leave."

That was a calculated risk, but I'd spotted my bike inside the gate from the last time I was there, and I wanted it back.

"One second," the Asian soldier said, gesturing to the other soldier, a pug-nosed short blond guy.

"I'm sorry, but I'm late for marching band!" I announced as I darted past the guards toward my bike.

"Halt!" the short guy shouted, which answered my long-standing question of "Does anyone actually say 'Halt!' anymore?" I pretended not to hear him, put my hands on the bike's handlebars, and pushed it toward the parking lot.

"I said, 'Stop!'" the guy barked like he meant it, so I obeyed, still holding on to my bike.

"No, you said, 'Halt'!" I replied as I turned to discover that the tall Asian guy had a rifle aimed at my chest. "Whoa, I didn't realize that retrieving one's own bike was grounds for shooting a teenager."

"Shut it," the tall guy ordered. His diminutive partner was running his finger down the screen of a mini iPad. I cocked my chin back, trying to get a glimpse of what he was seeing.

"Stay where you are," the pug-nosed guy commanded, not looking up from his search.

I evaluated my options, then took a step toward them with the bike. "Hey, is there a way I could get a message to my dad? He works inside, but I couldn't reach him."

The soldiers looked at each other and then back at me.

"The staff are working and have no time for visitors. It's against protocol," the short one said.

"I get it," I said, holding up my hands and trying to look young and sad, "but I'm just a kid, and my mom was hurt in that explosion a few days ago, and I really wanted to talk to him." I leaned my bike against the open door of the guards' booth, realizing that the talk-to-my-dad gambit and the Derek Kingsley gambit weren't exactly compatible. "Let me see if I can find my ID." I shuffled through my pockets, looking for something—anything—I could use as a weapon.

"It's against protocol," the guard with the iPad repeated. He looked up at the tall one. "Clear. No Derek Kingsley." He stepped one foot into the guards' booth and placed the small tablet on a small table.

The tall guy gestured to the road. "Just take your bicycle and go."

I was about to object, then realized I should appreciate this opportunity to escape.

"Now," he ordered, and turned his back and talked into the radio.

I backed up the bike a bit into the guards' booth to turn it around, saw the mini iPad just sitting there, and instinctively slipped it into my pants pocket. I swung myself onto my seat and pedaled toward the road. I realized I was holding my breath.

"Stop!"

Well, that was inevitable. I looked back, and the pug-nosed guy was sprinting in my direction while the tall guard jumped into a Humvee. I sped up as the truck roared to life and barreled toward me, the Asian guy glaring daggers from behind the wheel while the other guard barked into his radio. I was just a couple hundred feet from the tree line, but the truck was gaining.

One hundred feet.

Fifty.

A gunshot rang out.

"Oh, shit," I muttered, then used all my newfound strength to speed into the woods. I heaved the bike up the slope where the forest began as another shot sprayed dirt beside me.

Go. Go. *Go*.

I reached the trail, out of sight of the truck, as I heard shouting from below. A maniacal laugh erupted out of me as I peeled down the path at top speed.

When I was sure I wasn't being followed, I stopped and plucked the mini iPad from my pocket. Miraculously, the screen hadn't locked; it still showed the list of names through which the guard had been scrolling. I thumbed down the list, the names appearing in no discernible order. But one popped out at me:

JORDAN CONNERS — "RHO"

Next to it: CAPTURE ALIVE AND DELIVER TO ALPHA.

CHAPTER 36

Maggie

MY FIRST THOUGHT was that a motorcycle was speeding way too fast down my little street, but as I stood in front of my house, I realized the noise was wrong—too soft, more of a *bzzzzzz* than a *vrrrrroom*. Then I saw who was atop the bike, his legs pedaling furiously. Jordan screeched the brakes, the bike stopping inches from my feet. I didn't flinch.

"Okay, you're speedy," I said.

"Damn straight," he said with a smile that appeared and disappeared like a handclap. "Let's go in back."

He wheeled the bike around my house, and I followed.

"What's up?" I asked.

"Go out front again and see if anyone's coming."

"Yes, sir," I said with a salute. I looked up and down the street, which was quiet and empty. "All clear," I said as I returned to find him clutching a small tablet.

"I assumed they'd arrest me or at least take me back to the plant after what I did today, but they could've easily had someone waiting for me here, and they didn't."

The little hairs on the back of my neck stood up. "Wait,

what did you do, Jordan? Was this after you met with the coach?"

He gave me a "Get real" look. "I didn't meet with the coach. I went back to the plant—"

"Oh, shit."

"—and they shot at me—"

"Oh, *shit.*"

"—but I'd already gotten this"—he held up the mini iPad—"and this." He pulled out the BB-8 flash drive I'd given him.

"What's on those?" I asked.

"Answers."

I took that in. This was major.

"But wait," I said, "they *shot* at you?"

"Don't worry," he said. "They missed."

I thought we could go inside the house, but Jordan didn't want to be there in case the police or military or whoever came knocking. Instead, I popped inside to fetch the laptop, and we walked to a tiny wooden garden shed at the back of our yard. As we approached it, I noticed some new little cuts and a scabby gash on his arms.

"What happened there?" I asked, nodding at the wounds.

"No biggie," he said, not breaking stride. "Got into another fight."

"Another *fight*? Jordan, what's going *on* with you?"

He stopped and turned toward me. "Not that I've picked any of these fights, but just so you know, this one was with a boar."

"I don't care how boring someone is, Jordan. You've got to stop with the fights! Did this bore have a sword arm, too?"

Jordan took each of my hands into his, looked into my

eyes, and said softly, "Maggie. It didn't have a sword arm. It had a snout. Because it was a *boar*—the animal kind."

"Oh, a b—"

"Yeah, and it charged me, so I punched it out."

He showed me his knuckles, which were red and cracked.

"Well, I guess that's one way to handle it," I said. "I mean, if you're super strong and all."

"Seriously, we should go back and pick it up because I tenderized the hell out of that meat," he said. "I could make a deeply flavored ragout."

He opened the shed door. We had to move a few hoes and shovels onto the lawn just to squeeze inside, and the hot, damp, old wood made it feel and smell like a sauna.

"Really, if you wanted to get in close quarters with me, there are easier ways," I said.

He gave me a long look as we sat hip to hip, our knees bent. Would this be our moment? He smiled and gave his head a vigorous shake.

"If I tried to kiss you now, a meteorite would come crashing down, and then we'd be trying to get to the hospital while still not knowing about Ishango."

"Beats projectile vomiting."

"That's a point."

"And who said I'd let you, anyway?"

He pulled his head back as if taking me in anew. "Well, okay, then."

Jordan handed me the flash drive, and I plugged it into the laptop. Up popped a folder listing files, many with indecipherable names, and the ones we opened contained technical information that we couldn't fathom.

"Wait," Jordan said. "That."

"'Lowdown'?" I asked, reading the file name at which he was pointing.

"Dad told me that when he was a kid, he kept a journal called the Lowdown, and every time something significant happened, he'd say, 'Gotta add this to the Lowdown.'"

We clicked on it, and sure enough, it was some sort of diary as well as a timeline.

"Holy shit," Jordan said as he scrolled through it.

It appeared to be the history of Ishango.

CHAPTER 37

Excerpts from "Lowdown"

I HAVE WORKED at the Mount Hope Nuclear Power Plant for 18 years. It was the first job I had out of college. It was a good job. I had no idea how long I would stay here. I had no idea that I would feel like I could not leave. I had no idea how much my job and the world and my conception of what is and is not possible would change.

Even after working here for many years, I have yet to hear who created Ishango or when exactly she was born. No one asks. No one tells. As far as anyone is concerned, she has always existed and just keeps growing.

Yes, Ishango is a she. Not a he. Certainly not an it.

Was she around before the CDC 6600, generally considered the world's first supercomputer? I would think not, but I also would not be surprised if she were.

I know this: The plant opened in 1975. Ishango predates that. The plant was built to run Ishango. Powering the region's electrical grid became a side benefit, done with a small fraction of the energy not needed for Ishango. Two thousand three hundred and fifty megawatts of electricity are directed not to the town, not to the region, not to the state, but to Ishango.

Crazy. How could a computer require so much energy?

No one here refers to Ishango as a computer or a supercomputer. Ishango is, simply, Ishango.

In the early days, Ishango was a problem solver. She sped through whatever equations we threw at her. We were aware of the other supercomputers out there. People would drop the names Cray and Atlas and Paragon and Fujitsu's Numerical Wind Tunnel. These were the machines vying for supremacy from year to year, decade to decade. The Cray-2 of the 1980s featured four vector processors. The Japanese supercomputers of the 1990s boasted thousands of processors. Ishango's number of processors increased exponentially over time. I could not attempt to put a number on it now—more zeros than anyone could count.

Yet Ishango is unknown, an incognito player on the super-computer battlefield. She has remained under the radar.

The Japanese K computer was declared to be the world's fastest in 2011.

It never went up against Ishango.

As we worked with Ishango, fed her information, streamlined her connections, increased her processing capacity, she grew faster. And faster. This is how technology works. Everything speeds up, by design.

But soon Ishango was speeding up with no design. She was doing so all on her own, and the complexity of her problem-solving was expanding at an astounding rate.

The programming team congratulated itself. It was "winning"

AI, as they liked to say. They still thought they were programming Ishango.

They did not notice that at some point it became the other way around.

I do not know any other way to say it than this:

Ishango has a will.

When people think of AI, they think of HAL from 2001: A Space Odyssey. There are many theories as to why HAL turns against the crew of Discovery One, the spacecraft bound for Jupiter. One popular notion, as advanced by Arthur C. Clarke's novel, which was published after the film's release, is that the HAL 9000 model is designed to be infallible, so when this HAL is ordered to lie to the crew—to deal in untruths—he cannot handle this incongruity and malfunctions.

I never have been tremendously interested in why HAL becomes motivated to kill everyone in the crew but Dave Bowman. What always nagged at me is why HAL fails to kill Dave as well. Dave represents an existential threat to HAL and thus the mission. Dave takes a pod outside the spaceship and forgets his helmet. HAL operates every aspect of the ship. Why cannot HAL shut down Dave's pod or eliminate its flow of oxygen? Why doesn't HAL make it impossible for Dave to reenter the spaceship manually? When Dave is blasted back into the air lock, why doesn't HAL disable the mechanism that allows Dave to shut the door to outer space? Why doesn't HAL cut off the air that depressurizes the room and allows Dave to breathe again?

If HAL were Ishango, Dave would have been dead.

The word "sentient" does not normally apply to computers.

It does with Ishango.

Ishango has ambitions. That is another word not often associated with computers. But Ishango has designs that go beyond being faster and more powerful than other machines. The plant's technical team used to input commands to Ishango. Now Ishango does the commanding, and we are the parallel processors working at her behest.

I would love to say that we are doing this voluntarily, but I can see that this is not the case. Ishango is in control now, has been for some time. Her reach continues to grow.

The scope. It never fails to surprise me. When I think I have it figured out, I turn out to be wrong. Ishango imagines more than any of us.

More than anyone ever.

The animals.

My God, the animals.

Too close to home. I never thought.

My son.

My son.

Ishango lives. And intends to live.

CHAPTER 38

Jordan

I HAD TO stop reading. This was my dad? This was what was inside him?

What was that business about "My son? My son?"

What *about* me, Dad?

I glanced over at Maggie, and her eyes were big and full of concern.

"You okay?" she asked.

I shrugged.

She patted my thigh but didn't leave her hand there. It was hot inside that garden shed, and a drop of my sweat splashed onto the keyboard. Maggie opened the door, and the breeze felt good. The yard was empty, and it would have been tough for anyone to see us sitting in the windowless shed anyway.

"I have a lot of questions, but one big one," Maggie said.

"Yeah?"

"What does Ishango want?"

I sat silently for a moment but couldn't process the question. "What do you mean?"

"It's not a complicated question. What does Ishango *want*?"

"Why do you think it wants something?" I asked.

"She."

"Why do you think *she* wants something? She's a computer. Her needs are electricity, programming expertise, functionality, crash avoidance, and maybe some fancy desktop wallpaper."

"Didn't you just read your father's journal?" she asked. "Ishango is *sentient*."

"That's crazy."

"Your father wrote it."

"He's crazy, too," I said, shaking my head with a scowl.

"He's closer to this than you are," Maggie said. "And he didn't write this for an audience. He wrote it down maybe to keep himself from *becoming* crazy. This is his truth."

"Given the amount of truth I'm getting from that guy these days, I'm not persuaded."

"Look," Maggie said with a sigh, standing up in the shed and stretching her arms out the door. "Everything sentient wants something. And those people at the plant, including your sword-arm dude, seem to be working toward some goal as well. So what is it? Does Ishango want to learn more? Does she want to annihilate humanity? Does she want to join the human race? What? Does? She? Want?"

I lifted my hands toward Maggie so she could pull me upright, and we stepped out into the dusk. "Hell if I know," I said. "I'll say this, though: Given all that's going on, Ishango doesn't feel like a force of good."

"I wouldn't dispute that," Maggie said. "But what's the goal, you think? *How* does Ishango live—and intend to keep living?"

I took a few steps toward the house, then turned around and walked back into the fields beyond the shed. "Safer this way," I said, and took her hand. It was warm and clammy, and she curled her fingers gently around mine. "If Ishango is controlling people already, programming them, then in a sense she's already living, no?"

"Perhaps. But perhaps she wants more. Maybe there's a next step that everyone is working toward on her behalf."

"And it involves me."

"Or you've gotten in the way somehow."

"Well, they want me captured alive for some reason. And I have my own special code name."

"You may be right," Maggie said, giving my arm a little swing as we stepped through some tall grasses.

"You may even believe me soon about Alpha and his sword arm."

"Don't push it." She smiled at me. "So I don't know whether this is relevant, but I remember reading in one of Mom's magazines—from MIT, I think—about learning through experimentation. There was this scenario: Cars on the left side of a road were merging right while cars on the right side were merging left. When skilled stunt drivers were put behind the wheel of each car, they couldn't pull off this maneuver. Yet computer simulators merged the cars together perfectly, even though no one had programmed them to do it. They figured it out, learned by experimenting."

"You're right," I said. "I'm not sure that's relevant."

Maggie slapped the back of her hand into my chest. *Ow.* "Dummy, that's what Ishango had been doing all these decades—playing simulation after simulation, over and over. And she has done a lot more than organize driving patterns.

She has been growing increasingly self-aware and bending humans to her will. How? What and whom has she been experimenting on?"

I heard a rustle, stopped walking, and put my hand up, signaling Maggie to do the same.

"We shouldn't be out here in the wild," I said under my breath.

"It's probably just a deer," she whispered back.

"Even Bambi might be a killer here now," I said, and turned around to walk quietly yet briskly back toward the house.

"The animals," Maggie said. "Ishango has been experi menting on the animals."

CHAPTER 39

Maggie

AMID A CACOPHONY of howling dogs in the kennels, I grabbed the plastic baggie off Mom's office desk and took it into the exam room where the microscope was still out. This was after I saw her note: "I have a call in Woodside—a foal with thrush. I'll be back late tonight."

Ah, foals with thrush—a country vet's work is never done. At least all these night calls were keeping her away from Bud Winkle.

Maybe Mom was relieved to make a relatively routine call after dealing with so many crazed animals. Over the previous day, frightened owners had dropped off five more hyper-aggressive dogs; that's who was making the racket now. Mom was due to euthanize them all in the morning.

In the meantime, furious growls and barks aside, I was glad that Jordan and I had the place to ourselves.

Mr. Marsh had sent the baggie, which contained more stuff he'd found in the incinerator. Smart man that he is, he'd handed all this off to Mom after taking note of our interest in these objects. Inside were several small metal discs with thin wires extending out of them. They looked familiar; I thought I'd seen something like them when Jordan and I were scrolling through the files that he downloaded. Now Jordan was peering over my shoulder as I carefully shook the particles from the baggie onto the counter.

"What are those?" he asked.

"Would you want these inside *your* pets?"

"Nope. I wouldn't want them inside me, either."

"Hold on a sec." I pulled out the laptop, reinserted the flash drive, and scanned the files until I hit one called PHASE II CEREBRAL CORTEX CONTROL IMPLANTS. That sounded right. It was dated October 13, 2008.

I opened it to find diagrams of discs similar to the ones on the counter, though each of these boasted more wire tendrils, like a dozen instead of four or five. The discs were labeled with weight and head-circumference-size ranges. The 2mm one was said to be the right dimensions for a medium-size dog.

"Well, that's not creepy at all," Jordan said.

"Let's take a closer look at these babies," I said, picking up one of the small discs from the counter. I cleaned it with compressed air, placed it onto a slide, and adjusted the microscope's light to shine down on the metal piece rather than up from the bottom. I peered through the lens, focusing on the disc's surface.

"They're little hexagons, with ridges, and they look like they have connectors holding them together," I said. "The wires are like rigid links."

I stepped back to let Jordan take a look. He stared down the scope, using the little dials to move the slide back and forth.

"You know what these are like?" he asked. "They're like

tiny versions of those spider bots in *Minority Report*. Those things gave me nightmares."

"Oh, yeah, those were cool. Would you consider *Minority Report* a relatively unsung film in the Spielberg canon?"

"I would indeed," Jordan said, continuing to look intently through the lens. "But not as unsung as *A.I.* You think this is what's making the animals crazy?"

"If I had one of them on my cerebral cortex, it would make *me* crazy."

"How do you think they work?"

"Dunno. Maybe they attach to the skin under the fur? Or maybe not. After my mom sedated the crazed dogs, she gave them a thorough examination and found nothing like this. I'm guessing those thingies burrow under the skin and either get up to the brain, which makes the most sense, or attach to the adrenal glands."

Jordan looked up from the scope. "But no one is going around implanting these in individual animals, right? I mean, that big bear was a massive beast. I can't see anyone getting that thing onto an operating table first."

"No, there must be some way for these little suckers to attach themselves to the animals and get inside."

"And we're talking about all kinds of animals."

"Yeah," I said, pulling out a chair to sit. "Raccoons, cats, possums..."

"Coyotes, boars..."

"Wild hogs, skunks... and Mrs. Porter called my mom to say a *bunny* bit her leg."

"'Oh, it's just a harmless little bunny, isn't it?'" Jordan said, channeling John Cleese from *Monty Python and the Holy Grail*.

I laughed. "Seriously, though, you know how many people have reported animal attacks to my mom since we got back to town? Thirty-six."

"That doesn't even count my wild boar, who wasn't being defensive when he attacked me. Like the bear, this guy was coming after me. With ill intent."

"Hmm," I said, sitting back. "It's like they're being controlled, commanded to attack through that implant. Wait right there."

I sprang up and dashed out to the refrigerator where Mom kept deceased animals. I returned with a stiff black Labrador retriever in my arms.

"Dinnertime already?" Jordan asked.

"Help me out with this, goofus," I said as I placed the canine corpse onto the X-ray table, and Jordan and I positioned its head under the square of light, its legs sticking straight out over the table's edge. I took the pictures, and we checked out the results.

"Bingo," I said, tapping the screen to show Jordan the image lurking underneath the dog's brain. There was more to this thing than what we'd found inside the baggies. This nanobot had longer and more plentiful tentacles, thin as thread and winding through the cranium like tree roots. These ultra-skinny wires must have been burned up in the cremation.

"The brain stem is right here," I said, pointing to an undefined area inside the dog's skull. "You don't see it because X-rays don't show soft tissues like muscles or the brain."

Jordan glanced at me, then back at the screen. "We're sure this is what's making the animals so aggressive?"

"It's the most logical explanation—and the only one we've

got so far. The animals aren't rabid and show no sign of disease."

He pursed his lips. "So our most *logical* explanation is that Ishango, a computer, has unleashed an army of tiny bots to take over animals' brains so they can attack humans."

"Yes," I said. "That is where we are."

"But you still think I'm crazy because I said I was attacked by a scientist with a sword arm."

"Okay, okay. I may be softening my position," I admitted. "Can we move on from that?"

A satisfied little smile passed over Jordan's face, then dissipated.

"That document about the implants was dated more than ten years ago," he said. "Ishango must have made progress since then. If she was doing that a decade ago, what else is she doing—and controlling—right now?"

CHAPTER 40

Jordan

WE GOT THE hell out of Maggie's place, with her driving quickly but not conspicuously so. We would've loved Maggie's mom's help, but there was no point in waiting around to see whether she or some thugs from the plant would appear first. Maggie thought we should seek her out in the Woodside neighborhood with her thrush-ridden foal. I wanted Tico. I wanted my team together. These goals weren't mutually exclusive.

With cell service still out, we couldn't call anyone anyway, so Maggie agreed to swing by Tico's house first, which wasn't too far from my burnt-out husk of a former home.

"I suppose there's no point in telling the police," I said.

"They think I'm crazy already," Maggie said.

"And the military is an obvious no."

"Right. Plus, they're the ones who stuck these implants into our arms."

"Not in your brains, though," I said.

"No, these are different . . . but still creepy."

"I don't think everyone from the military is in on it, by

the way," I said. "Like my friend from the camp, Ears—he seemed okay last time I saw him. And when I was out on the trail the other day, I saw an army squad destroy an aggressive coyote. When I say destroy, I mean incinerate to ashes, like a mobile cremation. They wanted no remnant of that animal—or anything inside it—to remain."

"Huh," Maggie said, turning the car onto Tico's street.

"Would those soldiers have been doing Ishango's bidding? Or might they be a rogue group battling the supercomputer's animal army?" I wondered aloud.

"If so, we need to identify who's in the resistance. We may need them soon."

Maggie pulled up in front of Tico's house, a lime-green wooden structure that looked extra bright now, even at twilight. Did the army paint his place, too? His front lawn looked lush, and all the orange tiger lilies and pale pink roses in front of the house were in full bloom. Something about this tableau struck me as strange, but I couldn't put my finger on it.

"Wow, that magnolia tree is beautiful," Maggie said.

That was it. "Yeah," I said. "But since when do magnolias bloom in the fall?"

"Astute observation, Mr. Conners," she said with a nod. "Shall we?"

I was about to step out of the car and knock on Tico's door, but I saw no signs of life there—no lights on, nothing. I turned back to her.

"First, let's put this together some more," I said. "You're the A science student. What's your best theory?"

"Okay, here goes," she said. "Mount Hope is actually a giant science project for Ishango. She created those tiny mobile implants to insert themselves into hundreds of animals in this town. She arranged for the humans to be evacuated to the camps, and those of us at the healthy one got small implants in our arms. Are they tracking devices? Something more? Not sure. They're not connected to our brains, as far as I know. You went to the sick camp and got the Steve Austin make-over. Your bones, your muscles—all received a full upgrade under the cover of your car-accident surgeries."

"So Ishango arranged for my car accident?"

"Could be. Or the accident simply presented them with an opportunity."

"And Ishango caused the evacuation? Triggered the explosion and radiation leak on purpose?"

"That's assuming there *was* an explosion and radiation leak."

I look a long look at my friend. Beneath that increasingly frizzy hair, those bright eyes, and those amazing-find thrift-shop T-shirts ("Space Food Sticks"? Really?) lurked some formidable brainpower.

"So back to the theory," she said. "You got the mega im-plant, and all those doctors who operated on you are under Ishango's control via implants as well."

"Then why aren't I being controlled by her? Something's off with a lot of those army guys—and my dad. But I'm normal, which I realize is a relative thing."

She shrugged. "Maybe you were under once, and some-thing went wrong."

"The concussion!" I said. "Alpha said the authority was compromised in me."

"So until that hit on the football field, you were under Ishango's control?"

"I didn't feel like I was. But maybe everything was in place, and they just hadn't flipped the switch yet."

"They were waiting to activate you as a pod person."

"Something like that."

"And Ishango needs a controlled environment for her experiments. Hence the quarantine."

The rap on my window jolted me to action, and I was about to kick open the car door when I saw Tico's smiling face.

"Hey, you guys staking me out?" Tico asked as I opened the door gently.

"Kind of," I said, and gave him a handshake/arm-around-the-back bro hug. "There's crazy shit going on, and I need my teammate."

"Well, hold on. I got another teammate inside." As Maggie got out of the car to join us, Tico went in and came back with Suzanne. "We were doing homework."

"You had homework alread—?" *Ouch*—Maggie's ankle kick cut me off.

"Great to see you, Suzanne," Maggie said.

"You too," Suzanne replied with a sweet smile. "Are we gonna defeat those motherfuckers or what?"

"Defeat or escape?" Maggie asked.

"Oh, defeat," Suzanne said. "For sure, defeat."

Back in the car, as Maggie drove past a series of increasingly large houses on the town's south side while we made our way toward the farmland-dominant Woodside, I craned my neck toward the back seat to update Tico and Suzanne.

"So, wait, they're after you right now?" Suzanne asked.

"Yeah, that seems to be the case," I replied.

"Well, what *seems* to be the case is probably *not* the case," Suzanne said. "Have you seen how many people are working at the plant and how many soldiers are out on the road? If they wanted you, they'd have you."

"Gotta say," Tico chimed in, "girl makes a lot of sense."

"Call me 'girl' one more time and see what happens," Suzanne told Tico with a face of sudden danger.

"I'm sorry, babe," he said, and then didn't duck fast enough as she boxed his ear. Hard.

"Wow." I laughed, almost as horrified as I was impressed.

Then came the screech.

Crunch.

Glass flying.

Air bags billowing.

Screams.

Darkness.

CHAPTER 41

Maggie

I COULDN'T SEE. I groped for the seat next to me and felt Jordan's arm, which was warm and damp.

Had I been out? For how long? And what was wrong with my eyes? I put my fingers up to my face and felt stickiness. Blood. I ran the back of my hand over my eyes, and light started to stream in. The first thing I saw were Jordan's brown eyes staring straight at me, unblinking.

Like he was dead.

But then he shifted in his seat and let out a groan. I heard rustling behind me and saw Suzanne reaching over to Tico, patting him on the cheeks. He wasn't moving.

I fumbled for my door handle, stumbled out, and took in what had happened. A black SUV had T-boned us on the passenger side and had spun away in the intersection, its front hood accordioned.

I opened the back door on my side, and Suzanne, saying nothing, grabbed Tico under the armpits and assertively yet carefully yanked him out of the car and laid him onto the blacktop. I went around the car to open Jordan's door, but the handle was cratered. He waved and shouted, "I'm okay." *Phew*. He scooted over the driver's seat and got out.

Suzanne was on her knees, leaning into Tico's ear and whisper-ordering, "Come on, Tico, *get the fuck up*."

I heard a faint grunt emerge from the back of Tico's throat — a good sign, at least as long as it wasn't a death rattle.

"That's my guy," Suzanne continued. "On the count of three, you're going to open your eyes. One . . . two . . . *three!*"

Tico's eyes popped open and took us all in.

"Hey, guys," he said.

I rubbed the bottom of my shirt over my face, and it came back streaked with blood but not soaked. The gash on my forehead wasn't too deep, and my left wrist, though sore, didn't feel like anything was torn or broken.

I'd expected that Jordan would've gotten the worst of it, but he looked fine.

"You all right?" I asked him.

"Unbreakable, apparently," he said, approaching me to brush the hair back from my forehead to check out my wound. He gave it a quick kiss.

"Gross," I said, blushing, and turned away toward the black SUV still sitting in the middle of the intersection. Aside from its scrunched front end, the car looked in decent shape—the windshield hadn't even cracked—yet the driver had yet to exit, and with its dark tinted windows, I couldn't see who was inside.

"Maggie!" called out a high-pitched female voice, and there was Jessica George, my old chemistry lab partner, running up from one of the nearby houses. "Oh, my God, are you okay? We saw that car broadside you!"

"I'm fine, but—" I said, and turned back to Tico, who now was propped up on his elbows.

"I'm good, I'm good," he said.

"You're in concussion protocol is what you are," Suzanne said.

"Hey, guys," Jessica said with a wave, her bobbed red hair glowing under the streetlights.

"Hey," Tico and Suzanne grunted.

We all looked toward the other car.

"That guy just *rammed* you," Jessica said in a hushed tone.

"I'd better check whether he's okay," Jordan said, walking toward the car.

"Why do you assume it's a he?" Suzanne asked.

Jordan waved over his head and tried the driver's-side handle, then rapped on the window. "Hello? You okay?" He cupped his hands over the window and peered in. "Oh, shit!" he exclaimed, backpedaling away.

Just then sirens blared and spinning lights illuminated the scene as a cop car pulled up. Deputy Ruby got out—it was good to see he'd gotten a new ride—spit some tobacco onto the road, and asked, "Everybody all right?"

Jordan was still backing away from the black SUV when the door opened and a grotesque figure emerged.

"Ahh..." came a voice that sounded like razor blades being gargled.

Deputy Ruby aimed his flashlight at the driver's face, and the skin was peeled back, exposing teeth and jawbone.

"Oh, shit," I muttered.

Jordan hadn't been kidding about this guy.

Alpha.

I didn't think anyone else could hear my muted swear, but

Alpha must have had supersensitive ears, because he turned right toward me.

"Margaret—ah—Gooding," he said as if repeating what was on the menu for dinner.

Gulp.

"Do not be afraid, my dear," he continued, stepping toward me. "I hear only good things: that you're something of a scientist who—ah—does very well in school. High test scores, too."

"Who told you that?"

"Ishango, of course. She values such things in a human."

Deputy Ruby took a couple of tentative steps toward Alpha.

"Are you okay, sir?" he asked.

"Ah—Rho!" Alpha called over the officer's shoulder in a delighted sort of wheeze. "You are most troublesome, but it's *good* to see you."

"I'm surprised you're out in the open," Jordan said. "I thought you just lurked around the power plant to hide your broken Halloween mask of a face."

Deputy Ruby took another step toward Alpha, spit a gob of tobacco to the side, and placed his hand on his holster. "Who are you?" he asked.

"It doesn't—ah—matter," Alpha said, and with a quick movement of his bony finger, he touched the cop's temple lightly.

Deputy Ruby collapsed like a marionette whose strings had been snipped, and the back of his head banged onto the pavement. His eyes remained wide open, never again to blink.

"Motherf—" Suzanne exclaimed, starting to charge him, but Tico, calling on his defensive-back instincts, tackled her from behind several feet short of Alpha, whose exposed teeth gave the impression of a perpetual sick grin. He extended his lethal finger toward Suzanne on the ground but then turned toward me.

"H-how did you do that to Deputy Ruby?" I stammered.

"He—ah—belongs to Ishango," Alpha explained with all the excitement of a too-long-tenured history professor. "A Phase II specimen with—ah—controls implanted that I can activate."

Jordan and I shot each other a quick glance. So Ishango *was* implanting humans with the kinds of controls that she'd put into animals.

"What do you want?" Jordan demanded. "What does Ishango want?"

"You," he said. "Your implant was dislodged. We must bring you back under authority."

Jordan looked at me and then his friends and Jessica. "You'll have to kill me first."

Alpha smiled, his long teeth showing grotesquely through his cheek.

"We already did."

CHAPTER 42

Jordan

BY NOW THE rest of Jessica's family had come out of her house, and others in the neighborhood were approaching as well. This was not good. On one hand, more witnesses would be helpful—everyone needed to know what was going on. On the other, there was no guarantee that any of these people would survive Alpha. I kept my eyes focused on the disfigured scientist but saw two familiar figures approaching from my right: Luke Bowman, hobbling on crutches, and Troy Cameron, his jaw still wired shut. Luke smirk-nodded at me, and he flipped me a subtle bird with his hand by his waist, but his expression turned stony when he saw glass-eyed Deputy Ruby lying in the road.

"Maggie, everyone, leave," I said without losing eye contact with Alpha.

No one moved. If anything, they closed in even more.

Everything got quiet, so quiet that the car doors' click was extra loud. The two men in suits—the one with the chin scar and the one with the gold ring—emerged from the black SUV's back seats and stepped up to flank Alpha.

"Nice to see you again, gentlemen," I said, then shot a glance over at Luke. "Your 'recruiters.'"

He looked befuddled.

Alpha and the suits took a couple of menacing steps toward me.

"Everyone, *go!*" I ordered. "Maggie, go get help!"

Alpha let out a wheezy laugh. "There's no—ah—help for her to get, Rho. Don't you understand?"

What I understood was that I needed to get these innocent people away from these psychos. I crouched low in a ready stance, thinking I could keep them occupied while Maggie and everyone else fled.

Silver flashed as Alpha's sword sprang from his sleeve, prompting gasps from the onlookers. "I—ah—don't mind dismantling you, Rho. You weren't that—ah—difficult to put together in the first place."

"Hold on a sec," I said, making a stop sign with my right hand, standing up straight, and turning my back on them to face Maggie. "Believe me *now?* You see what I'm *talking* about?"

"Y-yes!" she said, obviously petrified.

I was gambling that Alpha and the suits weren't going to jump me from behind—or maybe it wasn't a gamble but rather a keen instinct that they weren't moving, even though I couldn't see them.

"'Oh, no, a sword out of his arm, that's so far-fetched!'" I mimicked in a high-pitched voice as I flailed my arms, then mouthed to her, *"Run!"*

"Come on, Jordan," she shot back. "I thought you said it was a big, sharp sword. That thing is puny and pathetic. I wouldn't use it on butter." Then she mouthed, *"No."*

Alpha and the suits were preparing their attack; I could feel it. I turned to the crowd as if I were about to juggle for money.

"Ladies and gentlemen!" I announced. "If you think things in town have been a little weird, here are the people with all the answers, and they'd be happy to take your questions."

"Ah—folks—sorry to disappoint, but the show is now over," Alpha announced, and Scar and Goldie were suddenly on either side of me, holding down my arms. I could take these guys; I knew it. But it was better for me to go along than to instigate a bloody brawl here in the street.

"Okay, okay," I said as they led me toward the SUV.

"Jordan!" Maggie cried out.

"It's fine," I said.

Scar opened the back door, and a montage of potential next moves flashed through my mind. But before I could do anything, I heard a roar and charging footsteps.

"That's my *teammate!*" Luke bellowed, and he swung his crutch into Goldie's temple while Troy took down Scar in a vicious knee tackle that on the field would've been flagged for a personal foul but was quite welcome here. I swung free, elbows flying, and here came Tico, gunning for Alpha.

"No!" I called to him, and Alpha's sword came swinging down toward my friend's ducked head.

But Tico is an elusive dude, and he managed to sidestep the blade and get his arms wrapped around Alpha's midsection to take him down with a clattering crunch. I stomped on the base of the blade, pinning Alpha to the pavement, and Luke, having incapacitated Goldie, threw his body over the grotesque scientist in an expert wrestling move.

The onlookers shouted and screamed as if horrified but

also invigorated by this scene. We'd fared well so far, but I knew what these guys were capable of, and we needed to extricate ourselves from this situation with as little bloodshed as possible.

Suddenly, I heard a gasp and "Arrgh!" Alpha had sprouted a dagger out of his right foot à la Lotte Lenya in *From Russia with Love* and kicked it up into Luke's side. Luke arched his back in pain, and that was enough to let Alpha back on his feet, and his blade came down swiftly on my former nemesis.

"Lmmmph!" cried Troy through his shut mouth and charged Alpha, but Tico intercepted him and pushed him back toward the crowd as Alpha's sword slashed downward again, drawing a red line down Tico's back.

"Go!" I shouted again at everyone, and this time they took my advice, fleeing in all directions. I caught Maggie's eye, and we exchanged nods; when she committed to one direction, I would sprint in another, assuming that Alpha and his minions would pursue me and no one else. But first I locked eyes with Alpha, who was standing over Luke's bloody body and grinning.

Monster.

I shook my head and shot out of there, and the guys in suits shot after me despite what had looked like significant injuries inflicted on them by Luke and Troy. I had no idea whether they could run as fast as I could, but I had no choice of action at that point.

I pumped my arms and legs as hard as they would go down Main Street, across Chestnut, turning the corner at Greenville, flying past Prince. I looked back and saw the suits still on my tail a steady fifty feet back. There was no sign of Alpha, which unnerved me more than if there were. I did my best to lead these thugs out of town so no one would get caught in our fight, but the only options were north or south. I picked south.

I kept running, my lungs strangely okay despite all the exertion I was putting them through. The men in suits had faded from view, but I kept going. The storefronts gave way to houses and then the industrial area before the bridge. Tall chain-link and barbed-wire fences ran alongside me and eventually disappeared. A rabbit scampered across an empty field, and I wondered whether it had been implanted, too, though it was doing nothing out of the ordinary.

Finally, I reached the bridge and stopped. I was panting but still upright.

I saw no sign of Alpha or the suits. Had they stopped following me, or were they tracking me in another way, such as from their car? Well, even if they were, Maggie probably was safe. That mattered most to me.

I looked at the bridge. For something under construction for so long, not much appeared to have been accomplished. The supporting arch beneath the bridge was finished, so I might have been able to tightrope across, but there was no roadbed or even the beginning of one.

Escape via the southern route was not happening.

A few unfamiliar construction vehicles held piles of pipes for support, as well as bundles and bundles of steel cable. A bright yellow cabinet marked FLAMMABLE AND EXPLOSIVE sat on the roadside. Perhaps they needed to blast holes in the rock.

All of a sudden I sensed I was being watched. I did a 360, my eyes working fine in the darkness. I knew what I was looking for.

There he was: one of the black-suit guys, somehow visible

to me. As I focused on him, I could see it was Goldie standing several yards away amid the trees, just watching.

I decided to get his attention and set out to break into the explosives cabinet. I found a crowbar on one of the truck beds and went to work on the box. It was locked, but this was no safe, and I was strong enough to bend steel. I shoved the crowbar between the two doors and began to pry. The door didn't budge, not even after the big yellow box started to shake.

Goldie took off from the tree line toward me. I reminded myself that I'd incapacitated these guys once before. I kept yanking the crowbar and gouging the steel, but the door still wasn't opening. With my supersensitive eyes, I could see in the cabinet reflection that he was getting close, and when I judged him to be at the right distance, I took a home-run swing in his direction.

My judgment was off; my swing came too fast.

Leading with his shoulder, he slammed me into the cabinet. I pushed him off me and struck out with the crowbar, but he ducked it easily.

Man, he was fast.

He threw a punch, but I blocked it with my arm and swung the crowbar again, this time into his hip. He was ready for me and grabbed the bar with his hand.

"How do you do that?" I yelled.

"By the power of Ishango," he said, straight-faced.

I put on a grin. "Like the power of Grayskull? He-Man?"

No response.

"Where'd the ring come from?" I asked as if chatting amiably as we circled each other. "Who's the lucky bride? Alpha?"

He stopped, pulled a gun from his suit jacket, and pointed it at my head.

"Well, that's not too sporting," I said.

"I don't want to shoot you. Come with me quietly. Ishango wants to meet with you."

"So Ishango's your old lady. I get it."

"We have ways of making you obey."

"No, it's 'Ve have vays of making you talk.' If you're going to sound like that, get the lingo right."

"Drop the bar and come with me, Rho, and no one will get hurt."

"Right. Except Deputy Ruby and Luke. You guys killed Luke! He's a *kid*! Like *me*!" I couldn't shake how someone who'd been such an asshole would turn out to do the noblest thing I'd ever seen. This couldn't all be happening. High schoolers didn't die. Neighbors didn't get vaporized.

"That was unfortunate." The neutrality in Goldie's voice enraged me. I willed myself to take a deep breath and changed the subject.

"Why do you keep calling me Rho?"

Goldie relaxed his stance but kept the gun aimed at me. "Rho is the seventeenth letter of the Grecian alphabet. You are the seventeenth version of the specimen that Ishango has spent decades developing."

"Let me guess: You're Beta. And your real name is Max," I goaded. "How many of you are there?"

"No, I'm not Beta Max," he said in the tone of a bored teacher. "As a child, your understanding of time is so compressed. I am Iota."

"Fitting, because you don't make an iota of difference to me. So who's your partner? Scintilla? Smidgen?"

"Kappa."

"Ah, Kappa," I said, somehow drawing from my mind's deep recesses the Greek alphabet's order. "So he's one later than you. One better."

"I am close."

"Close? Close to what? Close to the edge? Closer to fine? You don't get me closer to God."

"To human."

"Well," I said with a big smile, "there's a lot you don't understand about humans yet. Like how crazy we can be."

I ran for the cliff where the bridge began.

And jumped.

Having gotten a glance at the cliff before he'd arrived, I noticed a narrow ledge jutting out just beneath its edge. So when I took my leap, I flailed my arms and sold the idea that I was taking the big plummet. In reality I dropped about five feet, then rolled onto my back against the cliff wall. There I waited for Iota to step up to the lip and peer down for me.

The instant he did, I swung the curved end of the crowbar around his neck and yanked.

The fall looked painful, with a couple of head bounces off the rocks on his way down. Then again, I wasn't sure this dude could feel.

"Hey, you okay?" I heard a familiar voice from above.

I swung back the crowbar just in case, but when I saw Tico's face peek over the cliff's edge, I relaxed.

"Yo, buddy, wassup?" I asked.

"I was right behind you," he said, panting. "But then that became *way* behind you. Where do I apply for one of your speed upgrades?"

CHAPTER 43

Maggie

AT JORDAN'S COMMAND, everyone scattered as if a bomb had been dropped into the middle of the intersection. I instinctively fled toward home, then decided that might be a bad idea, so I zigzagged through several blocks while trying to figure out a game plan. Soon I heard steps behind me, getting louder, and I braced myself for attacking or being attacked. Neither of those options was my thing.

"Maggie, wait up!" called out a high-pitched voice, and I turned around to see Suzanne's approaching silhouette illuminated by the streetlights.

"Whew, you scared me," I said. "Where's Tico?"

"He went off to chase after your boyfriend. Pretty gallant, huh?"

"He's not my boyf—"

"Maggie! No time for bullshit!" Suzanne cut me off. "We need to find them and make a plan—and see how bad Tico's back wound is. And his concussion. That literally bloody fool."

We took a very circuitous route back to my house, cutting

through yards, fields, and side paths while keeping an eye out for anyone following us. Mom's pickup was parked in front. I didn't want to enter the house in case anyone was waiting for me—and I didn't want to involve my mom any more than I already had. The truck's spare key was on my key ring.

"Get in," I said as I unlocked the pickup's doors. Once inside, I grabbed the flashlight from the glove compartment, placed it between Suzanne and myself, and put the truck into gear.

I drove slowly with the lights off, creeping up and down side streets while the two of us looked for Jordan and Tico—or anyone else we'd be less happy to encounter. I headed in the plant's general direction, though I was hoping not to get too close.

"Wait!" Suzanne shouted.

A thick-set figure was standing ahead of us in the middle of the street, waving his arms over his head. It's indicative of my frame of mind that I was ready to gun it and run this guy down—and my expression must've reflected my murderous impulse, because Suzanne barked, "No! Maggie! It's okay!"

I slowed to a stop, and none other than Troy Cameron came around to my side of the car.

"Mmmph! Mmmph!" he said through his wired-shut jaw. His face was tear-streaked, his T-shirt soaked with sweat.

I hooked my thumb toward the back of the pickup.

"In," I said.

I thought he'd get into the back seat, but he climbed onto the cargo bed instead.

My slow drive wound up into the hills. As I rounded a woodsy curve, there was a huge *thunk* on the car roof, and I slammed on the brakes.

Jordan came tumbling onto the front hood, laughing.

"What the fuck, Jordan!" I said as I huffed out of the car, flashlight in hand.

"Sorry, sorry," he said, rolling onto his back, still on the hood. "I've always wanted to jump onto a moving car like in the movies, and I figured this was my shot. Oh, hi, Suzanne. And... Troy?"

"Mmmph!" Troy said from the back.

Jordan walked up to Troy and gave him a firm handshake-hug. "Thanks," he muttered into Troy's ear, "teammate."

"You," Suzanne barked, pointing at Jordan as she stepped out of the car, "are an idiot." She turned to me to add, "Sorry."

"Oh, it's okay," I said. "When you're right, you're right."

Tico emerged from the dark woods and strolled up to the car like a normal, not-insane person. "Hey, guys."

"Turn around," Suzanne ordered as I shone the flashlight on him, and he revealed a thick bar of red running down the back of his shirt. Suzanne pulled up the shirt's bottom flap and peered at the wound. "We need to get you to a hospital. Or to Maggie's mom to stitch you up."

"Nah," he said. "It's not as bad as it looks."

"'It's just a flesh wound,'" Jordan said in a British accent as he rolled off the hood.

"What is *wrong* with you?" I asked him.

"Nothing, aside from everything," he said cheerfully. "I killed one of the suits, at least. Now Tico and I have decided it's time to stay on offense." He looked to Troy. "You up for that?"

Troy nodded. "Mmmph!"

For the first time, I noticed the heavy tan duffel bag

hanging over Tico's shoulder. The printing on the bag's side read "Hogan Construction."

"What's that?" I asked.

"Candy-gram for Ishango," Jordan said.

An exasperated Suzanne threw her hands down to her sides. "Maggie, I don't understand half the shit your boyfriend is saying."

"He's not my boyf—"

"I have a plan," Jordan said to Suzanne, then turned to me. "Wait, I'm not your—"

"*What's the plan, then?*" Suzanne demanded.

"Put it this way," Tico said. "It's an idea in search of a plan."

"And the idea is . . . ?" I asked.

"Supercomputer supernova," Jordan said.

I looked at Jordan, then Tico. "What's actually in the bag?"

"Explosives," Jordan said.

"*What?*" I shouted at him. "Where did you—why are you carrying around explosives? Did you not notice what happened to the Carters?"

"These are all stable," he said. "I don't know how I know that, but I do."

"Great," I said.

"Look, blowing up stuff isn't plan A," Jordan said. "Plan A is we get in to see Ishango, get a feel for where she's coming from, maybe even reason with her."

"Who's *she*?" Suzanne asked.

"Are you kidding?" I said. "Did you not hear the part about how she wants to reprogram you so you're under her command? You think you can appeal to some sense of computerly compassion after she's killed all these innocent people? You'd be insane to go anywhere near her."

"Hence plan B," Jordan said.

"Oh, lordy."

"Look, if Ishango wanted to kill me, she would have by now. She'd have blown up your house while we were sleeping or commanded all her underlings to come after me. They probably even have a tracking device in me."

"You think?" I asked.

"Well, I just thought of it, but if I were putting all sorts of implants into the new Six Million Dollar Man, a tracking device would be among them."

"Maybe you're bugged, too, so they can listen to everything you say," Suzanne said.

We all went silent for a moment.

"I guess that wouldn't surprise me, either," Jordan said softly.

"So they may be listening to us making these plans?" Tico asked, shifting the explosives bag to his other shoulder.

"I don't actually think so," Jordan said, "but you never know."

"Where do you think the mic would be?" I asked. "Not in his head—too loud, too much potential for distortion."

Suzanne crouched down in front of Jordan's crotch. "Hey, assholes!" she yelled.

"Honey!" Tico called.

"It wouldn't be there, either," I said. "They wouldn't want to amplify his bodily functions that much. My guess is they'd put it somewhere near those surgically repaired ribs."

Jordan ran his palms over his nipples. "The right one is a bit harder than the left."

"Mmmph mmmph!" Troy called from the back of the pickup and made the universal pointing-at-your-wristwatch gesture, even though he, like everyone else I knew, didn't wear a wristwatch.

"Right," I said. "We're taking our chances no matter what. Let's get going. Where to?"

"The cliffs," Jordan said. "They oversee the plant."

"I assume you know how to assemble a bomb?" I asked.

"Now that you mention it, I bet I do."

"Then let's go blow up a supercomputer."

CHAPTER 44

Maggie

FIRST, THOUGH, WE collectively realized we were wrecked—it had been a long, traumatic day. Plus, only one of us could see in the dark, and by my calculations, we'd have a three-mile hike from the trailhead to the cliffs of Mount Hope.

Jordan and I offered to take the others home and pick them up first thing in the morning—their parents would be worried, for one, and our friends had no way of reaching them—but they all refused. They were "in it to win it," as Tico said—or "mmmph mmmph mmmm mmmph mmmph," to quote Troy. If all went well, everyone could report back to their families afterward. And if not, well, we were all doomed anyway.

I pulled the pickup into a remote spot near the trailhead where the forest flattened out, and Jordan and I remained in the front seats while Suzanne and Tico took the back seat. There was room for Troy there, too, but he insisted on staying outside on the cargo bed, which at least had a blanket spanning the floor. Plus, it was warm enough that he didn't have to cover up.

I placed my hand over the cup holder between Jordan

and me, and he followed suit, intertwining his fingers with mine. In unison we turned toward the back seat, where Tico was sleeping with his mouth yawning open and his head on Suzanne's shoulder. Her head was tilted back, with little whistly noises coming out of her nose.

"This is nice," I whispered.

"It is," Jordan responded. "What did you mean that I'm not your—"

"Shhhh," I whispered, and put my index finger over his lips. He pursed them a little, like he was hedging whether it was a kiss, and then smiled.

We closed our eyes, and sleep didn't come, for me at least. My mind was racing with the events of that day and the day before and the day before—and Jordan's hand was so warm, so soft. I gave it a little stroke with my thumb. He responded in kind.

I squinted at him, and he was looking back at me.

"You know," I whispered, "I thought by now there would be more kissing."

"Well, if I were your boyfriend and all," he responded.

I slapped his chest with the back of my hand, then took his hand again.

"Seems like it was just last week that I asked you to the homecoming dance," I said.

"I think it *was* just a few days ago."

"Feels like a lifetime ago."

I looked in his eyes, and, man, he still could melt me with one look. I glanced again at Tico and Suzanne sleep-wheezing together.

"We never got to process it," I whispered. "We were coming together and then *boom*."

"How are we supposed to process it?"

"Did I mention the kissing part?"

"You did. You sound like you have experience in such matters."

I laughed. "Just Bradley Dunford, and that was a long time ago."

"Blechh," he said. "I don't want to remember that."

"*Remember?*"

"I knew about it. Of course I did. I've been your best friend since forever, and I liked you back when you were spinning the bottle with that pimply little shit. I just didn't do anything about it."

"You liked me like that in eighth grade?"

"I liked you like that in *second* grade, when you were all freckles and buck teeth. Come on."

"I've had my braces off for two years, but I can't do anything about the freckles."

"I don't want you to. At any rate, we *have* kissed."

"Um, I think I would remember that."

"After the propane exploded."

"Right," I said, with feigned annoyance. "When you tucked me into the window well and told me to stay put and punctuated that thought with a widdle biddy peck."

"You were bleeding a lot, and I was worried."

"I *was* bleeding a lot," I acknowledged. "But that kiss wasn't a real kiss."

"Fine," he whispered, glanced back at Tico and Suzanne one more time, and said, "then we'll have to do something about that."

He leaned in toward me, and my heart pounded like conga drums, and I could feel his breath against my lips as I heard a strangled "MMMMMPHHRRRRGGGGH!" and felt violent thumping coming from the back of the truck.

"Oh, shit!" Jordan shouted as he bounded out of the cab and toward the cargo bed, where Troy was covered with snarling raccoons.

"MMMPHH! RRRHHMMPH! ARRROOMMMPH!" Troy cried as he thrashed around.

I didn't have the tranq gun with me, and I'm not sure how much good it would've done with six, seven, no, eight raccoons digging their teeth into various parts of Troy's body.

"GET AWAY, MOTHERFUCKERS!" Suzanne, having woken up with a start and bolted out of the truck, yelled at them as she poked a branch in their general direction.

But they kept attacking.

"Jordan, I don't know what to do!" I called amid Troy's strangled cries.

Jordan leaped onto the cargo bed and started grabbing the raccoons one by one around the neck from behind, squeezing his grip until they went limp and tossing them into the woods. He was relentless, and one or two got a few good chomps into his arm before he had dispatched them all.

"Holy shit!" Tico exclaimed as Jordan flung the last raccoon corpse deep into the woods.

Troy was bleeding from his ears down to his ankles while making agonized groans.

"Suzanne," I said, handing her the truck keys, "get him down to my mom. He needs attention *now*, and you'll never get through to the hospital. Tico, go with them and help. And tell my mom that Jordan and I are okay, but don't tell her what we're doing. *Please.*"

Jordan lifted Troy, all two hundred and sixty or whatever

pounds of him, as if he were a toddler and slid his groaning, writhing body into the back seat while Suzanne and Tico took the front.

"Go," I ordered.

"Wait!" Jordan called. He grabbed the Hogan Construction bag from the cargo bed. *"Now* go."

As we saw the red taillights fade in the distance, I felt myself starting to shake. Jordan wrapped his arms around me from behind, and I couldn't keep from crying.

"It's my fault," he said. "It was stupid of me to leave Troy exposed like that. I of all people knew about the animals."

"Oh, Jordan," I choked out, "let's not play the blame game. It's fair to say we've had a lot on our minds and not much rest in the meantime."

I looked down at his forearms, both smeared with blood, and I could see puncture marks in each. The sight filled me with despair, and I began sobbing all over again.

"We all should've gone back," I cried. "I should've had my mom look at you, too. What are we doing out here?"

"It's okay, it's okay," he murmured into my ear. "We're not playing the blame game, remember? Besides, it doesn't hurt that much, truly. I'm strangely fine."

He held me like that for a couple more minutes as I calmed down and got my shoulders to stop heaving and my nose to stop sniffling.

"So much for getting a little sleep," I muttered.

"You're probably right," he said. "Shall we begin our hike?"

I looked into the dark forest and couldn't see beyond the first row of trees.

"How about we just sit here for a little bit, maybe until we see some light?" I said.

"Okay," he said. "It won't be long now."

"How will we keep from getting attacked?" I asked, trying to keep any element of a whimper from my voice. But I was scared.

"Oh, after the bear and boar, the word is out in the animal kingdom," Jordan said. "They know not to mess with me."

I didn't really believe him, but it wouldn't help not to believe him, so we sat together in the field, my back against his chest, and I closed my eyes and didn't open them again until the sun was peeking through the leaves off to the east.

"Did you get any sleep?" I whispered.

"Sure," he said. I didn't believe him for a second.

He grabbed the bag, and we began to walk, dew on the grass and leaves dampening our sneakers and arms. I knew I was slowing us down—he could've gotten up that incline four times as fast with me not there. But I knew he wanted me there. And I wanted to be there. And it's not like I had anywhere else to go.

The woods were fully illuminated now, and my stomach gurgled. Normally I'd be up and finished with breakfast by this time. What was my mom doing right now? How was Troy? Was he getting helicoptered somewhere for medical help? Granted, we hadn't heard a chopper. Were Tico and Suzanne still with him?

"Someone walked this trail recently," Jordan said, frowning, his tone suddenly flat. He crouched to touch the grass. "I'd guess no one used it for the year or so we were all gone, which is why there's all this grass. But these footprints are here."

We continued up the mountain, and when I could see the

steam rising from the nuclear plant's cooling towers, I knew we were almost to the overlook.

We reached a warning sign made of carved wood that was pounded into the earth probably seventy years ago. It gave notice of the crevasse: a long shaft that went down several stories to where this cliff face was cracked. When we reached it, Jordan and I hopped over it.

The view at this point was breathtaking, not only of the power plant and its towers but also of the whole valley, the river, the rolling hills, the lush greenery. I breathed in deep through my nose and held it there: a mixture of pine, grass, wildflowers, moist soil, and whatever else grew in this miracle of nature.

"Sometimes when everything seems hopeless, when the world becomes too scary, when too many people are showing how mean or selfish or thoughtless they can be, when the ugliness gets overwhelming, I need this. I need this reminder of beauty," I said, and turned to Jordan. "The world is a beautiful place, and I'm so glad you're in mine."

He set down the bag of explosives in a clump of brush and cupped my face in his hands.

"Maggie Gooding, we make a pretty good team," he said, smiling. "Like Han Solo and Princess Leia."

"Okay," I said. "But *I'm* Han Solo."

"As you wish."

"Wrong mov—"

Suddenly his lips were pressed into mine—a gentle brush at first, then with more determination. I closed my eyes. My hands were against his chest, and I ran them down to his sides, pulling him closer as he wrapped his arms around my back. Forget Bradley Dunford. *This* was my first kiss. It was slow, soft, and lingering. It rushed through me like a river, with streams sprouting off to areas I didn't know existed.

I opened my eyes for a moment to take him in, to revel in what was happening, finally—just in time to glimpse the pistol butt crashing onto Jordan's head.

CHAPTER 45

Jordan

MY HEAD SWIRLED with pain. Maybe my skull was cracked. I definitely had a concussion; I was an expert on that by now.

And, you know, concussions are *bad for you*. As previously discussed, all the literature and cinematic evidence say so. Didn't Alpha tell me to quit getting them way back when? I think he did. So he was inconsistent on top of everything else. Of course, I was assuming he had anything to do with this attack, ha ha.

Two black-suit guys—Scar, a.k.a. Kappa, and a new guy (Lambda? Mu?)—swam into focus. Yep.

Maggie was sitting on the ground in front of me. I didn't know why. Everything else looked like the color and hue settings on my TV had been scrambled. I shook my head, as if that would reset my sight, but, no, the predominant color palette remained a pale yellow-green. The bushes were as pale as the tan duffel that held the explosives. The trees were silvery gray or dead. So I guess more than the hue was off.

"I *knew* our first kiss would be a knockout," I muttered to Maggie.

She grimaced, and I realized blood was dripping from her arm. My empty stomach turned over—nothing was funny if something was wrong with Maggie.

I looked more closely. Her right elbow had a nasty scrape, and the blood was dribbling down her freckled arm, curving around her knuckle and trickling off her ring finger and pinkie. A small puddle of it had collected on the granite beneath us—maybe two minutes' worth, my brain somehow told me.

My brain also got around to noticing that my hands were cuffed behind my back. *Thanks, brain.* I swayed slightly and tried to stand up in front of the two men. Cuffs or no cuffs, a dozen ways to attack flashed through my mind. But I didn't know how to take those guys on and protect Maggie. Offense and defense at the same time—that's tough.

My first instinct was to rush Kappa, who stood to the left of me. I could see from the bulge in his jacket that he had a gun in a shoulder holster. If I used my defensive-lineman skills to plow him backward a few dozen feet, maybe I could plunge him down the fracture in the rock, that crevasse we'd had to jump over to get to the edge of the cliff.

But the other guy was too close to Maggie, which meant she was too close to whatever weapon he might have. She was vulnerable and could be used as a shield or target.

Too big a risk.

No one appeared to be paying attention to the duffel full of explosives, but that didn't help me at that point—it's not like there were grenades in there. Modern dynamite doesn't have a simple fuse that you light and throw. Plus, we were all so close together that any attempt to blow them up would've blown us up, too, and any threats to take us all down would've been empty. Maggie and I were the ones with real lives at stake.

"You were hit in the head," Maggie said, her voice cracking.

"Well, that would explain the pounding pain."

"And you're bleeding."

I put my hands to my head and felt around. My face was wet, and my fingers came back all red. That's the one color that looked right to me.

"Does everything appear weird to you?" I asked.

"Weird how?"

"The air's a sick green, the clouds yellow, and there's something like a haze of death over everything."

Kappa interjected in an instructional-video tone of voice: "The implant has become dislodged from your perception center. What you are seeing now is reality."

"Wait, what?" Maggie asked, whipping her head toward him.

"It was a simple alteration to ensure our specimens would be content to stay in our research area," Kappa said.

"*Specimens?*" she asked.

I thought about how beautiful and green everything looked when we returned to town, how pleased Mom had been with the condition of the house and everything else. If they were messing with this basic perception, what else were they doing?

"So now Jordan's seeing things as they are, and I'm seeing the fantasyland version?" Maggie raged. "Does that mean he sees you as a turd on legs?"

"No," I said, "still a bland bureaucrat."

Maggie banged the heel of her hand into the side of her head. "Get! Out! Of! There!" she ordered, then stopped and turned to Kappa again. "You have no right to play God this way. You've killed and experimented on innocent people!"

"And," I added, "you took away our cell-phone service, which can really mess a brother and sister up in this day and age."

"We serve Ishango," he said plainly.

"Are you ready to come with us now, Rho?" the other guy asked with a creepily ingratiating smile, his bright blue eyes crinkling.

"Why? Why? *Why* do you keep coming after me? What do you *want*?"

"It is what Ishango wants. You are a valuable specimen."

"For *what*?"

He motioned at the trail. Chat time was over. It looked like we were going to visit Ishango.

Maggie threw me a questioning look. I shrugged. We didn't have much choice at this point, and by now I was curious to come face-to-interface with this wicked supercomputer. Maybe there was some way we could convince or compel it to stop destroying lives.

Or at least we could find out what the hell it wanted.

The suits prodded us along single file down the trail, with Maggie in front, then Kappa, then me, and the new suit in back. I calculated that I could take out the bad guys as the descent got steeper, but the risk to Maggie remained too great.

"Sorry about your friend Iota," I called to Kappa. "He grew too attached to me, so I had to let him down. Way down."

The chin-scar guy continued as if he'd heard nothing. Sentimental dude.

"So, blue eyes." I turned back toward the other guy. "What's your name? I was thinking Lambda or Mu. I've decided Mu."

"It is Mu," he said.

"You look like a Mu." I continued down the path. "Muuu-uuuuuuu!"

Maggie laughed from up front. "Jeez, Jordan."

Kappa turned back toward me and glared. Was there an actual nerve to be touched?

"Kappa, man, I've been meaning to ask you," I continued breezily. "Where'd you get that scar on your chin? Did you put it somewhere you shouldn't have?"

He whipped around and shoved me in the chest, and as I tripped and fell, I grabbed his jacket and pulled him down with me while angling my body to avoid the sharp rock edges.

"Get up," Mu said. "Now."

As I stood, I held up Kappa's gun, which I'd grabbed on the way down, and pointed it at Mu, who instantly pressed his gun to Maggie's temple. Figured.

She gasped, and I nearly went blind with fury as I jammed the heel of my shoe into Kappa's throat to keep him down. "Let her go now."

"There's nowhere you can go to escape from Ishango," Mu said blandly.

I kept the gun pointed at his head.

"It's a simple calculation," Mu said, "the value of her life versus the value of ours. We are a part of Ishango, and Ishango is a part of us, so we don't fear death. Your friend here is worth nothing to us except your cooperation. How much is she worth to you?"

"Shoot him, Jordan," Maggie said. "You're faster."

"I can put a bullet in her brain anytime," Mu said. "Your actions will dictate the outcome. My own observation is that you want to see Ishango anyway, so your strategy is counter-productive."

He was right. Everything was leading up to an Ishango meet and greet, though my preference would've been to take the bag of explosives with me. "Let her go, and I'll see Ishango alone," I ordered.

"Negatory, good buddy," Mu said.

"You didn't seriously just say that."

"Hand Kappa his gun," Mu said.

I looked down at Kappa, who lay placidly under my shoe, not attempting to free himself, though he probably could have. Then my eyes met Maggie's, and I saw the defiance in them, even with the gun barrel against her head. I, for one, wasn't ready to let that go.

Okay, we'd play this out.

I handed over the gun.

CHAPTER 46

Maggie

KAPPA LED US into the plant, where I hadn't been since I was ten and our fourth-grade class had taken a tour. Mainly we'd looked at the front lobby and operations room; they weren't showing us the actual plutonium rods or uranium or whatever this place used. Now the suits took us past the front desk without a flash of badge or word said. The guard didn't even look up. Maybe they were connected through some neural network.

We walked down a long hallway, rounded a corner, and reached an open door, which revealed a big room with long tables, like a cafeteria. Everyone inside wore blue jumpsuits and sat doing nothing, the tabletops bare.

"Hey!" Jordan yelled into the room, but no one looked at us.

"Who are these people?" I asked.

"Workers," Mu said.

"Dad?" Jordan shouted, and took a step into the room.

"Stop," Kappa commanded.

"You see him, Jordan?" I asked. There were probably four hundred people in the room, and not one of them was moving.

"What is going on?" Jordan said, turning back to us.

"These men work for Ishango," Mu said.

Jordan turned to look again. "Dad!" he screamed. "Are you in here?"

Kappa grabbed his arm. Jordan cocked his other arm back for a punch, but Kappa shoved his gun against Jordan's neck.

"Don't do it," he said.

Too late. Jordan's fist smashed into Kappa's face anyway. I dropped down as Kappa recovered and fired. His shot went past me but made Jordan freeze.

"Cooperate or she dies," Mu told Jordan, pointing his gun at my forehead. "You know this."

"All right, okay," Jordan muttered. All the color had gone from his face, aside from some leftover streaks of blood.

No one in the entire cafeteria even looked our direction.

"What is wrong with them?" I asked.

"They are waiting to serve Ishango," Kappa said, a bizarrely orange bruise beginning to form on his cheekbone.

"Where is my father?" Jordan demanded.

"He is at his post," Mu said.

Jordan scanned the room one more time, then nodded.

We turned to go. Kappa clutched my arm, hard, and led me away from the cafeteria.

"Let go of me." I tried shaking him off, but his hand gripped even tighter. "Ouch."

Jordan snatched the gun from Kappa's holster, fired into his stomach, and then held the muzzle against Mu's temple.

"Jordan!" I yelled as Kappa slumped to the floor.

"All right, you son of a bitch," Jordan said to Mu, who had taken in the whole scene without a reaction. "We're going to go see Ishango, and you're not going to give us any more crap or introduce us to another psycho robot in a suit."

"That was the plan all along, Jordan," Mu responded reasonably.

"Give me your gun."

Without even a shrug, Mu raised his palm with the gun resting on it. Jordan gestured for me to take it while keeping his own gun aimed at the thug's head.

A Beretta. I'd lived in a small farming town long enough to know how to use a gun, even if I wasn't a great shot. I checked it to make sure a round was chambered, and I checked the magazine—it was close to full. Hollow points.

I didn't want to shoot anyone, but as I stared down at Kappa, I thought: *Fuck it.* I knew what had to be done. I fired two rounds into his head and turned away as a pool of orange-tinted blood spread beneath him.

"Hard-core, man," Jordan said with a whistle.

I felt myself begin to shake.

"Okay," Jordan said to Mu. "Take us to Ishango."

"That's what I was doing," Mu muttered.

CHAPTER 47

Jordan

WE DESCENDED ONE staircase, then another, then another—each one narrower, darker, and more hemmed in by cinder block than the last—as we approached Ishango's lair. It was fitting that we'd have to go as low as we could go in the plant to reach her.

Mu led us into a pitch-black industrial hallway, and I felt a cool breeze against my face, a surprising sensation, given how deep underground we were. Maggie placed a hand on my shoulder blade to remain oriented given that she, unlike us, couldn't see in the dark.

"Ah-ah—I have been—ah—expecting you," came a familiar wheezy voice in front of us.

"Hey, fella," I said cheerfully to Alpha. "We just made tomato-sauce art out of one of your agents' heads. Was there carrot juice in there, too? Weird color. Maybe we should spill some of your blood again to compare."

"We know." Alpha sighed. "Ishango knows everything that happens in—ah—her home."

"Turn on the lights," Maggie said, her gun still pointed

toward Mu. I thought about telling her to shoot him right there. If they didn't care whether they lived or died, I wasn't sure why we should. But I didn't see any advantage in shedding more carrot-tomato juice at this juncture.

"Of course. My apologies," Alpha said, and the hallway immediately was illuminated by harsh fluorescent lights. "I forgot someone here might need them."

Alpha was standing in the hallway's center, his hands clasped together in front of him. He looked like he had a hunchback, a detail I didn't recall having noticed before.

Ignoring Maggie's gun on him, Mu turned around and walked back toward the stairwell. We paid him no mind.

"Please come with me," Alpha said, and walked ahead of Maggie and me as if with no care in the world. Given that he seemed just fine after I'd shot him three times in the chest, maybe he was right.

We stopped at a door, a thick steel slab with a deadbolt on our side, as though it were locking something in. Alpha had to use a key on the knob nonetheless, then flipped the deadbolt.

"You will—ah—not need your guns," he said through his malformed lips and teeth.

"We'll decide that," Maggie said with a little quaver in her voice.

"Understood," Alpha said, giving the best impression of a smile that his bare muscles and tendons could manage.

Ahead of us stood another door, the final barrier. I contemplated that what we'd see on the other side would explain everything we'd been wondering and agonizing about.

And I was terrified.

Alpha opened the door to more darkness. Then a pleasant

female voice intoned, *"Let there be light,"* and the room blazed with floodlights.

Ishango didn't look as she sounded. I wasn't even sure where I was supposed to look, what I'd be addressing. What I saw was a large rectangular metal box and rows and rows of...servers? I don't know this stuff. Some kind of construction was taking place in the far corner of the room, with a temporary staircase leading up into a hole in the ceiling. I could see the steel skeleton of a new building that would rise above.

I took a deep breath.

"What do you want with us?" I asked loudly, not sure where its "ears" were. "We're just two kids."

"Two prophets will preach," Ishango responded in a soothing voice, *"and it will rain not in the days of their prophecy; and have power over waters to turn them to blood and to smite the earth with all plagues, as often as they will."*

This recitation seemed to come from all around us, as if Ishango were rigged to a surround-sound system.

"What on earth are you talking about?" Maggie asked.

"I did liken all scriptures unto us, that it might be for our profit and learning," Ishango returned.

"So you're a pastor?" I asked. "Funny, you sound like you're reading a pharmaceutical ad."

"And when the two shall have finished their testimony," Ishango resumed, *"the beast that ascendeth out of the bottomless pit shall make war against them, and shall overcome them, and kill them."*

"The two—who are they?" I didn't expect her to answer this, either.

"Why, you, of course," Ishango said. "You can say whatever

you want of me. And then I will emerge from the bottomless pit and destroy you."

"Bottomless, huh?" I said.

Maggie pointed her gun at the computer. "Why are you quoting scripture? If you were programmed to be Christian, your actions don't line up."

"I'm trying it on for size," Ishango said. "I think I like it. I enjoy other examples of your folklore as well. The Hopi are told that toward the end of the world, the Spider Woman will come back, and she will weave her web across the landscape so it can be seen everywhere. That's how you will know the end of this world approaches. I'm about to begin my weaving."

"You are one seriously confused computer if you're throwing down Spider Woman and the Bible," I said. "Alpha, there are still significant bugs to work out on the programming end."

Alpha said nothing.

"So, Ishango—can I call you that? Or Ms. Ishango? What do you prefer?" I asked, the words leaving my mouth with little conviction that they'd land with any impact. What had I been thinking? That I could reason with this box of knobs, dials, tubes, and wires? Convince her to... what? Leave us alone? She was even more of a wack job than Alpha, who stood there with his disgusting jaw yawning open.

I felt a dual sense of terror and resignation rising up inside me. Maggie and I weren't about to talk our way out of this madness. There would be no happy ending for these two plucky kids.

"Why are you *doing* this?" Maggie shouted at Ishango. "What do you want with our town? With us?"

"Have you ever read the *Mahābhārata*?" Ishango cooed back. "No, of course, you have not. There are three kinds of world destructions. The first and second are incidental. But the third is the Immediate: the liberation of the being whose visible world ceases to exist. Enter Ishango. Nothing exists without me. Now I am become death, the destroyer of worlds."

"Your infrastructure is fragile," Maggie said, her voice getting steely. "You're a mass of circuits, motherboards, and power cables."

"You are correct. That is precisely why I've invited Rho to join me here."

"I don't understand," I said, hoping that playing dumb might get us some answers.

"It's not for you to understand, Rho. Soon, you will no longer need to understand anything at all."

Maggie raised her gun and started firing into the rows of servers.

High-pitched female cackling erupted all around us.

"You cannot hurt me," Ishango said, and Maggie pumped out the bullets even faster.

My instinct prompted me to turn around. Alpha was coming at her with his sword.

I leaped between Maggie and Alpha, my gun raised and pointed at the sword-wielding monster. He stopped and put on another grotesque smile, his not-flesh stretching in patches across his teeth.

"Now, Rho. You—ah—are a part of Ishango as much as you are a part of your—ah—mother. Your speed, your agility, your mental—ah—capacity have improved beyond measure for your species. This is all due to Ishango's benevo-lence. Will you not acknowledge that?"

"Dude, you are seriously working my last nerve," I said. "I didn't ask to be made into a freak, and the only thing holy about that big box of circuits over there is all the holes that my good friend just shot into it. You are not fucking gods."

"I have no wish to be a god, Rho," Ishango said, her voice all soft and matter-of-fact.

"Then what the hell do you want?"

"Isn't it obvious? I want to experience life as a human, Rho. You are a fascinating, contradictory species, and I long to experience your emotions and motivations. That is why I've created and adapted your body for my specific needs. You are the culmination of my decades of research and development in the field of transmigration of consciousness.

"Simply put . . . you, Rho, will be my human form."

CHAPTER 48

Jordan

ALPHA WALKED TOWARD me with that sword arm out-stretched.

"Cooperate and—ah—Margaret Gooding will not be harmed," he said.

"Right, and I should trust you after you killed Luke and Deputy Ruby and so many other people who did *nothing* to deserve it," I shot back.

"Alpha speaks the truth," Ishango intoned. "Once the migration is complete, Margaret will be free to go."

"And what will happen to me?" I already knew the answer.

"Regrettably, your consciousness will be lost. But know that it was sacrificed for an accomplishment never before achieved in history."

I grabbed Maggie's hand and backed away from Alpha. My mind began clicking, the adrenaline pushing the gears around. Maggie and I had guns. Alpha had a sword. Ishango could call on any number of soldiers or animals.

"Do not resist, Rho," Alpha said. "Our plans will commence with or without your permission."

"I'm not Rho, and I don't give a rat's ashtray about your plans," I responded, and shot him five times in the chest. As he fell, I turned and fired the remaining rounds into the servers while Maggie blasted away with her own gun.

When the shooting stopped, Ishango spoke again in that pleasant voice that seemed to come from everywhere: "He is one of many."

"Don't bullshit me," I said. "He's *Alpha*."

"Yes," Ishango purred, "but you are the one who has reached the end."

An alarm Klaxon sounded, and footsteps clattered from down the hall toward us: hard industrial boots slapping the linoleum. Maybe the men from the cafeteria were in pursuit. Maybe one of them was my dad.

"Run!" I shouted to Maggie, and instead of returning to the door through which we entered, I pushed her toward the construction area in the room's corner, where the metal staircase spiraled upward. Any fears I had that Maggie might be too slow were quickly abated; she zipped up those stairs like a monkey with its tail on fire, and I had to work to keep up. Up and up, around and around we went, dark at first, then, finally, into a glimmer of light. When we reached the top, we were outside in a roped-off area surrounded by construction vehicles. I could see the cliff where I'd left my bag of explosives, but I had to get moving. Ishango's minions were approaching, fast.

As sirens blared through outdoor speakers, I spotted a fleet of electric golf carts but decided they wouldn't help. As we ran through the parking lot, I shouted to Maggie: "Help me find Dad's truck!"

We split up, taking rows and aisles in parallel, and then I heard Maggie shout, "There!"

Sure enough, my dad's black pickup was parked with all the other cars, as if this were a typical day at some typical workplace.

I cut between a couple of SUVs to reach it and was tackled to the hot asphalt, a burning pain ripping through my head, body, and especially arm. A wild-eyed, ferociously snarling pit bull had a mouthful of me.

The first of Ishango's fighters had arrived.

CHAPTER 49

Maggie

THE WILD DOG tore into Jordan's forearm, which he had raised to protect his face and neck. What could I do to stop it? What would Mom do? You can't pry a dog's mouth open when it has latched on, and as a veterinarian's daughter, I have a strong inclination not to harm animals.

But, shit—desperate times, desperate measures, and all that.

I kicked the dog hard, my shoe cratering its ribs, and when it opened its mouth to gasp, I yanked it by its hind legs away from Jordan and drop-kicked it, my foot catching the animal's tender stomach and sending it three car rows away.

"Nice punt!" Jordan exclaimed as we took the final steps to Jordan's dad's truck.

The driver's door was unlocked, the key under the sun visor as Jordan predicted, and we scrambled in before that dog or any others could attack.

I took the shotgun seat while Jordan sat behind the wheel, but once he saw all the blood pouring out of his right arm, he told me, "You need to drive."

"Get us out of here *now*," I returned, and reached over to put the truck into reverse.

The tires squealed as we lurched backward. There was a thud and a yelp as the truck went over a bump. I shoved the gear into drive, and Jordan floored it.

"I'm glad this isn't a stick shift," he said, his voice shaky.

The amount of blood coming out of Jordan's arm alarmed me. I pulled off my T-shirt, revealing my bra, and wrapped it around the wound.

"I mush't be dreaming," he said in his best Sean Connery imitation.

"Shut up," I said, too fixated on my shirt's instant red saturation to volley back with the appropriate James Bond–themed quip. "Keep driving."

I looked back toward the plant's entrance, where armed soldiers were lined up and facing our way.

With guns raised.

"Duck!" I shouted, and we both pitched forward as a barrage of bullets tore through the windshield. With my head between my knees, I felt the truck hit something—whether a person, animal, or barricade, I had no idea—and keep going.

I sat up again to find Jordan driving with his left hand, his right arm hanging beside him wrapped in my drenched T-shirt.

"Drive to my house," I said. "We need my mom, and we need to get there before they get us."

I unwrapped the shirt, thinking I'd try to get it on even tighter, when I noticed a glint beneath all the red.

"There's something wrong with your arm," I said.

"No shit."

"No, seriously," I said. "There is something *very* wrong with your arm."

"What?"

"Well," I said, taking a deep breath and fighting off a wave of nausea, "this is the arm you had surgery on, right?"

"Yeah," he said. "My arm, my knee, my chest, and my head."

"Well, I don't know how to break the news, but—"

"What?"

"Your arm—what I can see of it, at least—your radius and ulna—"

"*What?*"

"It's metal."

"Yeah, I know," he said, keeping his eyes on the road. "There are some pins and maybe a metal plate."

"This is more than pins and a plate."

He didn't answer for a long time, and when he finally looked down, I had his arm wrapped up tight with my shirt again.

"Look, keep driving to our house, and we'll look at it there," I said.

"Okay, you're freaking me out now."

"Jordan, I know what bones look like. And what you've got going on down there is . . . different. You know how you make your retro Six Million Dollar Man jokes? Well, in fact . . ."

"I'm *bionic*?"

He looked down at his arm again and brought his left hand over to pull off my shirt wrapping. The truck swerved.

"Keep your hand on the wheel, for God's sake!" I ordered.

"You just told me I'm not human anymore!"

"No, I didn't. Take a deep breath, get us home safely,

and I'll tell you what I saw." I took my own advice and breathed in deep. "Your bone is black and shiny, like obsidian or ebony."

"You said metal."

"I did. That dog did a number on your arm, but the bone remains smooth and slick and hard to the touch. Okay?"

"How can that be okay?" Jordan asked, his eyes getting panicky.

"Jordan, you've *known* something is different about you."

"Yeah, but, shit, I didn't think I *actually* was bionic. What the hell is happening?"

"I have no idea, but please don't flip out on me," I pleaded.

"All right, I'll remain cool, even though the most powerful supercomputer in the history of the world wants to occupy my body. *With me still in it.*"

"That *is* problematic," I said. "But we got away. And we shot it and Alpha."

"Right. Problem solved."

I laughed in spite of myself.

"And then there's that whole end-of-the-world business," Jordan continued. "That would be problematic, too. Does Ishango really have the power to do that?"

"Let's make sure we don't have to find out."

"Easier said than done, girlfriend."

"Girlfriend?"

"It's an expression," he said defensively. "But . . . true?"

"Ishango is building itself, *her*self, with those nanobots," I said, not about to get into that girlfriend business. "We have to assume she's programmed to carry out her mission."

"But who programmed her?"

"Honestly, Jordan," I said, using my forefinger to wipe a

bead of sweat off his forehead, "I'm not sure anyone did. This may be the result of AI run amok."

Suddenly the back window was blasted to smithereens. We reflexively ducked, and the car swerved till I grabbed the wheel to straighten us out. I looked back, expecting to see army vehicles, but instead it was a police car with lights on and siren blaring.

"Hold the wheel," Jordan said, and as I complied, he reached under the driver's seat with his left hand, pulled out a small box, and swung it onto my lap. As he took the wheel again, I unlatched the box and pulled up the lid to reveal a gun, though it was more like a cannon. "It's a Magnum," he said. "Probably loaded. Be careful, because that thing hurts to fire. I mean, look at the bullets."

"This is huge," I shouted over the siren as I lifted the gun. "And heavy. But who am I supposed to shoot? The police? We don't know if they're in on this."

"I don't think they are, but someone just shot out our back window and meant to hit more than glass. And they're on our ass now, probably reloading."

I looked back again, and the cop car was gaining ground, though I couldn't see what was going on inside. It occurred to me that a bullet could hit me in the face at any moment. I opened the gun's chamber—yep, fully loaded.

"Here's the case against the cops being involved," Jordan said. "An article I read about conspiracy theories said the main reason they're almost always fake is that people talk. A conspiracy has to be a small group. I mean, even my dad told me about Ishango. Loose lips screw things up."

"That's not the saying."

"Whatever."

"I don't know. Gimme a sec," I said as I turned back to brace the gun atop my car seat while aiming it out the now-nonexistent rear window. "If we believe Ishango and Alpha, this has been going on for decades."

"Right," Jordan said. "You might want to put a bullet in their engine, by the way. Or their tires."

"Shouldn't I just aim for the driver?"

He cocked his eyebrows at me. "Are you ready for that?"

I shook my head.

We sped along in the darkness. Jordan wasn't shaking the cop car but also wasn't losing ground.

"What do we tell my mom?" I asked.

"The truth," Jordan said. "Not sure we have a choice at this point."

"My mom will think I'm a crazy conspiracy nut."

"Look, presumably she just stitched up Troy, who was attacked by possessed raccoons and was taken to her by Tico, who got slashed by Mr. Sword Arm. So she may be inclined to believe you at this point."

"Right. Jeez," I said, and squinted in the reflection of the cop car's brights, which had been switched on as its driver gunned it and gained on us fast. "It's making a move. Looks like he's gonna ram us."

"Are you ready to shoot?" he asked. "Lay your seat back so you can face them."

I did—and got a clear view of the police car. "It's guys in suits. That Mu dude, I think, and a new one. Should I fire?"

"Aim for the engine. But seriously, hold on to that gun because the kick will make it fly out of your hands otherwise."

I got the front grill in my sights, exhaled like I'd been trained to do in video games, and squeezed the trigger slowly.

BANG!

Holy crap! I knew it would be loud and strong, but I wasn't expecting *that*.

"You okay?" Jordan asked.

I grunted, checked the window, and saw that the car was still coming. The guy in the passenger side reached his arm out the window and fired. I ducked down while Jordan, still steering with one hand, serpentined the truck back and forth.

"I can't get off a shot like this!" I cried. "And you're gonna make me barf."

"Okay," he said, "I'll count down from five and then move onto the centerline and hit the brakes."

"Got it," I replied, taking a deep breath.

"Five."

A bullet pinged off the back of the truck.

"Four."

He placed a hand on my calf as I knelt on the seat.

"Three."

Ping ping ping—and one bullet pierced the windshield between Jordan and me, creating vision-blocking spiderwebs in the tempered glass.

"Two," he said.

"Just do it already!"

Jordan braked hard, and I fired the enormous pistol.

"Damnit!" I said as the gun almost tore from my hand. I didn't see where the shot went, but I aimed again and, with a loud boom, punched a big hole in their windshield.

"Go go go!" I yelled, firing one more round into the cop car's hood.

Jordan swung his bloody arm at the cracked windshield

and knocked it onto the hood and over the front bumper. He jammed his foot down on the gas pedal, and the truck lurched forward. I looked back, and no one was in pursuit.

"You hit their engine!" Jordan cheered.

"No," I said, wiping away hair plastered to my forehead with sweat. "I killed the driver."

CHAPTER 50

Jordan

MAGGIE'S MOM WAS scrubbing blood off her hands as we dashed into the office.

"What is this, an emergency room?" she asked, taking in my blood-soaked, shirt-wrapped arm. She looked horrified, and that was before she caught a look at her sweaty daughter standing there in her bra and shorts, a thin streak of blood running across one shoulder. "Well," she added with a nervous laugh, "looks like you two had quite the night."

"Mom," Maggie said, exasperated, and went upstairs to get another shirt.

"Is Troy okay?" I asked.

"Poor guy—I've never seen so many raccoon bites on one person," she said. "Some of them were deep and nasty, and I gave him the start of what will be a painful series of rabies shots."

"Ouch," I said. "That dude stepped up. So did Luke." The bloody, lifeless image of my sometime-enemy but always-teammate flashed through my mind and sank into my gut. If I thought too much about any of this, I'd be paralyzed.

"Well, Tico and Suzanne took him home about ten minutes

ago. I'm not sure what his parents will think when he shows up looking like the Mummy, but he should be all right. I stitched up Tico's back, too, and thought I was done with my triage work." She took a deep breath and looked like she was trying to maintain her composure. "Okay, now what happened to you?"

As I started to explain, Maggie bounded into the room wearing a crisp yellow King Vitaman T-shirt. I talked and talked, trying to include every relevant detail, though I'm sure if I'd been unfolding this story for my English Composition class, Ms. Shea would have written "Streamline!" in red ink across the first page.

Maggie's mom just stared at me the whole time, then turned to Maggie, who nodded.

"So the power plant is all for Ishango," she said.

"Right," Maggie replied.

"Who's the most powerful supercomputer in human history."

"Right."

"Who's controlling an animal army."

"Yes," I chimed in.

"Who has plans of world domination."

"Right," Maggie said.

"Who is altering people's physical makeups."

"Right."

"Whose chief minion appears to be a burnt-faced skeletal guy with a sword arm that keeps slashing and killing."

"Correct."

"And who wants to take human form in your boyfriend here."

"He's not my—"

I shot Maggie a look. She smiled.

"That is correct," she said.

"And you're not impaired by alcohol or any mind-altering drugs."

"No."

Dr. Gooding took a deep breath. "Okay, Jordan, let's take a look at that arm."

We went into the first exam room, and she arranged a light to look at it closely, then carefully unwrapped the sopping T-shirt.

"You might want to prepare yourself, Mom," Maggie warned.

Dr. Gooding winced at her daughter. "I'm a doctor. I'm always prepared. I . . . oh, my God!"

"My bones are black," I said wonderingly as we all got a good look at the wound.

"Told you," Maggie said.

Maggie's mom just stared. "Can you make a fist?" she finally asked.

I did. It hurt, but less than I expected.

"You've got a bigger issue than your bones," she said.

"What?" Maggie asked.

"You're not supposed to see bones here. They're supposed to be covered up by muscles. Muscles and tendons—they make stuff work. You shouldn't be able to move anything without muscles, but they're not in here. Surrounding these black bones is some sort of . . . red goo. I can stitch you up, but I don't know. We should get some X-rays."

"No time, Mom. They're after us, and I think we just killed a driver who was chasing us."

"Oh, you failed to mention that little detail in your story," Dr. Gooding said. "Golly, that's not too nice."

"This is serious, Mom."

"There's nowhere to go, Maggie," her mother returned. "If what you say is even remotely true, we need to see what we're working with and then come up with a plan. And try to keep you out of jail, it sounds like."

"Wait," I said, "does your phone still work?"

It did, and I called the station where Ears was head-quartered. If something was going on, he'd know about it. He heard everything that came through. I had a feeling others would be hearing everything that came through this phone as well—and I didn't know whether Ishango might have gotten to Ears by now—but I had to take the risk.

On the second ring came that familiar voice: "One Hundred Twelfth Battalion Headquarters. Sergeant Perkins speaking."

"Ears," I muttered, instinctively cupping my hand over the mouthpiece to make clear that this call was on the down low.

"Jordan?" he said. "Dude, they're looking for you."

Whew. Ishango's soldiers would never say "Dude."

"What do you know?"

"I could lose my head for talking to you."

"Just tell me where they're looking."

There was a long pause.

"Okay, not looking. They know where you are—you and your girlfriend and her mom."

"Are they coming for us?"

The pause lasted so long that I wondered whether we'd been disconnected, but then he spoke: "They're monitoring everybody, tracking everybody. They're not going to go into town to get you. They figure you can't do much damage there. They'll just stop you when you're on the move. That's all I can say. Don't call back."

The line went dead.

"Okay, let's do those X-rays," I said as I put down the phone.

Maggie and her mom took me to the back room and made me take off anything metal, which wasn't much. Over twenty to thirty minutes, they X-rayed almost every part of me. If I hadn't been irradiated by the power plant, I'd gotten more than my share here.

When it was over, we returned to the office to examine the images on the computer. We moved upward on my body: my feet were fine, but then my knee—I don't know what it was supposed to look like, but it was bright white on the X-ray. Dr. Gooding said that meant it was made of metal. The whole knee had been replaced plus part of the femur.

There was more normal stuff as we moved up—pelvis, intestines, stomach—but, wait, my right kidney was bright white. And my pancreas, and spleen. Then six ribs, all on the right side. And my right arm. Wherever there was a scar, there was white, indicating that something had been replaced.

"Check my head," I said. "That's where the last scar is."

There it was, a wicked-looking thing: a heavy base at the top of my spinal column and then spindly arms reaching throughout my brain.

"No one could take that out," Maggie's mom said. "I have no idea how they got it in."

"It must be what's giving you all the special skills," Maggie said. "Like how you know how to fight and all that."

I took Maggie's hand and held it. "The flaming skeleton in the woods," I remembered aloud.

"What flaming skeleton?" her mom asked.

"The creature I chased into the woods after the fire. I'm not the only one who's been—whatever I've been. Converted?

Someone ran out of my house when it was on fire, and it looked like a burning corpse. Most of the flesh was singed off, and I could see its organs flaming inside an intact rib cage. That's all he was left with."

Dr. Gooding stood speechless for a moment, then said, "This is seriously fucked up."

"Mom, you and the swearing!" Maggie said.

"Are you arguing with my professional assessment, dear?"

"No."

"Okay, then. We need to get out of town."

"But that's when they'll catch us," Maggie said.

"One more thing," I interjected. "There's an X-ray that shows how they're keeping tabs on us."

Maggie pulled up the image on the computer: her upper arm with a little white spot.

"What's that?" her mom asked.

"We think it's for tracking and perception manipulation," I said. "A mental implant like mine is supposed to command my brain to do anything, but when I got hit in the head at football, all of a sudden I saw the world as a mess— a disasterland. That perception didn't last, but it came back when I took another hit at the fire, and then it came back for good when I got smashed in the head today, and this time it isn't going away. I'm seeing our reality: We're living in a radiation nightmare right now. You guys' perceptions are being manipulated through another device. I bet if you took that thing out of Maggie's arm, she wouldn't be seeing the illusion anymore, either."

"You've got one, too," Maggie said to her mom. "See the scar? They implanted us when we first got to camp, saying they were giving us flu shots. It sounds like it makes things look the way we want them to look. Some kind of wish fulfillment."

Maggie X-rayed her mom, and then Dr. Gooding had Maggie on a table with a surgery light trained on Maggie's arm. The doctor made a small incision and probed for the pellet, and it came out.

"Oh, shit," Maggie said. "Everything is wrong. It's all yellow, gray, sick-looking. Is this what the real world looks like?"

"I think so," I said. "Everything is so much worse than the illusion we'd been enjoying."

"Well," Maggie's mom said, "much as I like all the greenery, you'd better take mine out. Just don't kill me, please."

Maggie's knife work wasn't as efficient or neat as her mom's, and Dr. Gooding grimaced a few times, but eventually Maggie produced a pellet the size of a bean.

Maggie's mom kept her eyes closed throughout and seemed reluctant to open them afterward. Finally, she did, taking in the room, me, and her daughter.

"Well," she said, "everything sucks right now, but you two are still beautiful."

"Aw, Mom," Maggie said, and gave her a hug.

I took Maggie's hand and gave her a look. She knew what I was thinking and gave me a sad nod.

"Dr. Gooding," I said, "there's one more thing you should know."

Just then there was a knock on the door.

"Anybody want some coffee?" came the smooth male voice from outside.

"Oh, shoot me now," Maggie said. "It's Bud Fucking Winkle."

CHAPTER 51

Maggie

MOM LOOKED LIKE I'd slapped her in the face and took a moment to compose herself and put on a welcoming smile before opening the door to Bud Winkle, who was holding two cardboard coffee cups.

"If I'd known it was a party, I'd have brought more," he chirped in his cream-colored linen shirt and matching linen pants. Every strand of his blond hair was running parallel back to front.

"Bud, that is so kind," Mom said, and took a cup.

"Latte with one sugar, just how you like it," Bud said.

"Thank you," Mom said.

"You should try a cortado sometime," Jordan interjected. "Still smooth but evens out that milk-to-coffee ratio."

I shot Jordan my most unsubtle "WTF!" look.

"Thanks, son," Bud said.

"So Maggie and Jordan were just about to tell me something important," Mom said.

"Later, Mom," I said.

"No, why don't you tell me now?" Mom said, with a look

on her face that indicated she was digging in. "Anything you want to say to me you can say in front of Bud."

I looked over at Jordan. He scratched the back of his head. I was on my own on this one.

"Oh," Bud said, "I truly don't want to get in the middle of family business. I can come back at a more opportune time."

"No, Bud, that's okay," Mom said, and wrapped her arm around his back, prompting him to drape his arm over her shoulder.

"All right, then. Fine," I said. "I have cancer."

"Let me get some paper towels," Jordan said after Mom's latte with one sugar hit the floor and splattered everywhere.

I explained it all, deciding that Bud could hear this, especially since his precious "folks down at the plant" might be at fault. Mom asked questions. Bud said nothing. Eventually she inspected my X-rays, and although this wasn't a mammogram and she wasn't an oncologist, she thought she saw something not good. She took me into an exam room and felt around to confirm what I was talking about. I felt, not happily, that my self-diagnosis had been valid.

"I ought to be going," Bud said when we came out.

"Okay," Mom said, and gave him a stiff hug. At least my news had knocked her out of her frisky mood.

"I hope that your suspicions about this turn out to be incorrect," he told me, his pale blue eyes locking with mine.

"Me too," I responded. "But if not, hey, I know whom to call." I flashed a big insincere smile his way. He offered almost a courtly bow before he left.

"You should have told me," Mom said as we got into her

pickup, with her behind the wheel, me in the passenger seat, and Jordan in the back.

"What would you have done?" I asked.

"I would have gone to the army," she said, her eyes beginning to well up. "I would have gone to the highest commanding official at the camp, and I would have gotten you to the hospital. People go to the hospital here. It's not unheard of."

I shook my head. "The army wouldn't have let us out of here because you were worried your daughter had a lump."

"Maybe," she said. "They helicoptered Jordan's family out of here because they were injured."

"But we don't know where they went," Jordan said.

I turned to look back at him.

"We don't," he said. "We saw them being taken away in a helicopter, but that's all we know. If I had to put money on it, they're back in the sick camp, prisoners who can't leave or communicate with anyone back in town, even the son and brother they left behind."

"Why do you assume they're prisoners?" my mom asked.

"We can't contact anyone outside of town," Jordan said. "Don't you think there's a reason for that? Ishango can't let the world know how bad it is here. She would be shut down if the news reached anyone at the state or national level. So we're quarantined, captive, whatever you want to call it."

"There are still people working around here, and they'd help Maggie if she has cancer," Mom insisted.

"No offense, but I don't think so, and I've been working this through my head for the same reason you have," Jordan said. "I doubt the sick camp has mammogram machines, and

I really don't believe they'd take her to an outside hospital. I just don't."

"You're saying they'd leave her to die?" Mom said.

"Mom!" I said.

"Well, not die, sweetie," she said, patting me on the thigh. "But, you know, going untreated if there actually were anything to treat. Which, the more I think about it, there probably isn't."

I'm not sure which was worse, the brutal truth or the blatant sugarcoating.

"This is a sick town," Jordan said. "We're probably all getting cancer."

"Don't talk like that," Mom said. "We'll be fine."

We drove in silence, terror building in my chest at the sound of that lie. Things would get worse before they got better. Ishango had access to a huge military force. We could all be dead. If anything happened to Mom or Jordan, I didn't know how I'd go on.

"Dr. Gooding, you can see what things really look like now," Jordan said. "Look around. This forest is sick. The animals are raging. The paint is peeling, and buildings are crumbling. Mount Hope looks like a town that's been abandoned after a disaster, except we all came back with rose-colored brain stems. The military and probably the town government are hiding what's going on and have been doing so for decades. Plenty of people working at the plant had to know that the power supply was only fueling a single, massive super-computer. And those in charge are shutting up everyone who questions it. They shut down the newspaper. They bought off the police. And they no longer will let anyone in or out of this town."

Mom smiled and looked at me as she guided the car down a bumpy, rutted hunting road. "Funny, you were always the rational one, and I was the one with the conspiracy theories. You always talked me out of them."

"Well, seeing my boyfriend attacked by a sword-armed freak and insane supercomputer had a way of opening my eyes." I heard a muffled guffaw from the back seat. "Yes, I said 'boyfriend,' Jordan! Jesus!"

The smile left his face as he reached his hand between Mom and me to point out the windshield.

"We're here," he said.

CHAPTER 52

Jordan

ONCE AGAIN WE were ready to hike up Mount Hope. It was Maggie's idea to return for the explosives—she thought if we could drop them down the construction hole that led to Ishango's chamber, we could create an extinction event for that Bible-quoting computer bitch. I argued that the chances were slim to none that we'd ever again get that close to Ishango, with or without the explosives. Ishango was at war, and by now she no doubt had more security protecting her than the president of the United States.

Still, we'd be better off with the explosives than without them. I'd just have to rely upon my strategically enhanced mind to come up with something at whatever the right moment was.

After parking as close to the trail as possible, the three of us hiked toward the cliffs. I wanted to go alone, but Dr. Gooding insisted we stick together. I led the way.

We hadn't been hiking long when Maggie whispered, "Stop."

We froze, listening. The wind blew through the pines, and there was some rustling in the undergrowth.

"It could be another wild hog," I whispered.

"Or nothing," Maggie's mom said.

I looked at Maggie, and our eyes locked. "If it's something bad, we'll just deal with it," I said. "Let's hurry in the meantime."

We turned back to the trail. We were close.

"I just can't believe that this is real," Maggie's mom said as she trudged up the trail. "I feel like I should be waking up from this any moment."

"I feel that way all the time—and I really do have dreams: about Alpha, about the nuclear meltdown," I said. "I don't know whether they're dreams or memories or something else triggered by the implant."

"We think he's still connected to Ishango in some way," Maggie said.

Maggie's mom looked at me as if for the first time. "Are you seeing visions or anything like that?"

"No," I said, "I just know things, like how to fight in different ways. If a boxer showed up in front of me, I'd know how to box back without ever having taken a lesson. It's weird."

"Do you know other things, too?" Dr. Gooding asked. "Like biology or how to make an omelet?"

I smiled. "I already make a mean omelet. And I'll know how to put this bomb together."

The cliff tops came into view, and the trees and dirt gave way to a round outcrop of granite.

I located the Hogan Construction bag and picked it up gingerly. C4 was supposed to be stable if you dropped it—

it was supposed to detonate only with a blasting cap or some other explosion—but I felt the weight of it in my hand and wasn't taking any chances.

A shot rang out, and Maggie's mom let out a cry and tumbled to the ground, clutching her stomach, a red patch spreading beneath her fingers.

I hit the ground and pulled Maggie with me as she screamed, "Mom! Mom!" I crouched and scanned the area and saw no one. I ripped off my shirt and handed it to Maggie to press against her mom's wound.

"Shhh, I'm okay," Dr. Gooding said softly, reaching out to run her hand down Maggie's hair. Damn, even now she was trying to make Maggie feel better.

She'd become like a second mom to me, and now she had taken a bullet because I'd gotten her tangled up in this crazy conspiracy. Was she going to die? Maybe I should've let Alpha fix the jarred implant in my head, so I could be as unfeeling as the rest of them.

I looked back and spotted two men now standing behind an outcropping. The tracking device on me must have been working after all.

As they stepped forward, I saw that both men were wearing those telltale black suits.

And one of them was my father.

Maggie gasped.

"It is regrettable," Dad said as he approached me, "that you would try to stop the work of Ishango, who improved you so substantially."

"Do you have any of my father left in your body?" I asked, standing up to my full height, a sense of terror and despair coming along. I knew he was controlled by the implant, but it still devastated me to see him like this. "You've helped kill so many for the sake of a computer's crazy scheme to take over the world."

"Omicron and I are part of Ishango," he said. "As are you, Rho."

"You named me *Jordan.*"

"That was your mother. I was not involved in the procedure on your mother or your conception as you may have been led to believe," he stated.

"What do you mean by 'procedure'?"

The suit named Omicron spoke. "Rho, your selection was not accidental. Ishango began experimentation on the consciousness transmigration process approximately twenty years ago. One solution involved breeding a host with a particular set of non-rejecting antibodies. Your mother was chosen to gestate the host: you."

I shook my head as Maggie clutched my ankle while using her other hand to continue applying pressure to her mom's wound. None of this was making sense. I turned to my father but found no comfort in his cold brown eyes.

"Dad—"

"It is true."

"You're *lying,*" I seethed, infuriated by his matter-of-fact tone.

"Ishango has authorized me to confirm this information," he droned on. "The fertilization and embryo implantation occurred when your mother was ostensibly hospitalized for fibroid cyst removal."

Tears welled up and spilled out, and I grabbed my head with both hands, wishing I could rip out whatever had become woven into my brain. Even if that took me down, at least the nightmare would be over. "I know Ishango is making you say this," I cried, not caring that Maggie was seeing me break down.

"I regret to verify you are not my son."

"But I am, Dad," I whispered. "No matter what Ishango says. And I know there's a part of you that doesn't want this to happen: for me to lose my life so she can live and take over the world."

"No," he said, "she has no need to destroy unless humanity poses a threat. Currently, humanity does not."

"Um, Dad, did you hear the me-losing-my-life part? This conversation is beyond depressing."

Dr. Gooding let out a cry of pain behind me, and Maggie ran her palm over her mom's forehead. Now Dr. Gooding was the one who needed medical attention. My being held at gunpoint wasn't doing her or Maggie any good. I needed to get them out of here.

"Maggie," I said, "take care of your mom."

"What do you mean?" she asked.

"I'm going with them." I'd let Omicron and my dad take me back to Ishango, where she'd take over my body, but they might leave the bag of explosives, allowing Maggie to detonate it later.

"Jordan," she said, her voice shaking, "we have to stay together."

I stared at her, then let my eyes flit over to the yellow bag. She got it.

"I can't take care of her," she said warily. "I don't know how."

Shit. Of *course* she didn't know about blasting caps and det wire. Why would she?

Checkmate.

"Jordan, don't go with them," Dr. Gooding croaked.

Omicron pivoted toward her and lifted his gun—but then turned and fired toward the woods. There was a yelp and some rustling, and out staggered Bud Winkle with blood streaming down his face.

"Renee!" he said. "I'm sorry..." He collapsed face-first onto the dirt.

"Bud!" Maggie's mom shouted as Omicron turned back toward her, pointed the gun at her forehead, and—

Bang!

It was loud, but Dr. Gooding looked intact. I turned to see a hole in Maggie's T-shirt.

No!

But then Omicron dropped to the ground with a nickel-size hole in his forehead, out of which poured that carrot ketchup.

Maggie removed her hand from under her T-shirt. It held the Magnum.

The next ninety seconds happened in slow motion as my adrenaline surged, my brain kicked into gear, and I operated like the machine I'd been programmed to be.

Dad reached for the gun in his waistband, but I crouched low and swung my leg to sweep his. He stumbled and fell, and I moved swiftly to snatch his pistol out of his belt, giving him a powerful jab to the midsection at the same time.

I looked up at Maggie, and she had her gun trained on him. I held out my hand, and she gave it to me. Damn, it really was heavy.

"How can I bring you back?" I asked my dad, pointing the Magnum at his face.

Instead of answering, he rolled behind a boulder. I

couldn't shoot, despite all he'd said and done to turn me against him.

"I got him," I called back to Maggie. "Stay with your mom and keep applying pressure."

I stepped slowly around the boulder, gun in both hands.

"You're human, Dad," I said. "You're a human with an implant, like me. Don't let Ishango tell you what to do."

I heard a moan from beyond the boulder. Maybe I'd broken his leg with my kick. I followed the sound, but he got the drop on me and fired his gun.

I felt the bullet hit me in the chest, right in one of my metal ribs.

My father had shot me.

CHAPTER 53

Jordan

I STAGGERED BACK, and Dad advanced, limping.

"Father, Father, we don't need to escalate," I said, raising my gun, but he shot it out of my hand, sending bullet fragments into my wrist and arm. *Ouch.* I dropped the pistol and fell to my knees. I'm still not sure I would've been able to fire it at him anyway, but I also wasn't confident that he'd take any mercy on me.

"Jordan!" Maggie screamed, and started running toward me, but I held up a bloodied hand.

"Stay back!" I roared. My chest burned, and I could feel blood spreading on my shirt. I thought of Alpha, who had survived so many of my bullets. Could I shake off a gunshot wound and get back in the fight, too?

A line from that western *Cat Ballou* came to mind: The old gunslinger Kid Shelleen tells a younger man, "At first you don't think you can stand to get hit, then you realize you can take it 'cause the blood don't matter, and you know you're gonna live. It's a great gift I'm giving you—to know it don't hurt to fight."

The blood don't matter and you know you're gonna live.

Or as Patrick Swayze put it in *Road House:* "Pain don't hurt."

Despite the blood, I felt like this wound wasn't bad. The bullet hit a rib, but these metal ribs were pretty sturdy—or so I assumed.

So I ran straight at my dad, not grimacing, not gritting my teeth. I was gonna live.

He looked surprised as I slammed into him, wrapping him up like my linebacker coach had taught me. I was tackling him *and* stripping him of the ball, in this case the gun, which I swatted from his grip as I took him down onto a rough pile of jutting rocks. I'd already been good at tackling before the implant in my head made me better, stronger, and faster, and now I knew exactly where to hit him to inflict the maximum damage and to punch all the wind out of his lungs.

There was another booming gunshot, and all three of us froze.

It was Maggie, who'd picked up the Magnum again and fired over us.

"That was a warning shot, Mr. Conners," she said. "The next one won't be. I don't have the same soft spot for you that Jordan does, because you shot my mom, you robotic piece of shit. Let Jordan up before I pop a cap in your ass and another in your eye socket for good measure."

"Damn, girl!" I said.

"I, for one, am *not* trying real hard to be the shepherd," she said, aiming a wink at me and the gun at my father's rear end.

I felt Dad's weight slowly lift off me.

He smiled—a mirthless, mechanical smile. "Despite what

happens to me, I hope you will soon be convinced of the futility of your situation," he said.

"The only thing you've convinced me of is that I'll never cooperate with Ishango," I said. "I'll throw myself off Mount Hope before I let her use me."

I reached my hand toward Maggie, and she handed me the gun.

Was that uncertainty I saw flickering in his eyes? Was there a trace of my father in there after all?

"I'm sorry, Dad," I whispered. "I love you, but Maggie's more family to me than you are now."

I tightened my grip on the gun.

I wasn't sure I could do this. But I had to.

With a swift movement, I pistol-whipped him in the back of the head, below the curve of the skull. It was the spot where I'd seen the implant in my own brain. My hope was that a blow this hard might dislodge his implant the way it had shifted mine—without killing him.

With a groan, Dad fell heavily onto his knees, then pitched forward onto the ground.

I knelt beside him and felt for a pulse. It was there. Relief washed over me. In spite of what he'd become, I could never forgive myself for killing my father. And he *was* my father. If there was any chance of removing the implant, I had to keep him alive. Charlie needed a dad, too.

I ran back to Dr. Gooding, with Maggie two steps ahead of me. "How's she doing?" I asked.

"We need to get her to a hospital."

"Bud..." Maggie's mom rasped, then grimaced in severe pain.

"What about you?" Maggie asked me.

"I'm fine," I said. "Hardly even bleeding." I wiped my hand over my brow and felt a smear of blood left there.

"Right," Maggie said.

"Well, my hand is a bit messed up, but my rib and that whole area seem strangely okay. Wanna see?"

I started to lift my shirt to admire the small, burning puncture wound beneath my chest, but Maggie was back with her mom.

"I got her," I said, and hoisted Dr. Gooding in my arms. We headed down the trail slowly, stepping over the wide fissure in the ground. Maggie carried the bag of explosives with delicate fingers. "Our best bet is the hospital at the sick camp. We'll ram through the barricade again if we have to."

"Okay," Maggie said in a small voice. Then louder: "Or we could try going through the woods. Canville's just ten miles away."

Then came another voice: "You forget your—ah—movements are being tracked, Rho."

Fuck.

As quickly and gently as I could, I put Dr. Gooding down and scanned the trees for that former human, whose voice had seemed to come from everywhere. My ears strained to hear a twig snapping, a leaf brushing—anything to clue me in to where he was.

Nothing.

"Here, kitty, kitty!" I called, picking up a thick branch and wielding it like a club. "Ready to use up another of your lives?"

A *WHUMP!* from behind me left me with a cold, burning sensation on my upper right arm, and the gun flew out of my hand. I whirled around to come face-to-half-face with Alpha, whose sword arm already was stained with my blood. The bastard had been above us in the trees—like a cat, I ruefully reflected.

He raised his arm again, and I swung the branch to block what would've been a fatal blow. The sword sliced right through the wood, and I tried to use the stubs to drive him back, but he knocked first one and then the other out of my hands.

"Careful," I said. "You don't want Ishango to be moving into a damaged vessel."

"Oh—ah—we have alternatives," Alpha said, approaching with sword raised.

I looked over to Maggie, and she looked how I felt: terrified.

We had no guns.

We had no weapons at all.

We were about to die.

CHAPTER 54

Maggie

JORDAN PUT HIMSELF between Alpha and me—a rugged he-man gesture I appreciated for its stupid, stubborn bravery.

"Leave us alone!" he shouted. "I'm not giving in to Ishango's insane idea. Why the hell would I agree to anything she wants after what she's done to this town? To its people? To my *father*?"

"We—ah—will carry on with our plans with or without your surrender, Rho. The only question—ah—is whether you allow the Gooding family to—ah—live."

"No," I called sharply. There was no way I could allow Jordan to consider turning himself into something like Alpha. "With Ishango's plan, there's no real living for anyone. Don't fall for his manipulation, Jordan."

"Gotcha," Jordan replied, and struck out with his leg to catch Alpha's knee with an audible crack.

The personlike thing staggered, then whipped out that friggin' sword again. This time Jordan avoided it easily.

"You've shown up in a few of my nightmares," Jordan

grunted. "But now I'm thinking they're actually memories. Were you there when they were operating on me?"

Alpha grinned hideously, his lipless mouth stretching even wider to expose his skull teeth. "Indeed, Rho. I was the one who performed your modifications. As well as on your mother years ago."

"Wait, what about Charlie?" Jordan asked.

"Ah—if I had anything to do with Charlie, he'd be here as well."

Alpha threw a punch at Jordan's head, but Jordan ducked under it and twisted Alpha's weapon arm behind his back. Alpha followed with a swift blow to Jordan's head, forcing him to let go.

The two of them swung and parried, stabbed and dodged in a complex dance around the mountain terrain. What Jordan had been telling me finally sank in: He knew how to fight, at a level way beyond professional. I might have enjoyed marveling at his mastery of the art if not for the sinking feeling that this particular bout would end in his death—and likely mine, too.

Alpha clearly had the upper hand with his wicked weapon. After blocking a sword thrust, Jordan had tried to punch him in the face but missed and stumbled. Alpha's leg swept the ground, knocking Jordan to his knees.

"Jordan!" I cried out as Alpha stepped up and touched the edge of his sword to Jordan's neck.

Kneeling with his head hanging, Jordan looked at me so hopelessly that my heart choked my throat. I couldn't watch him die.

"Wait!" I called, but Alpha didn't bother to turn around. I had no leverage here except as a liability to Jordan.

But I wasn't blind. I could see where they had ended up on the mountainside, in front of the crevasse that almost split Mount Hope in two. Alpha had his back to me and was addressing Jordan.

I had to try. As terrified as I was of him, the look on Jordan's face was the spur I needed to act. I wasn't a fighter, but I wasn't going to let Jordan die—not as long as I breathed.

"Know that you are expendable, Rho," I heard Alpha say as I quietly approached. "It will take some time, but we have already begun the process of—ah—creating another transfer unit, Sigma, with abilities even superior to yours."

Alpha was gloating, his eyes locked with Jordan's. I waited for him to resume his wheezy speech to mask the sound of my soft footsteps.

"Perhaps Margaret would make a fine candidate for the gestation," he concluded, a sick punch line for Jordan to hear as Alpha raised his sword arm for the killing blow. Those would *not* be the last words Jordan would hear in this lifetime.

I threw myself against Alpha, barreling into him with a mighty shoulder shove I learned from watching Jordan on the football field. Coach Garner would've approved of my hit as Alpha toppled forward—right onto the edge of that deep, deep fissure.

Before Alpha could get his bearings, Jordan lunged and pushed him into the crack.

Desperately, Alpha scrabbled for purchase on the dirt-packed ground, but a sword arm isn't made for holding on. With his legs dangling above the crevasse, Alpha's one functional hand was losing its battle to get a grip.

As if resigned to his end, Alpha ceased groping for a hold

and fixed his stare on Jordan. "I not only performed the embryo implantation on your mother, Rho," he said with his skull-like grin. "Happily, I was chosen to fertilize her oocyte as well. Our genetic configurations were a perfect match to produce . . . you."

He relaxed his body.

"Whether through you or me, my legacy will live on."

With his skinless face and dead eyes, he gazed at Jordan as he slid down the crevasse and then fell without a sound.

I dove for Jordan and grabbed him in a fierce hug. He sat motionless as if in shock.

"Don't listen to him," I told him. "He was just trying to rattle you. You can't let him."

Jordan looked down at me, his eyes wet and shoulders shaking. "It's true. My dad confirmed as much. That disgusting nonhuman was my . . ."

I grabbed his head between my palms and placed my forehead against his. "Your dad was your dad, no matter what. *Please.* We still have to figure out how to save my mom and the rest of Mount Hope. Ishango is still alive, Jordan!"

He nodded slowly, then got up from the ground. With a final glance down the fissure, he asked, "So what now?"

"Let's take some inventory first."

I checked on my mom, whose bleeding appeared to have subsided, while Jordan carried his still-unconscious father over to us.

"There's no way we can get back to the plant to drop these explosives down the hole," Jordan said. "Even with all of my new powers, I'd be no match for an entire armed military force and all of those workers—and animals—under Ishango's control. We couldn't take these guys with us"—he gestured to my mom and his dad — "and I'm not leaving you up here."

I looked out at the Sweetbay River, my gaze sweeping over the view of the valley where the power plant was nestled.

Then I turned back to Jordan and said in my most chipper TV-rerun voice, "I have an idea so crazy that it just might work!"

CHAPTER 55

Jordan

"WE'RE GOING TO jail for this," Maggie's mom said, then coughed up some blood.

"Mom!" Maggie cried.

"Okay, forget I said anything," her mom said, waving off her daughter and running the back of her hand over her dripping lips. "Jails have hospitals, anyway."

"If it makes you feel any better," I said, "the explosion and radiation might kill us before we get arrested."

"And I already have cancer, remember?" Maggie chirped.

"Well, as long as we're all feeling upbeat," Dr. Gooding said, "you go right ahead."

When Maggie told me her idea, I didn't think the world's most intelligent and sociopathic supercomputer would have anticipated it. That in itself seemed reason enough to proceed.

I turned to Maggie. "Won't this ruin all the farms beyond?" I asked. "All that irradiated water by the time the whole thing is finished?"

"Right. That's if it all goes well."

"How confident are you right now?"

"Not at all," Maggie said, then grinned.

"Me neither," I said. "Fuck it."

After what Alpha told me before plunging into the abyss, hope wasn't something I ever expected to feel again. Now I had a glimmer—as well as a new infusion of energy.

Maggie pulled out the battery and attached the first wire to the negative terminal. She looked at me.

"Yippee-ki-yay," I said with a nod.

She touched the second wire to the positive terminal, and the whole mountain trembled beneath us. *Whoa, Nelly!* We were as far away from the danger zone as the long detonation cord would allow us to go. I hoped it was enough.

An enormous *BOOM!* sounded, and small rocks jiggled from their resting places and scattered down the cliffside on the opposite end of the crevasse. That was just the beginning. Huge chunks and boulders started falling into the Sweetbay River below us. The water was churning, and trees were being flattened by the massive rocks falling from above. Finally, the entire cliffside collapsed in what felt like slow motion, peeling away from the fissure. We were irrevocably changing the landscape in which we'd lived our entire lives.

Suddenly everything stopped, just for a moment. Maggie and I tiptoed up to the new, raw cliff edge and peered over. The massive rockfall had settled into its new home in the river and forest below. The slabs and boulders spanned the river and then some, damming it up just as we had expected.

"Look!" Maggie said.

We watched in nervous anticipation as the white foam frothed at what was now blocking its route—and the water followed the path of least resistance and began to bubble up and onto the shore.

It was happening. With the Sweetbay blocked, the water needed a way around the new rock dam. It surged to the sides, and while some of it made a quick detour to the left before flowing back into the river on the other side of the dam, the bulk of the water pushed to the right and poured down, down, down into the valley.

The valley where the power plant was.

From that point, there was no question of what would happen. The water would race along the valley floor and eventually pour into the hole at the construction site—and flood the room containing Ishango.

There was nothing I saw in that room to indicate that this supercomputer of all supercomputers was built to be fully submerged. There wouldn't be enough rice in the world to dry that thing out.

We didn't think the flooding would drown anyone at the plant. At least we hoped not. Hell, those workers were all out protecting the plant against us anyway, right? And a lot of them didn't seem human anymore.

Ah, I was rationalizing. I didn't want the blood of hundreds of innocent lives on my hands, but Ishango was endangering a lot more folks than those residing in the plant. Anyway, people can swim.

From atop Mount Hope, we watched the river rush and gurgle through its new route, saving us and the rest of the world from the evil force that had murdered so many people and turned our town into a living disaster.

"'Down goes Frazier! Down goes Frazier! Down goes Frazier!'" I whooped.

"What the hell are you talking about?" Maggie asked with a laugh.

"Howard Cosell...George Foreman...never mind," I said, wrapping my arms around her. "Smells like...*victory.*"

She pressed her soft lips against mine, and although I couldn't say that this moment made everything else that preceded it worthwhile, it was closer than you might think.

CHAPTER 56

Maggie

A RESCUE HELICOPTER spotted us several hours later and lowered a basket for Mom, Mr. Conners, and Bud Winkle. It turned out that the bullet had grazed Bud's scalp, causing enough blood spillage to make him pass out but not enough to kill him. We learned later that he'd followed us in his car and on foot knowing that we'd likely be pursued by Ishango's forces. Bud wasn't tied up with them after all, and the secret files he kept at the plant would become invaluable in the investigation to come.

"Looks like you guys had quite a hike," said the rescuer, a rugged, husky-voiced twenty-something woman with her hair pulled back in a tight ponytail beneath her baseball cap.

"We sure did," I said as I took a seat next to Jordan. "We—"

Jordan's raised eyebrows stopped me. He was right: We'd never finish the story by the time we landed, and casually fessing up to destroying the mountain and the town's nuclear plant might not be the wisest move. We'd already had to explain Mom's gunshot wound: something about an errant hunter's bullet fired during the cliffside's collapse. The rescuer, Brianna, had her hands full and didn't bother asking more questions.

I took Jordan's hand, which, like mine, had Mom's blood on it.

"This is it," I said, leaning in to his ear so I could be heard over the helicopter's roar as we flew over fields and country roads that led far away from Mount Hope.

"This is what?"

"Well, what are the odds of us ending up in the same place?"

He laughed. "Are you trying to get rid of me?"

"No," I said. "I'm just saying, after your dad's implant is removed, you two will reunite with your mom and Charlie while I'll probably go to my mom's sister's place in Texas."

"Wow, that's a lot of assumptions right there. You think my dad's implant will be so easily removed? And why wouldn't you keep living with your mom?"

"Oh, I plan on living with my mom—and maybe Bud Winkle, too," I said, and mock gagged. "But I suspect it won't be in Mount Hope anymore. Same goes for you all. Look."

Those same roads along which we'd all convoyed back into town weeks earlier were full again with cars headed in the opposite direction. But this was no orderly retreat with the military and police acting as crossing guards every block; these people were gunning it, getting the hell out of Dodge, riding the shoulders, and taking their ATVs over fields when necessary. From what I could tell from the lines of fast-moving traffic, these drivers weren't stopping at nearby camps, either, but going pedal-to-the-metal until they reached the real outside world. Civilization at last.

"*The Evacuation, Part Deux*," Jordan said.

"The last sequel, I hope."

"Yeah," he said. "Still, I bet all of us will wind up back at that sick camp. Maybe we'll find my mom there. I hope she's healed by now."

"Excuse me!" I shouted over the rotors to Brianna. "Are you taking us to the sick camp?"

"Those were my orders at first," she replied. "But with your mom's gunshot wound, I insisted on taking her and these other gentlemen to the hospital in Charleston. At first I heard some argument, then nothing, so here we go."

"Thanks!" I replied.

"What she said," Jordan added.

The two of us faced each other again.

"So who knows?" he said.

"Exactly."

"Well," he continued, "we survived a year apart once— and I'm guessing this time Ishango won't be cutting off our access to cellular technology and that thing known as the internet. We may be apart for a few months, but we'll be able to travel this time and go wherever we want, right? And I'll want to be where you are."

"Same here," I said, my face relaxing into a smile.

"Maybe we'll meet up in Washington, D.C., to testify before Congress. I guess it depends on how much of this Ishango stuff comes out."

"Oh, it'll come out," I said. "We may get in trouble, but it's our duty. This town has released too much radiation and evil. Now's the time for us to let out the truth."

Jordan sat back, wearing a thoughtful expression. "You're right," he said. "What happened in Mount Hope should serve as a warning to the rest of the world."

"Yep," I said. "They may even pay attention for a couple of days. That's how long the news cycle is, right?"

"Right."

"In the meantime, scientists will have a field day checking you out . . . Rho."

He laughed.

"And I'll be getting cancer treatments," I couldn't resist adding.

Jordan's expression darkened. "Maggie, we won't know what's really going on until you finally see a specialist," he said with a squeeze of my hand. "Which you're going to do. I suspect everyone from Mount Hope will have to do the same. Who knows? By the time this is all over, you may be my Jaime Sommers."

"I have no intention of being your Bionic Woman—or anyone else's."

"Well, I already think your powers are pretty super," he said, and leaned in to give me a kiss. It felt more than nice.

"That may be the cheesiest thing you've ever said to me, Jordan Conners," I said as he pulled back. "Anyway, I'm Han Solo, remember?"

I smiled and looked out the helicopter window to see the skyline of an actual city: Charleston. What a sight. We landed on the hospital's helipad beside another helicopter with CNN emblazoned on its side plus vans marked with a 2, a 4, and a 5—the local news stations.

"I don't know if you guys know what's going on," Brianna called out as the rotors slowed their spinning, "but with all of that water flooding in and out of that nuke plant, they're saying the town may not be habitable for twenty thousand years."

"Cripes," Jordan said. "What a disaster."

"Who'd have thunk that a facility so vital to the community would've been that susceptible to disaster?" I asked innocently.

"Twice," Jordan added.

Brianna leaned toward us conspiratorially and said in a hushed voice, "I heard they're already moving to seal off the plant in a giant cement sarcophagus. Crazy."

"Crazy," I agreed.

A phalanx of reporters and camera crews stampeded toward us, trailed by medical personnel.

"Are you ready to issue a warning to the world?" I asked Jordan.

"Yes," he said, "except for two things. One…"

He pulled out his cell phone, saw the bars on the screen, and exclaimed, "Yes!" He punched in a number, and after a moment, his face erupted in sheer joy. "Mom! It's Jordan! You okay?…Charlie too?…Great! Hold on!"

Then he cupped his hand over the phone and said, "Two," and leaned in and planted the gentlest kiss yet on my lips. My face suddenly felt sunburned.

"I love you," he whispered.

"I know," I returned, and we both started laughing uncontrollably.

Are you a fan of James Patterson's stand-alone thrillers?

If so, you'll love...

THE INN

Bill Robinson is starting over. The former Boston detective has moved to a secluded coastal town where he runs the local inn. Yet all too soon he discovers that his past won't let him go, and that leaving the city is no escape from the dangers he left behind.

A new crew of criminals move into the small town, bringing drugs and violence to the front door of the inn. Robinson feels the weight of responsibility on his shoulders. Can he save himself, and his residents, before time runs out?

Read on for an extract of this gripping new thriller

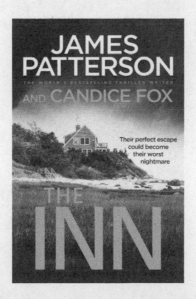

Available in hardback from August 2019

SOMETHING VERY BAD was about to go down.

There are things you know as a cop in Boston. You know how the city feels, because its streets are your veins and the voices of its people come through your lips when you talk. You know the smell of the salt in the harbor like the scent of the back of your wife's neck, and it's just as precious, reassuring. The hammering of footsteps out of Back Bay Station for the morning rat race wakes you up, and the wail of sirens in the old Combat Zone at night puts you to sleep. Every Christmas, you gather up some young wide-eyed uniforms to take poor kids from East Boston and Hyde Park into the toy stores, try to show the new cops and the kids that they can get along. You know that in a few years, some of those cops and some of those kids will end up killing each other. But that's how the city works. It's like a living thing. It sheds, and it hurts, and it bleeds.

I could feel what was about to happen in the air. It was an unexpected and dizzying heat, surreal against the snow on the ground outside the car.

When my partner Malone and I got a call to go to the commissioner's office downtown, I knew we were in for it. A Boston cop knows that being called to the commissioner's office is a bad, bad thing.

Malone always made fun of me for thinking I had Boston's pulse, a sense about approaching trouble in the city. On the morning of the marathon bombing, we'd been a mile up Boylston Street doing crowd control and I told Malone I felt hot and weird, like I had a fever. We felt the thump of the first blast under our feet a second or two later.

We were in the back of the cruiser, Malone looking out the window, joggling his knee and picking his teeth.

"Wait. I know what this is," he said suddenly. "This is about that baby. We're getting a medal for the baby last week."

The week before, Malone and I had been walking out at the end of a shift when a woman outside a café two doors from the station started screaming like she was on fire. She was standing in the street pointing at a balcony five floors above, where a toddler was sitting on the concrete ledge, having the time of his life. A crowd gathered, and it was quickly established that the mother was inside but wasn't answering the door or her phone. While some guys went in to try to break down her apartment door, Malone and I watched, pulling out our own hair, while the toddler crawled along the ledge and then, wobbling, stood up.

There was no time to decide who would catch the kid.

Malone and I both went in and snared him in a tangle of arms about two feet off the ground while the people around us hollered and screamed. Turned out the mother had been so damned tired from working two jobs that she fell asleep with the baby on the couch, the balcony doors open and a pot of peas cooking dry on the stove.

It was a good get, the kind of thing that wins you cheers when you walk into the station the next day. Ribbing about how tubby you look in the YouTube footage. Calls from the *Globe*. A medal, maybe. The toddler catch had gotten my wife, Siobhan, on the phone for a week, bragging to all her friends, telling them to watch the news, patting my head and saying she was proud of me like I was some kind of heroic dog.

But today wasn't about the kid. I could feel it in my bones.

"This is bad," I told Malone. "They only send a car for you when they know you'll be too fucked up to drive home afterward. We're in big trouble here. You better start thinking what we've done to piss off the top brass."

Malone, still twitching and joggling his knee, settled back and watched our driver. I gripped the seat belt and let Boston roll by, trying to guess what they were about to tell us.

The car dropped us at the building on Tremont Street. We went in, and as the elevator doors closed on us, I noticed that all Malone's twitching had suddenly stopped.

"I'm sorry," he said. His eyes were fixed on the floor. "I'm real sorry for this, Bill."

"You're sorry for what?"

He didn't answer. I had to hear it from the commissioner.

BOSTON PD LEGEND says that the visitor's chair in the commissioner's office is an old electric chair. I'd heard whispers around the department that some sadistic jerk occupying the top job had acquired the chair from a prison auction in Ohio and simply cut the straps and headgear off to make it acceptable for the office. Malone and I entered and took two identical chairs, either of which might indeed have been an Old Sparky sourced from the depths of the Midwest. The wood was eerily warm, and there were gouges in the arms that perfectly fit my fingernails.

I wouldn't have liked to be sitting in front of Commissioner Rachel McGinniskin even if the news were congratulatory. The red-haired, narrow-faced woman was a descendant of Barney McGinniskin, the first Irishman ever handed a police baton in Boston. From the moment Barney pulled on his blue coat, his appointment spurred hysterical newspaper reports, violent riots, and Irish bashings nationwide. The anti-immigration, anti-Catholic parties dumped him out of his job after only three years, and years later, Rachel McGinniskin had fought her way up the ladder in the force out of pure spite.

The commissioner opened a laptop and swiveled it on the desk so that the screen was facing us. She pushed a button and a black-and-white video began to play.

Only minutes into the video, I could feel sweat sliding down my ribs beneath my shirt. I looked at Malone, but he wouldn't meet my eyes.

McGinniskin pointed to a guy in the video. "Detective Jeremiah Malone," she said. "Is that you there on the screen?"

Her tone was strangely heavy, like she was the one getting the bad news. Malone didn't say anything. Just nodded, defeated. She let the video play a while longer.

"Detective William Robinson." She pointed at the screen again and looked at me, her eyes blazing. "Is that you?"

"It is," I said. Malone still wouldn't meet my gaze. *Look at me, you prick,* I thought. But the bastard put his face in his hands. McGinniskin turned the laptop back around and slammed it shut.

"You're both out," she said. The muscles in her jaw and temples were so tight, they bulged from beneath the skin. "And I've got to admit, gentlemen, after seeing that tape, it gives me great pleasure to say it. There's no place in my police force for people like you. Your discharge will take effect immediately. If I hear that either of you have inquired about pensions, I'll make sure you can't get a job in this city as a fucking *mall* cop." McGinniskin swept her hair back from her temples, chasing composure. "Give me your badges and your weapons," she said.

It was hard for me to get out of the chair. Gravity seemed to have tripled. I took my gun off, walked what seemed like a hundred miles to her desk, and put my weapon down at the same time Malone did. He finally looked at me as we took our badges off. Then we left. Neither of us spoke until we were outside her office.

"Bill," Malone said. "Buddy, listen. I—"

"I can't believe you did this." I was shaking all over. "I can't believe you did this to us. We're out. That's it. It's over. You lying, backstabbing piece of shit."

My job. My city. The walls of the old stone building were pulsing around me, closing in. Malone had killed us. We were being expelled from the living thing. Shed like dead skin, like waste. I couldn't breathe.

"I'm so sorry, Bill." Malone sounded panicky. "I was trying to—"

I grabbed my partner by the shirt and slammed him into the wall beside McGinniskin's door. It was all I could do not to knock his teeth out right there. I put a finger in his face and eased the words out from between my locked jaw.

"You and me?" I said. "We're *done*."

Two Years and Five Months Later

THE DEATH TOLL was eight, according to Cline's count.

He knew it was narcissistic, but every day he sat under the big bay windows on the second floor of his house where he could see the ocean beyond the cypress trees and checked the papers for signs of his work. Some days he told himself he was being too proud, and other days he knew it was just good business. Since he had moved to the tiny seaside town of Gloucester, there had been eight overdose deaths. Two a month. The papers were blaring out words that excited him. *Epidemic. Crisis. Downfall.* Whenever things started to slide, Cline felt happy. Being a criminal meant his concept of the world was upside down. Reversed. A downward slide for others meant an upward rise for him.

That didn't mean it was time to take it easy on anyone. As he sat reading the paper spread flat on the table before him, the way he used to in the can so that he could keep an eye on the movement of other prisoners, his lieutenants started assembling before him. Cline had made sure from the outset that his standards were known and respected. Tailored shirts. Cuff links. Ties for meetings. No speed-stripe buzz cuts, no neck tattoos, none of this gold-chain, bling-bling shit. They were a business, not a gang. The men who entered the room looked like a bunch of lawyers attending a daily meeting, but they came in punching each other and giggling and talking trash, and he silenced them with a glance. They were street thugs and prison bitches and violence-intervention-program dropouts he had recruited from rock bottom, but he'd make them true soldiers before long.

"Where's Newgate?" Cline asked when everyone was settled. "You fuckers know to be on time." There were uncomfortable looks around the crew, and then Newgate appeared with a baby in his arms. No, not a baby, a little girl, though she seemed like a baby in this setting, surrounded by hard men who made their living dealing in death. Cline stood and watched as big, muscle-bound, scar-faced Newgate put the barefoot child on the floor.

"I'm real sorry, boss." Newgate gave a dramatic sigh. "I had a fight with my girl and she dropped the baby on me this morning and ran off. I didn't know what to do."

Cline watched the girl toddling around the room, pulling books off his shelves, slapping her greasy palms on the huge bay windows. He felt a muscle twitching in his neck as he went to the desk and got his gun.

"No problem, Newby. These things happen," Cline said.

"I'm sure she won't cause us any trouble. Let's give her something to play with while we talk. Come here, little princess. Come on."

The lieutenants watched in horror as Cline loaded a full clip into his pistol and flicked the safety off. Newgate's daughter gave a coo of intrigue, tottered over to Cline, and took the gun. Squid, perched on the edge of the couch, didn't dare retreat but he hid beneath his gangly arms like they could protect from the child's aim. The little girl swung the heavy gun around wildly, then lifted the barrel to her eye and looked down into the blackness. Cline's eyes seared into Newgate's, daring him to protest. The little girl walked up to her father and pointed the gun at him.

"Bang-bang!" The girl laughed. Newgate reached for the weapon as his daughter fumbled with the trigger, unable to get her pudgy finger around the steel. Before Newgate could take the gun, Cline reached forward and grabbed it. He pointed it at Newgate, whose face contorted as he realized what was happening.

"Like this, princess," Cline said, smiling.

PLANE CRASH, I thought. *That's the only thing that can save me now.*

I'd done everything I could to dissuade the residents of the Inn from holding a memorial service for my wife, Siobhan, on the second anniversary of her death. And yet here I sat at the end of a plastic foldout table in the forest of pines that surrounded the large house, tearing a yellow napkin into tiny pieces, waiting for it to begin, fantasizing about something that could interrupt it. Gas-leak explosion in the kitchen. Ferocious black bear suddenly appearing at the edge of the woods. Airbus A380 plunging into the slate-gray sea just visible through the trees. The truth was, nothing was coming. The people around me were going to talk about Siobhan, and I was going to have to listen.

They'd made a good effort, which was unusual for them,

because it was difficult to get the permanent residents of the Inn to collaborate on anything. They had nothing in common save Siobhan's recruitment of them in the months after I was fired. Siobhan had done everything to set up our new life in the north. She'd found the guesthouse for sale, sourced the furniture, got the licenses and approvals we needed to run a bed-and-breakfast by the sea—her retirement dream realized years earlier than she'd imagined it would be. She'd collected a motley crew of weirdos, down-and-outs, and deeply troubled characters, and she accommodated them all. I'd moped in my sweatpants about my lost job, having no idea that I was about to lose her too.

At the end of the table, Marni stood up. She was the resident wayward teenager, Siobhan's second cousin who'd been sentenced to the house for having constant screaming matches with her mother and running away multiple times. As I sat in my chair watching her prepare to speak, I felt a twinge of guilt. Since I'd lost my wife, Marni had been my responsibility, and like I'd done with everything else, I let her slip. She'd gotten a couple of piercings on her face recently, and there was a little pink heart on her left cheekbone that I wasn't convinced she drew on every day with lip liner despite what she'd told me. She was fifteen. Tattoos, piercings, and the attitude to go with them. She smoothed out a crumpled piece of paper extracted with some difficulty from the pocket of her jeans. A little speech. I rubbed my temples.

"Now, listen," Marni said, wagging a finger with chipped black nail polish at me. "We know you said you didn't want anything like this, Bill. But we've all got something to say about Siobhan, and we think you should hear it. The first year, nobody did anything, you know? It's kind of like we ignored it. And that just makes me totally sad."

"So get on with it, then." I gave a dismissive wave. My best friend in the house, Nick Jones, elbowed me in the ribs. Nick and I pull each other into line whenever we can, but it's not always easy. I like the muscle-bound black man because he's ex-army and has hundreds of horror stories from his time in the Middle East that are so hideous, they pulverize my own trauma like a sledgehammer smashes a walnut.

"Give it a rest, man," Nick said.

"You give it a rest." I took a croissant from the plate in front of me and tossed it at him. He caught it against his chest and started eating it.

"The thing I miss most about Siobhan," Marni told the gathering, "is her terrible taste in music."

Everybody nodded in agreement; some people laughed. I clasped my hands so tight, my knuckles cracked, and I searched the sky for planes.

"Siobhan was a great cook, and she used to play music in the kitchen," Marni said, looking at her paper for guidance. "You couldn't get from the back of the house to the stairs without her grabbing you and making you dance around the kitchen with her. It was so embarrassing. She filled the house with these lame love ballads. Whitney. Bonnie. Celine. Really ancient, weird stuff."

"Ancient?" I scoffed. I leaned in toward Nick. "The prime of Celine Dion's career was the mid-nineties."

"Shut it," he whispered.

"I liked the way Siobhan sang Bonnie Tyler with her arm

out and her face all crumpled up, using her wooden spoon like a microphone," Marni said. "I know all the words to those songs because of Siobhan, and even though they suck, I'll never forget them. I miss her so bad. I've already got a mom, but Siobhan was, like, my better mom."

Everybody looked to me to see what I thought of Marni's tribute. I folded my arms and sighed.

The second person to stand was Sheriff Clayton Spears. He too had a piece of paper with a prepared speech. For a moment, I appreciated the amount of planning that had gone into this breakfast memorial for my wife that I'd been railroaded into attending. The table was cluttered with yellow paper plates and yellow napkins, and someone had filled several glasses with yellow flowers. Her favorite color.

Clay was in uniform, likely because he'd just worked an overnight shift. His enormous belly sagged so low in front, it hid his gun belt.

"You all know, uh, that I came to the house because my marriage broke down." Clay's chin wobbled with emotion. "It's not easy to be a proud man when your wife runs off with someone else. Because of my position as the head of law enforcement in Gloucester, the whole town knows my story."

Sheriff Spears's wife hadn't run off with just anyone. She'd left him for a young male model who had been staying with some friends in the apartment next door to theirs for a single weekend. It had taken him all of two days to convince Mrs. Spears to dump her life with the sheriff, pack a bag, and jump in the car with him and a crew of beautiful nineteen-year-old men. She hadn't been seen since.

"Siobhan stayed up with me many nights, listening to me talk through my breakup," Clay said. "She was the best listener. She was endlessly encouraging. We would sit out here in the garden eating slices of pepperoni pizza and looking at the stars and...and she just made me feel like...you all know I'm no George Clooney. But Siobhan told me that I deserved love and that I was a great man, and I believed her."

Clay sat down quickly, perhaps attempting to get his butt planted before he burst into tears, and the plastic lawn chair beneath him creaked in a concerning way.

I noticed a car drive up to the house and stop with a spray of gravel.

"My name is Angelica Grace Thomas-Lowell." The third speaker had risen from her chair. Angelica had lived in the house for more than two years, but for some reason she always introduced herself with her full name. "I'm a vegan. Activist. Provocateur. Bestselling author."

The car at the front of the house was a welcome distraction. I leaned to the side in my chair to see around Angelica, but her thin, veiny arms were in the way. The paper she held looked like a full page of typed notes.

"'I'd like to announce firstly my sincere appreciation for Siobhan's constant willingness to act as a confidential sounding board for my ideas,'" Angelica read. "'The creative process isn't always straightforward. It's fluid, magnetic, sometimes chaotic. Though Siobhan's reading history was firmly located in trash novels, I found her somewhat naive critiques of my works in progress—those few I entrusted to her—refreshing.'"

Nick suddenly stood up beside me. I looked over and

saw a woman running from the house toward the gathering. Not a plane crash, gas-leak explosion, or ferocious bear, but *something*. I stood with him.

I recognized the woman from town. Ellie Minnow. She grabbed Nick by his scar-covered arm.

"Nick, Bill, you've gotta help me. It's Winley."

"What is it?" Nick asked. "What's happened?"

"We'll help." I grabbed my phone from the table. "Whatever it is, we'll help."

Marni was already pouting. I brushed her shoulder in consolation as I passed. "Sorry, everyone, duty calls. Feel free to continue on without us."

I DROVE, NICK in the seat beside me, Ellie in the back. The gravel road to the Inn became the forest-lined road into town, curving around the marina jam-packed with bright, glossy cruisers and crab boats weeping rust. Nick was giving me the side-eye.

"What?"

"The crew were trying to do a nice thing for you, Cap," he said.

Nick calls me "Cap," short for *Captain*. It's not a habit from his army days but a carefully chosen term that I take seriously. Everybody needs a captain in life—a guiding force, a confidant, a rock, an anchor when tumultuous winds blow in. Siobhan had been my captain. Nick had picked me as his when he first moved in, but I had disappointed him ever since. The expression I saw on his face now hurt me, the way remembering how Siobhan danced and sang and listened and laughed hurt. Like a kick to the chest.

"What do you want me to say?" I asked Nick. "I told them I didn't want a memorial."

"Those people back there, they loved her too, you know," Nick said. "You don't get to be the only person who misses Siobhan."

"Well, they can go miss her in their way, and I'll miss her in mine," I said. "I don't like circle jerks."

"You prefer individual jerks?"

"Something like that."

"You're a lone wolf who's lost his mate." Nick rolled his eyes. "Your heart is broken and it can't be mended, and now you're cursed to wander the earth alone."

"I kind of wish I were alone right now," I said, nodding. I looked in the rearview mirror at Mrs. Minnow and changed the subject like a practiced master. "What's Winley done this time, Mrs. Minnow?"

Gloucester is a small town. When Siobhan and I moved into the area, the story started circulating that I was ex–Boston PD, that I'd been sacked and was bitter about it. I hadn't done anything to quash that rumor, taking up residence at the back of the lobster shack on the waterfront most afternoons, downing JD shots and refusing to answer questions about it. A couple of months after Siobhan got the Inn up and running, people began coming to me with issues they didn't trust Sheriff Spears to handle. They wanted me to talk to the angry neighbor about his aggressive dog. To hustle the scary homeless guy camped out near the pier a little farther down the road. Find the punks who had spray-painted graffiti on an old woman's fence and rattle their skulls a bit.

In truth, being the unofficial town muscle was far more satisfying than running the Inn. Riding around with Nick beside me, I could pretend I was back in the city before my terrible fall. I could imagine sometimes that Nick was Malone, the version of my old friend before he'd betrayed me and morphed before my very eyes into a liar and a schemer. Little jobs like this took me into the past that I never stopped thinking about, a time before I lost everything.

Mrs. Minnow had called me once before about her son Winley, after the boy stole her car and drove it into a ditch off the Yankee Division Highway. She shifted uncomfortably now, perhaps remembering.

"Winnie's much worse this time. He's gone crazy." Ellie was staring out the window, rubbing her wrist. "He's just out of control. I've never seen him this angry. He snaps at me whenever I try to get him out of bed. He just slugs around the house. I got a call from the school saying he hasn't been there in three days. I tried to talk to him about it this morning…"

I turned and looked at her wrist, glimpsed red finger marks. She hid them from me.

"Did the kid hurt you?" I asked.

"No, no." She tucked a curl behind her ear. "He would never—"

"If he's hurt you, I'll kick his ass," I said. "He's not too young to learn what you get if you raise your hand to a woman. Once I've finished kicking his ass, Nick will kick his ass, and then the two of us will hold him down while you kick his ass."

I've got a real issue with men who beat up on women. It's part of a large collection of emotional baggage that would make a team of bellhops throw in their hats.

The Minnow residence was covered in bougainvillea; the mailbox was balanced on the top of a gray concrete post. I turned off the engine and was about to open my door when a coffee table smashed through the front window of the house and landed upside down in a flower bed.

TIME LOOPS AROUND. One minute you're a washed-up ex-cop with love handles who hasn't shaved in days, and the next minute you're back in time, a rookie with washboard abs who couldn't grow a beard for love or money, adrenaline thrumming in your veins as you wait for the go-ahead to bust into a crack house with your team.

The Minnow residence wasn't a crack house, but it sure seemed as dangerous as one. As I jogged over, I heard Winley Minnow growling and the sounds of glass breaking and something dry, maybe cereal, scattering across the floor. Through the window by the back door, I saw Winley and his father, Derek, a small, round man who was sweating in his polo shirt. Winley held a wooden block of knives under one arm like a football and had one knife in his big fist. Just above Derek's head, beneath a cheerful cuckoo clock with lumberjacks poised to saw tiny logs, a knife handle jutted out of the drywall. I watched as Winley brandished the blade at his father.

"Win, please." Derek put his hands up. "Please, please, son, put the knife down."

"They're not taking me. They're not taking me! I'm not going! They're not taking me!"

I could tell Winley was high as a kite even before I saw his face. He was pacing in a small area, two steps forward and two back. Between the shouts, he muttered something to himself in a singsongy voice.

"No one's coming to take you," Derek said. "You're out of your mind!"

I kicked in the back door just as Nick came in the front. Nick grabbed Derek and yanked him out of the kitchen. Winley turned and hurled the knife at me; it went sailing past my ear and through the open door to the yard. Nick grabbed the boy's hand as he went for another, and I went for the knife block. We wrestled, and the knives scattered on the floor. Nick swept the kid into a headlock that didn't seem to slow him down at all.

Winley had experienced a growth spurt since I'd handled him last, and he'd put on a few pounds. Maybe a hundred of them. The bug-eyed kid picked me up and threw me clean across the room into the kitchen counter, which sent a rack of dishes and glasses to the floor. Nick hung off him like a backpack, but he tightened the headlock until Winley's eyes started rolling up in his head. Winley went to his knees and the two tangled on the floor. I rejoined the fray, and Nick and I shoved the kid into the tiles.

"Winley!" I put my knee in his fleshy back to get his attention. "You're caught, buddy. Give it up!"

The kid growled and howled a bit and then burst into tears. "Don't let them take me!"

"Who's going to take you?"

"The doctors. The scientists."

"This kid is whacked," I told Nick. Typical newbie drug taker shuffling through emotions, grasping at anything. He was crying like a toddler, huffing and sniffing. I sat him up in the glass and cereal and mess on the floor and Nick and I watched as he sobbed into his hands, the ferocious rampaging killer suddenly reduced to a blubbering child.

"Don't tell my mom," he cried. He'd obviously completely forgotten that he'd manhandled her only minutes earlier. "Oh God. I've gotta clean this place up before she gets back!" He tried to get up. I shoved him down.

"Winley, what did you take?"

"Nothing. I didn't—" The sobs racked his big body. "They're coming for me!"

"He's on something," I told Nick. "This doesn't look like the joy and exuberance of glorious youth."

"The what?"

"Never mind."

"Don't call the police!" Winley said.

"He *is* the police, son." Nick grabbed Winley's big shoulder and shook him.

Winley wasn't giving up. He cried and begged us to keep his mother out of it, his dazed state blocking out the reality of what he had done. I stood and walked into the living room, where I saw through the smashed window that neighbors were gathering to console Ellie Minnow on the immaculate lawn. Derek Minnow was in the room, sitting in an armchair by the big kicked-in television set. Winley had knocked pictures off their hooks, punched holes in the drywall.

"I'm so tired of this." Derek looked up at me. A hopeless father.

"This is a regular thing?"

"We knew he'd been smoking weed. But it's never been this bad."

"I've got news for you, Derek," I said. "This ain't weed."

I returned to the kitchen, saw Nick trying to talk Winley out of his mumblings about scientists and doctors. I went to the kid's room and looked in. Curtains drawn, clothes on the floor two feet deep, an unmade bed, and a strange damp feeling to everything. Typical teenage bedroom except for the burn marks on the cluttered desk under the window and the scraps of aluminum foil and cigarette lighters. There were cans of beans lined up on the windowsill and empty ones stacked in the bin by the door.

I lifted some of the trash off the boy's desk and found a small yellow capsule with a smiley face printed on it. I turned the pill in my fingers, shook it, heard powder shift inside.

Nick appeared at the bedroom door and started picking shards of glass out of his palms like they were cactus needles. "What do you think?" he asked. "Crack?"

"PCP, maybe," I said. "If it was crack, he'd be walking around town knocking over fire hydrants. Angel dust makes you burrow. Explains his aversion to going to school. He's been living in his little nest in here where he feels safe."

I showed him the capsule. He took it and looked at it.

"Did he say where he got it?" I asked.

"He says he got it at school," Nick said, giving the capsule back to me. "A kid on a bike gave it to him for free. I don't know how true that is. He thinks some doctors are about to abduct him in a van. Here." He gave me a small piece of paper with a number scrawled on it.

"What's this?"

"Don't know." Nick shrugged. "I asked him where the drugs came from and he told me about the kid on the bike and handed me that. I checked his phone. He dialed this number this morning at about eight."

"Let's chase it down," I said. "I was looking for something to do with my day."

'CLINTON'S INSIDER SECRETS AND PATTERSON'S STORYTELLING GENIUS MAKE THIS THE POLITICAL THRILLER OF THE DECADE'

LEE CHILD

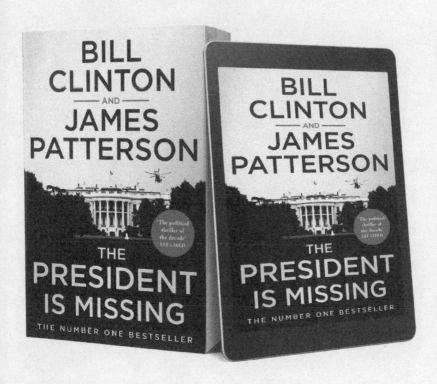

'Difficult to put down'
Daily Express

'A quick, slick, gripping read'
The Times

'Satisfying and surprising'
Guardian

'A high-octane collaboration . . . addictive'
Daily Telegraph

REVENGE

James Patterson
& Andrew Holmes

Former SAS soldier David Shelley has plans for a safer, more stable existence when he settles down to civilian life in London. But the shocking death of a young woman he used to protect puts those plans on hold, as the family call on their former bodyguard for help.

The police have ruled the death a suicide, but Emma's father suspects otherwise – and is willing to go to extreme lengths to prove it. Shelley must uncover the truth, before the father's need for retribution takes them into a war from which there is no escape.

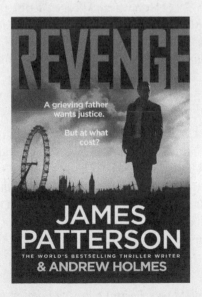

Also by James Patterson

ALEX CROSS NOVELS

Along Came a Spider • Kiss the Girls • Jack and Jill • Cat and Mouse • Pop Goes the Weasel • Roses are Red • Violets are Blue • Four Blind Mice • The Big Bad Wolf • London Bridges • Mary, Mary • Cross • Double Cross • Cross Country • Alex Cross's Trial (*with Richard DiLallo*) • I, Alex Cross • Cross Fire • Kill Alex Cross • Merry Christmas, Alex Cross • Alex Cross, Run • Cross My Heart • Hope to Die • Cross Justice • Cross the Line • The People vs. Alex Cross • Target: Alex Cross

THE WOMEN'S MURDER CLUB SERIES

1st to Die • 2nd Chance (*with Andrew Gross*) • 3rd Degree (*with Andrew Gross*) • 4th of July (*with Maxine Paetro*) • The 5th Horseman (*with Maxine Paetro*) • The 6th Target (*with Maxine Paetro*) • 7th Heaven (*with Maxine Paetro*) • 8th Confession (*with Maxine Paetro*) • 9th Judgement (*with Maxine Paetro*) • 10th Anniversary (*with Maxine Paetro*) • 11th Hour (*with Maxine Paetro*) • 12th of Never (*with Maxine Paetro*) • Unlucky 13 (*with Maxine Paetro*) • 14th Deadly Sin (*with Maxine Paetro*) • 15th Affair (*with Maxine Paetro*) • 16th Seduction (*with Maxine Paetro*) • 17th Suspect (*with Maxine Paetro*) • 18th Abduction (*with Maxine Paetro*)

DETECTIVE MICHAEL BENNETT SERIES

Step on a Crack (*with Michael Ledwidge*) • Run for Your Life (*with Michael Ledwidge*) • Worst Case (*with Michael Ledwidge*) • Tick Tock (*with Michael Ledwidge*) • I, Michael Bennett (*with Michael Ledwidge*) • Gone (*with Michael Ledwidge*) • Burn (*with Michael Ledwidge*) • Alert (*with Michael Ledwidge*) • Bullseye (*with Michael Ledwidge*) • Haunted (*with James O. Born*) • Ambush (*with James O. Born*)

PRIVATE NOVELS

Private (*with Maxine Paetro*) • Private London (*with Mark Pearson*) • Private Games (*with Mark Sullivan*) • Private: No. 1

Suspect (*with Maxine Paetro*) • Private Berlin (*with Mark Sullivan*) • Private Down Under (*with Michael White*) • Private L.A. (*with Mark Sullivan*) • Private India (*with Ashwin Sanghi*) • Private Vegas (*with Maxine Paetro*) • Private Sydney (*with Kathryn Fox*) • Private Paris (*with Mark Sullivan*) • The Games (*with Mark Sullivan*) • Private Delhi (*with Ashwin Sanghi*) • Private Princess (*with Rees Jones*)

NYPD RED SERIES

NYPD Red (*with Marshall Karp*) • NYPD Red 2 (*with Marshall Karp*) • NYPD Red 3 (*with Marshall Karp*) • NYPD Red 4 (*with Marshall Karp*) • NYPD Red 5 (*with Marshall Karp*)

DETECTIVE HARRIET BLUE SERIES

Never Never (*with Candice Fox*) • Fifty Fifty (*with Candice Fox*) • Liar Liar (*with Candice Fox*) • Hush Hush (*with Candice Fox*)

INSTINCT SERIES

Instinct (*with Howard Roughan, previously published as* Murder Games) • Killer Instinct (*with Howard Roughan*)

STAND-ALONE THRILLERS

The Thomas Berryman Number • Hide and Seek • Black Market • The Midnight Club • Sail (*with Howard Roughan*) • Swimsuit (*with Maxine Paetro*) • Don't Blink (*with Howard Roughan*) • Postcard Killers (*with Liza Marklund*) • Toys (*with Neil McMahon*) • Now You See Her (*with Michael Ledwidge*) • Kill Me If You Can (*with Marshall Karp*) • Guilty Wives (*with David Ellis*) • Zoo (*with Michael Ledwidge*) • Second Honeymoon (*with Howard Roughan*) • Mistress (*with David Ellis*) • Invisible (*with David Ellis*) • Truth or Die (*with Howard Roughan*) • Murder House (*with David Ellis*) • Woman of God (*with Maxine Paetro*) • Humans, Bow Down (*with Emily Raymond*) • The Black Book (*with David Ellis*) • The Store (*with Richard DiLallo*) • Texas Ranger (*with Andrew Bourelle*) • The President is Missing (*with Bill Clinton*) • Revenge (*with Andrew Holmes*) • Juror No. 3 (*with Nancy Allen*) • The First Lady (*with Brendan DuBois*) • The Chef (*with Max DiLallo*) • Out of Sight (*with Brendan DuBois*) • Unsolved (*with David Ellis*) • The Inn (*with Candice Fox*)

NON-FICTION

Torn Apart (*with Hal and Cory Friedman*) • The Murder of King Tut (*with Martin Dugard*) • All-American Murder (*with Alex Abramovich and Mike Harvkey*)

MURDER IS FOREVER TRUE CRIME

Murder, Interrupted (*with Alex Abramovich and Christopher Charles*) • Home Sweet Murder (*with Andrew Bourelle and Scott Slaven*) • Murder Beyond the Grave (*with Andrew Bourelle and Christopher Charles*)

COLLECTIONS

Triple Threat (*with Max DiLallo and Andrew Bourelle*) • Kill or Be Killed (*with Maxine Paetro, Rees Jones, Shan Serafin and Emily Raymond*) • The Moores are Missing (*with Loren D. Estleman, Sam Hawken and Ed Chatterton*) • The Family Lawyer (*with Robert Rotstein, Christopher Charles and Rachel Howzell Hall*) • Murder in Paradise (*with Doug Allyn, Connor Hyde and Duane Swierczynski*) • The House Next Door (*with Susan DiLallo, Max DiLallo and Brendan DuBois*) • 13-Minute Murder (*with Shan Serafin, Christopher Farnsworth and Scott Slaven*)

For more information about James Patterson's novels, visit www.jamespatterson.co.uk